THE Rainbow CLAUSE

BETH BOLDEN

PROLOGUE

COLIN O'CONNOR DIDN'T LOOK anything like the *Sports Illustrated* cover that Nick had spent the last three months trying not to drool over.

He looked even better.

Nick tensed, even though in his job as a journalist for *Five Points*, a sports and pop culture blog, he'd interviewed dozens of good-looking men. Sure, he hadn't felt that intensely visceral pull to any of them the way he did with O'Connor, but that didn't mean he couldn't stay professional.

"Thanks for dropping by. I see you're not too tired from those three touchdown passes against the Rams to talk to me today."

Colin blushed; it made him look even more attractive. Nick inwardly swore.

"I was at the game yesterday," Nick continued, trying to stay on topic, "and being the first home game back in LA, it was definitely spirited in the stands. How did it feel on the field? Any difference you noticed?"

When Colin had agreed to stop by *Five Points*, like any journalist, Nick had done his research. He'd been doing research on Colin O'Connor for years.

He'd read every scrap of information he could get his hands on. He'd watched homegrown YouTube footage of Colin's football games in Alaska. He'd hired Jemma Keane as his assistant based almost entirely on the college football profile that she'd written on him. She alone had managed to put together an article that seemed to finally tell the world something about the man who'd go on to win a Heisman Trophy, lead his team to the National Championship, and eventually be selected as the first pick in the NFL draft. And that was probably because she was also his best friend and Colin had *let* her write the article.

Colin gave the bare minimum of interviews. When he did give one, it was difficult to penetrate his reserve. He posed for *Sports Illustrated,* and while shirtless and undeniably handsome on the cover, his blue-eyed stare revealed nothing, and the accompanying article seemed to ask more questions than it ever answered.

The mystery of Colin O'Connor was the frustration of Nick's career.

Colin shrugged. "It was my first away game in the NFL. It's tough to judge. Seemed pretty exciting to the crowd."

When Colin had sat down opposite him, muscular thighs exquisitely framed by a pair of clingy khakis, Nick had sworn he'd seen those blue eyes checking him out, one long head-to-toe sweep.

Nick might not be a cover model like some people, but he knew he was decently attractive. And it seemed, incredibly, that Colin O'Connor might think so, too. That single, speculative glance threatened every promise Nick had ever made about mixing work with pleasure.

"Well, I was pretty excited," Nick said, with a smirk. His sexuality wasn't a secret, but he still rarely made mention of it during interviews. Mostly because the interviews weren't supposed to be about him.

It took Colin a second, but then he grinned back. "About the game or...?"

"You're definitely an exciting player, even when you're throwing three touchdowns against my home team."

Colin's smile grew. "Always happy to convert opposing fans."

"Do you feel like that's tough to do?"

"I'll be honest," Colin said, which was incredibly ironic because while yes, he was probably always honest, he was also a closed—and *locked*—book, "I find a lot of people don't like me."

Flirting was almost too easy when Colin kept throwing out such slow pitches.

"I like you," Nick said, shooting Colin the smile he usually reserved for cute men in clubs.

"Very reassuring," Colin said.

"Why don't people like you?" Nick paused, then gave Colin another long look up and down. "'Cause I'm not seeing a reason."

Colin blushed again.

"They don't like that I've won so many things. Heisman Trophy. National Championship. They think I'm all ego."

"Again," Nick said, a degree under a straight leer, "I'm sitting pretty close to you and I can tell you with certainty that you're not all ego."

"We've already established you're easy enough to win over," Colin retorted, but he was smiling.

It had never occurred to Nick that Colin O'Connor, the NFL's golden child, might not be straight. But Nick knew how straight men flirted with him—and bashful interest simmering in Colin's eyes now wasn't like that at all.

Nick threw his hands up. "Guilty as charged."

"But to clarify, no, I'm not all ego. I work hard. Really hard. Maybe that's not a popular or a mainstream opinion, but my success is all due to hard work and vigilance."

"Vigilance? That seems a bit extreme."

Colin shot him a strange look that Nick barely caught before it was locked down and away and that stupid, bland smile was back.

"Tom Brady eats the same thing every day, keeps the exact same schedule. He's the most vigilant and the most successful. I don't think that's a coincidence."

"Would you say you look up to Tom Brady?"

The strange look came back, for a split second longer this time. "I'm a quarterback in the National Football League. I think it would be hard to be that and *not* look up to Tom Brady in some capacity."

"Would you consider him your role model?"

"No." The answer was swift, sudden, and completely unexpected. Nick realized he must be getting to the man more than he'd realized. Colin retrenched. "No, I mean, of *course* I'd love to have the stat line he does. The Superbowl rings. But I consider Nelson Mandela to be my personal role model."

Nick, who had read every scrap he could find on Colin O'Connor, was almost one hundred percent sure that he'd never mentioned that in an interview before. He was also fairly certain that despite generally being a heathen, even *he* couldn't work Nelson Mandela into a flirtatious double entendre.

"So why Nelson Mandela and not Tom Brady?"

"He fought for something he believed in," Colin said with perfect conviction. "Something bigger than himself."

"Someone to emulate, then?"

Colin shot him that look again, longer and more puzzled than before. "While I'd love to bring about the sort of systemic change Nelson Mandela fought for, I don't think three touchdown passes against the Rams is going to do it."

"Right, right," Nick said. He felt off his game. Unprepared. Rocked, a little. He was resolutely *not* staring at the way Colin's bicep flexed when he clenched his fingers together, which he did each time he answered a question. What Nick needed was to funnel his distraction into something that could crack Colin O'Connor.

"Boomer told me after the game that you changed two of the touchdown plays at the line of scrimmage. You obviously became adept at running the no-huddle offense at Oregon. Is that something you're going to work for the Piranhas?"

Colin looked annoyed now, which made sense because the coach of the Piranhas, Daniel Mortensen, had explicitly confirmed that in his press conference two days prior. "That's the plan."

"Sounds like you're better at issuing orders than taking them," Nick purred, angling his body closer. This portion of the interview would never make the final cut, that much was inevitable, but Nick couldn't help himself.

Colin looked shocked and speechless for a moment. But it didn't take him very long to recover, and for someone who still blushed at female reporters' vague flirtations, he seemed very comfortable dishing it back to Nick.

"I can swing either way. It's all about the heat of the moment," Colin replied smugly, blue eyes twinkling, and a sly smile tilting up the corner of his perfect mouth. Looking straight at Nick. Daring him to take it one step further.

And that was it. That was the moment that sealed it. Nick Wheeler's body, and the part of his soul that didn't already belong to Stephen Curry, transferred semi-permanent ownership to Colin O'Connor.

CHAPTER ONE

REBELLION TASTED LIKE VODKA with a splash of soda and a sliver of lime, balancing precariously on the edge of Colin's glass.

Players were allowed to go out and party, mostly because nobody from the Piranhas organization could stop it from happening, but tonight at this particular club, Colin couldn't help but feel like he was pushing his luck.

It wasn't that he didn't go out, because he did. You couldn't live in a city like Miami and *not* go out, but he tried to avoid it because loud pulsing music, superficial standards, and free-flowing alcohol weren't things he normally enjoyed. But Teddy had insisted on him coming, and he'd even slipped in a hard-to-resist sweetener: "There's this new club," he'd said, "it's good for girls *and* guys, if you know what I mean."

Colin knew what he meant, and for that and many other reasons, Teddy was his favorite guy in Miami. Nobody else would have taken the time to find a place where Colin could theoretically mingle with both sexes, even though he was usually only interested in men. Nobody else would have cared. Truthfully, nobody else but Teddy *knew*.

Wasn't that the ironic cherry on top of the last few years? He was *usually* interested in men, but the one woman he'd fallen for hadn't liked him that way. Instead, she'd kindly but firmly kept their friendship platonic.

He was probably the only Heisman-winning quarterback to ever be friend-zoned.

Echoes of the tension headache he'd been fighting earlier throbbed in sync with the heavy bass. Colin took a long pull of his drink, and felt the vodka burn all the way down his throat.

Of all the things he'd done to try to move past his best friend, Jemma, he hadn't tried alcohol yet. Maybe it was time to try to drown his sorrows in more than too many reps and too many long, lonely nights studying the playbook.

Colin set his empty glass down on the VIP table in front of the couch he'd chosen, mostly because it had the best vantage point of the whole room, and also had the bonus of removing him from anyone who might want to talk to him.

He thought he'd been subtle about it, but when he'd sat down, Colin had seen Teddy's resigned glare.

The waitress appeared in front of him, like she had an alert button for when his glass emptied. His third, and all he felt was a mild, nauseous buzzing at the base of his stomach. Which was why he usually didn't drink.

Alcohol made him loose and looseness made him nervous.

"Another?" she asked, gathering the glass and the damp napkin sitting underneath it.

He didn't miss the way she'd been so attentive tonight, bending over further than necessary, flashing him long glimpses of her exposed cleavage. She was beautiful, with lots of smooth, tan skin and piles of dark hair on top of her head, exposing her graceful neck. No doubt the waitress had seen him, the rookie quarterback for the Piranhas, in her section and thought she'd hit the jackpot—and not for just the excellent tip she was assured. What she couldn't know was that while she was gorgeous, she didn't do a thing for him.

"I've already got it," a voice said behind her. Colin glanced up, and felt everything that he didn't for the nice waitress.

He was also gorgeous, with dark eyes and cheekbones to die for, a low-cut, black tank showcasing biceps that told Colin he knew his way around a weight room.

"Belvedere with soda, right?" the guy asked, his eyes twinkling. "I've been paying attention."

Colin looked at the pair in front of him, clearly competing for his attention, and hated the anxiety threatening to break through the comfortable numbness from the last three glasses of vodka.

Not for the first time, he wished he was just gay, because as hard as that had been in high school, that had seemed less a constant struggle to figure out what the hell it was that he really wanted. He'd known he liked men; he'd been absolutely sure. Then he'd walked into that first college class, seen Jemma's smile, and everything he'd accepted suddenly didn't feel as settled.

Of all the factors in the decision before him, Colin didn't think about what might happen if he took the drink out of this guy's hand, making his preferences clear. Yeah, this was an exclusive club, but people talked. Colin only wanted them to talk when he was ready for them to do so.

Every time before this, when he'd been confronted by a similar choice, he'd chosen nothing at all. Even Jemma hadn't been a choice, because she'd never chosen him. He could decline the drink and leave. But where had that practice gotten him? Alone and miserable, that's where.

Fuck it, Colin thought, and reached for the glass, giving the guy what he hoped was a flirtatious smile.

He didn't usually flirt, because everyone did it for him.

The guy smiled back brightly and shot the waitress a mildly triumphant glance of dismissal. She looked surprised, and Colin couldn't blame her; his preference for men was hardly common knowledge.

"Hi, I'm Matt," the man said, settling on the edge of the couch, his imbalance causing him to lean further into Colin's space.

Colin might have minded usually, but *this* was what he was supposed to be doing, right? Letting cute boys buy him drinks to help him forget about Jemma?

"Colin," he replied, fully expecting the guy to say, *of course you are.*

It wasn't easy being so recognized. There were a lot of perks to his success, but the constant revolving door of people who wanted something got old. Colin hoped this guy wasn't one of those because he was hot, and it had been so long since Colin had let himself think that a guy was cute.

But Matt gave no hint that he knew who Colin was. This wasn't exactly unprecedented, but it was nice. Maybe Matt was just a really good actor.

"I haven't seen you around here before," Matt said, leaning even further in so Colin could hear him over the music.

Or maybe he really didn't know who Colin was. Colin relaxed a fraction.

"I've never been here before," Colin admitted.

Matt's gaze swept over him and it was proprietary. Colin found he *liked* it; liked feeling being wanted for a change, and not because of all his accolades and accomplishments over the past few years. Jemma had liked him for other things, but then she'd never liked him the way Matt might.

"You're the hottest thing in this room," Matt confessed. "I would have definitely remembered you if I'd seen you here before."

Colin quenched the bubble of irony that threatened to escape his throat.

"I'm glad I came," he said, and to his own surprise, he meant it.

"Me too," Matt flirted back, one hand sliding up Colin's back and the other covering his knee. "You wanna dance?"

Colin made a face. "Not really. I'm a horrible dancer." He could move around the football field like a natural, but confronted with a person and any kind of music, he was a mess.

He was pretty sure it was more of an emotional hang-up than a physical one, but then he'd never really been motivated to find out.

Maybe he was motivated enough now.

"Oh, come on," Matt teased, his fingers moving up from Colin's knee to his thigh. He squeezed and Colin told himself to relax and *enjoy it.* But every instinct he'd had since high school was *hide, don't let it show, don't touch him the way you want him to* and it was hard to fight all that noise. "Athletic boy like you? I bet you're great."

Colin palmed his glass and hesitated a split second. Then he lifted it to his lips and downed the rest of the liquid. If there'd been any soda in there, he'd be really surprised. And for the first time, the noise in his head quieted a fraction. Not a lot, but it was enough.

He reached out a hesitant hand and brushed Matt's fingers, lingering on his upper thigh. "I'll dance if you want me to," he said, which was as good as he was going to get at flirting. He was beginning to think he was way too straight-forward for flirting. His natural instinct was to cut through all the bullshit teasing and get to what they both wanted.

Matt's dark eyes sparkled as he grinned. He really was gorgeous—open and charming and at ease with himself in a way Colin couldn't help but envy.

"Well then, let's go," Matt said, tangling their hands together and tugging him up, making no secret at all about his interest.

Colin let Matt lead the way out of the VIP platform and into the thick of the club. Nobody was looking at them and he felt a wild thrill at the anonymity of it.

He even found that he could move decently, especially because Matt was such a great dancer; sinuous and with hips that Colin wanted to grip. He had the thought and then he realized a moment later, he *could*. The idea blew his mind, and before, he'd never understood why closeted men sought out these clubs, but the idea of acting without thinking first was unbelievably appealing.

Colin's first touch was hesitant, but the way Matt leaned into it helped give him the confidence he needed to grip those slim hips and pull the man flush against him. Matt smirked, clearly pleased with himself for busting Colin out of his comfort zone and dragging him into Matt's own. Colin found he didn't really give a shit if Matt was the smuggest asshole on the planet. It had been so long since Colin had touched someone with non-platonic intentions. Even longer without that familiar pulse of guilt over Jemma. He was feeling good, and he was going to enjoy it.

The music pulsed in long, drawn-out beats around them, and Colin pulled Matt closer. Colin felt the familiar white noise static of pleasure beginning to take over his brain as Matt did something clever with his hips, grinding his dick right against Colin's with a mischievous grin.

Of course, that was the moment it all went to hell.

"Oh my god, you're Colin O'Connor!"

It wasn't Matt's voice, but the person over Matt's left shoulder definitely got his attention. Probably because whoever the dickwad was who'd decided to announce his identity, had screeched it loud enough that now everyone in the near vicinity knew.

Matt stopped moving and took an instinctual step back, confusion clouding his features. "You're *who*?" he asked and Colin was frozen in place, not sure whether to try to brazen out all this attention or to just run.

The blond man who'd yelled stepped around Matt and from the way they eyed each other, Colin figured out really quickly they knew each other.

"I can't believe you're dancing with a *football player*," the blond snorted with derision. As if Colin was the only player in the NFL to be queer. Newsflash: he wasn't. Nobody was out, but he knew of lots of players who didn't identify as straight privately.

"I *was*, until you interrupted, you asshole," Matt bitched right back. "And I was definitely going to take him home, too, until you interrupted." He turned away from the interfering blond, and luckily, most of the crowd had already forgotten about the altercation.

Matt reached out and his fingers brushed Colin's forearm, his muscles tense with panic. "Let's get out of here."

Colin swallowed hard. He wanted to. That much had been obvious from the bulge of his erection in his jeans. Matt was *really* cute. But he didn't want some meaningless fuck. He wanted late nights cuddling on the couch, and lazy, late-morning breakfasts and fancy dinners and *then* non-meaningless fucking. He opened his mouth to try to explain this, but Matt must have seen the answer on his face, because he threw up his hands and swore.

"See, you dick," he called back to the blond, who'd retreated but was still throwing plenty of snotty looks their direction, "you just cost me *another* hookup. *Fuck you.*"

"You wish," the blond called back, and that was Colin's cue to leave.

He retreated right back to the VIP section he'd left, and pulled his phone out of his pocket. He pulled up the text conversation with Teddy, and typed out: **not sure this is for me, maybe I should go.**

Glancing up, he searched for the waitress who'd been so eager to serve him earlier, but she was nowhere to be found. With too many emotions threatening to break through the vodka numbness, Colin stood back up and started making his way towards the exit. He felt a hand grab his shoulder right before he made it to the door, and jerked around, ready to tell some asshole off for touching him. But it was only Teddy, smiling back at him, eyes bright even in the darkness of the club.

He waved his hand towards the exit, and Colin took it to mean that if he was leaving, Teddy would, too.

A minute later, they were finally out of the hot and close air of the club, breathing in the night air, right off the ocean.

They walked around the corner, away from the line of people waiting to get in who might recognize either of them. Colin slumped against the brick wall, and he must have been drunker than he'd thought, because he felt about five seconds from word-vomiting everything up.

The boy from high school.

Jemma.

How football was both the best and the worst thing to ever happen to him.

The curse of his bisexuality.

Fucking all of it.

Teddy reached out and cupped his shoulder reassuringly. "It was never gonna be easy, man."

It exploded out of him.

"I could do *hard* in my sleep," he ranted, his voice rising, and he knew he'd lost it because he literally did not give a shit. He'd tell the fucking whole world right now. "I do fucking *hard* every single damn day. This isn't just hard. This is impossible."

Teddy's hand didn't move and he just gripped tighter. "I know," he said calmly, like he'd been expecting the outburst, even though it didn't make any sense because Colin had a reputation as a steel-nerved, emotionally-cauterized machine who didn't let things like fear or anxiety get in the way of what he wanted. He was Matty Ice Part 2, at least on the field. As for off the field, Teddy was maybe the only one in Miami who he'd let get close enough to see the rest. Definitely the only one who he'd told his secret to.

"I can't date. I can't take someone out. Because any guy who wants that doesn't want to be some dirty little secret. And the rest, they just want to fuck. And I can't do that. I want *more*."

Colin braced his hands on his knees, and tried to force the sob back down his throat. He'd never given up in his entire life, but this felt like surrender.

"It sounds like you know what you need to do," Teddy said, his voice still soft. Gallingly sympathetic, because they both knew what he was implying.

"Yeah," Colin laughed bitterly, because otherwise he might cry, "I was trying to avoid that. Sort of a last resort type of thing."

"If you want what you say you want, I don't think you have a lot of choice." Teddy paused, waiting until Colin had leveraged himself upright before wrapping his arms around him in a tight bear hug. "You gotta know, I support you, whatever you do."

Colin let out a sob then, squeezing his eyes and throat tight against the onslaught that was threatening to overwhelm him. Apparently when you'd held your emotions in check for so long, sometimes they just escaped out of you when you least expected it. "Thanks, man. You're the best."

"Let's get you home." Teddy let him go and fumbled in his pocket for his phone. He called a car. As they waited, he turned to Colin again. "I'm gonna say it again, not gonna be easy."

"No." An understatement. But the more Colin thought about it, the less it felt like surrender and the more it felt like staking everything he had on the outcome of the battle. And Colin knew he was in his element when it came to a fight.

The call with his agent went about as well as Colin expected it to go, even though his agent knew all about his sexuality, and had even negotiated a clause in Colin's contract with the Piranhas that would make this whole process easier now that he'd decided to move forward.

But it was one thing to ready the clause for a far-off day when Colin decided to come out, and another for him to actually decide to do it.

"All I'm saying is give it a few more years," Mark argued. "You've just finished your rookie year. It's going to go over better if you're more established."

Colin looked out on the moody Sunday morning sea, choppy and blue-ish gray. The water looked how he felt. "No offense, Mark, but I'm not doing this because of how other people will react. I'm doing this for me. So no, I don't want to wait a few years. I've waited long enough."

Like everything else, once Colin had decided on a plan of action, he was dead set on seeing it through. Which Mark knew, but since Mark was Mark, and a real jackass—albeit a jackass who was hell at the negotiating table—he argued anyway.

They both knew that Mark would be calling up the Piranhas organization today and setting everything into motion. It was only a matter of how much breath Mark planned to waste.

"If you're absolutely set on it, then I'll give Helen a call." Helen was the Piranhas' Director of Public Relations.

"Also tell her that I want *Five Points* doing the story."

Mark gave a groan. "I know they're all trendy right now, because of the Kimber Holloway story, but I think we can come up with an outlet that's a bit more high profile. Like, let's say *People*."

"No."

"You know that wasn't one of the negotiated points of the Rainbow Clause. Helen and the Piranhas might want *People*. I'm just saying."

The thing about Mark was that he kept Colin on his toes. He was sneaky in a way that Colin had been completely unprepared for, and still didn't really *like*, exactly. But his underhanded methods were very often successful, and Colin couldn't help but respect his success. He also thought Mark was good practice for learning to spot unscrupulous people, which was something he'd had to deal with a lot more since entering the NFL.

In the league, pretty much everyone had an agenda. The trick was to shift their agenda until it was *your* agenda.

"I think the Piranhas are going to want to stick with what makes me happy, Mark," Colin pointed out. "I also think that they'd be open to a suggestion from you."

"Fine, I'll let Helen know you want *Five Points*. That bastard Duncan Snyder better be fucking *thrilled* and realize he owes me until the end of time for this."

"I'm sure you'll find a way to let him know," Colin said.

"Damn straight. I'm sure they'll want to meet to hash all this out, and I'll send you an email when I know something."

"You'd better. You know how this works. Nothing without my approval." Colin let his tone take on a hint of warning. That was one of the first things he and Mark had agreed upon when Colin had signed with him as a client. Nothing was assumed; everything was checked through Colin first.

Colin might be ignorant about the seamier side of the NFL, but he wasn't going to let someone else run his career for him.

"Yes, yes, I know," Mark grumbled. Like Colin's successful rookie season wasn't responsible for the brand new, rose gold Rolex he'd been wearing.

"Colin O'Connor is *what?*"

Jemma looked up from the coffee she was soaking up with a paper towel. Coffee that Nick had knocked over because of the news Duncan had just brought to their morning meeting.

Shocked would be an understatement right now. Flabbergasted would probably be closer to the truth, and Nick had even wondered during the interview with Colin O'Connor all those months ago.

Of course, entertaining a vague idea that he might not be straight was not the same thing as, "Colin O'Connor is going to come out as bisexual and we got the exclusive story."

Thanks, Duncan. That was a $5 coffee I just spilled.

"Don't tell me you didn't wonder," Jemma scoffed under her breath. "I watched that interview footage. You practically surgically attached yourself to him."

"You knew," Nick stated, because of course she had. Colin O'Connor was one of those guys who would tell a woman—or a man, apparently—every piece of salient information when he declared his intention to woo.

Intention to woo. Nick knew he was reeling. That much was clear.

Jemma's glare was openly scornful, which she wouldn't have dared when she was still Nick's assistant. Unfortunately, she had more than earned her promotion during the Rio Olympics, when she'd substituted for Nick at the last moment. Nick found himself missing the days when she was still afraid to let him know exactly how she felt.

"Of course I knew." She hesitated. "I thought you'd be a whole lot happier about this."

"I am, I am, I'm just…"

"Acting like a total tool?"

Yes, he definitely missed the days when Jemma had been less comfortable being outspoken.

"*Surprised,*" Nick corrected with an equally venomous glare her direction.

"Children," Duncan, the owner of *Five Points*, said sternly, looking up from his laptop. "It's too early for this. Jemma—you're here because you wrote the most comprehensive profile on O'Connor to date. Nick—you're here because you're going to write his coming out profile."

It was a good thing that his coffee was already spilled, because Nick would have just knocked it over again.

Duncan glanced from Jemma to Nick. "No complaints about that? Nick is probably shocked silent, but, Jemma, I at least expected you to argue to replace him. I know you're good friends with him."

"He's my best friend. And that's why Nick is the right person to write the article." Jemma looked unexpectedly contrite. "Also, I know Nick has been waiting for an opportunity like this for a long time. He's got a personal angle for the material that I don't. No arguments from me."

"I'm glad you approve," Duncan said with wry amusement in his tone. "Nick?"

"I mean, yes, I mean, *god*, of course I've been waiting to write this. This article is why I majored in journalism. Opportunities to tell stories like this don't come around very often." He remembered when he'd started college and had imagined that there'd be chances around every corner to change the world.

He wasn't jaded and bitter—not entirely, anyway—but he could still acknowledge that he hadn't stumbled onto many chances to change the world during his career so far. He'd settled for arguing unpopular opinions, but it wasn't the same.

It wasn't special. Not the way this was.

Jemma glanced over at him. "Why does it feel like there's a *but* on the end of that?"

"There's not," Nick insisted, but Jemma was right. There *was* a but. He'd never let himself consider Colin really wasn't straight. He'd done so for practical self-preservation reasons.

Besides, he told himself, *even if by some bizarre happenstance, he happened to be interested in you, he's probably not as good-looking as you remember.*

It was a unique experience to walk into a room of people he worked with when his sexuality was no longer a secret.

Colin figured he'd better be okay with repeating it a lot in the next few months, but it still felt like a mini internal battle every time he had to meet someone's eyes around the conference table.

Then Colin looked up and to his surprise, didn't see Jemma on the conference call screen. Instead, it was that guy that had interviewed him last time he'd been in LA. Her boss, or ex-boss, or whatever.

He'd sort of, absolutely, definitely counted on it being Jemma. After all, she'd gotten where she was today partially because of another groundbreaking article on him, and then she'd written the one on Olympic swimmer Kimber Holloway and her mother, and so it seemed like flawless timing, at least to him.

Maybe not to Duncan Snyder, though.

The meeting started by a quick introduction around the table, including the screen at the far end.

Mark and Helen, the Piranhas' Public Relations Director, were supposed to be jointly hosting this meeting, at least from what Colin could tell from the meeting invite he'd received via email. But Helen was clearly letting Mark know who was in charge, pinning him with a steely glance from the opposite side of the huge, white, conference room table. Helen was the one to suggest they go around the room and introduce themselves, because, as she'd put it, "We'll be working closely together in the next six months."

Colin had naively always assumed that when you came out, you just *did* it. But apparently, in today's media-driven world, it wasn't nearly that simple. He'd discovered this particular fact when he and Mark had been negotiating his rookie contract. He'd wanted to put a broad clause in about coming out, giving him the power to do so if he chose to. The Rainbow Clause, as it had been nicknamed, had turned into a whole separate addendum.

At the time, Colin had hated the negotiations, terrified by all the mounting media speculation at how long it was taking him to come to an official agreement with the Piranhas. He'd worried that someone would find out about the real reason for the delay, but today he was grateful because it meant the difficult parts were already behind him. All they had to do was plan--however minutely--the actual details.

Helen introduced herself. Mark jumped in and introduced himself next, even though there were three underlings sitting between him and Helen. Colin barely refrained from rolling his eyes. Anyway, it provided a brief respite before he had to face the man at the end of the table. He looked like the Wizard of Oz, suspended on a huge screen, the tips of his dark, mussy hair fading into the ceiling, and his gray eyes piercing whenever Colin met them across the table.

He didn't really remember the man. All he had was a vague haze of pain and numbness when he remembered those weeks. The only thing that stood out to him was the way Jemma had smiled at her new boyfriend, Gabe, bright and earnest and painfully in love.

At least, it had been painful for Colin. As for Jemma, he'd known instantly how happy she was, and that was why he'd let her go with a stiff upper lip. Because really, she'd never been his in the first place. She'd been a pipe dream of normalcy, representing a hazy future where the Rainbow Clause was a distant thought, not an immediate need.

"Nick Wheeler," the man said. His eyes seemed to bore right into Colin, and Colin had to force himself not to squirm in his chair. He was vulnerable enough. He didn't need some interviewer savant to pick out all his insecurities right away. "We met at the beginning of the season last year."

"I remember," Colin lied. He hesitated then decided, *fuck it.* This was his Rainbow Clause, damnit, and he was going to exercise every hard-won section. "I assumed Jemma would be here. That she'd be writing this."

Nick leaned back in his chair, a glimmer of amusement in those stormy eyes that the magnification made impossible to miss. Colin couldn't decide if they were gray or blue, and already on edge, the inconsistency annoyed him.

"She's got another assignment," Nick said. "I hope I'm an acceptable alternative."

"Perfectly acceptable," Helen interrupted, shooting an apologetic look Colin's way. "We're all familiar with your work."

Colin wasn't, but he guessed he probably should be. He just didn't really like sports commentary, even when the commentators weren't talking about him.

"I'm sure you're very good at your job," Colin said stiffly.

A smirk tweaked the right side of Nick's mouth up. "You sure about that?" he asked.

Colin forced himself to look straight down the table. Lots of things in his life had been hard-won, but this felt like a bigger battle than it should have been. He should have felt like whoever was going to tell his story was on his side.

He'd always known Jemma was on his side. That's why he'd wanted so much for it to be her. He trusted that she wouldn't twist his words, or *him*. But Colin knew when he'd been called out. He knew how to win over an offense to his side. How to take control of a locker room.

"Maybe I'm not as familiar with you as Helen."

"Nick Wheeler. Thirty-one years old. LA native. Gay." Nick listed the points off perfunctorily, like there was some sort of checklist. And maybe there was.

But whatever Colin had expected, he didn't expect the last point.

"Ah," he stuttered, unsure what to counter with after Nick had dropped that particular bomb. "Well, it's nice to meet you." After the stupid phrase was out of his mouth, Colin remembered that they'd already fucking met, and he sounded like a first-class idiot.

"Likewise, Mr. O'Connor," Nick said smoothly, not pointing out his mistake.

Colin simmered at his end of the table as Helen took over the meeting.

She outlined a general timetable. Talked about leaking hints to certain reporters. Talked about LGBTA+ friendly programs that the Piranhas were going to introduce in the next year.

When she finished the "prep" phase, as she'd called it, her sharp gaze found Nick's. He'd been as silent as Colin during the last fifteen minutes, though clearly taking some sort of notes. Not that Colin had been watching him or anything.

"Let's talk about your feature, Mr. Wheeler," Helen said.

"I'd like a few weeks in Miami with Mr. O'Connor. Access to his residence, to player facilities at the Piranhas' compound, to his schedule, to his charitable enterprises. To all football and non-football activities, essentially."

Colin forced himself not to make a face. He'd completely avoided these sorts of "in-depth exclusives" for his entire football career. He'd let Jemma write the one article while he was still in college, but other than that, he'd tried to keep his private life private, and not just because he was afraid of what a nosy reporter might find.

He didn't like the spotlight, even if it loved him back.

"That's a lot of access," Mark piped up. Mark was probably seeing dollar signs, because more press meant more prominent exposure, which in turn meant more sponsorship deals. But Mark was also on a short leash, and knew what Colin didn't like.

Nick spread his hands out. "It's a very important story. I want to do it justice. Not just for Mr. O'Connor. Think of the impact it will have." *For people like me* hung unspoken over the conference table.

Maybe that was what swayed him. Later, Colin wouldn't be able to point to *why* he'd given in so easily. But he folded like a terrible hand of poker.

"Fine," Colin said. "It's fine."

He tried to ignore how pleased Nick looked, and also tried to ignore the jolt of awareness that shot right through him when Nick smiled. He had a gorgeous mouth, especially when he let some sunshine through the bitter, world-weary clouds.

It turned out the former was far, far easier than the latter.

CHAPTER TWO

"YOU DIDN'T WANT IT to be me." Nick leaned back in his chair, sipping his latte, and seemed pleased about throwing out such an unapologetically blunt conversation starter.

Colin was already on edge because he hadn't wanted to have this meeting. This man had essentially invited himself into Colin's life, and then had the gall to issue more demands. Like that he needed Colin to meet with him to finalize details of the profile while he was in LA.

Colin had nearly sent Mark. The only reason he hadn't was because he wasn't sure he trusted Mark with this, and he definitely didn't trust Nick.

"Of course, I didn't." Colin had cautioned himself in the car about letting Nick get to him, and already he was off-balance and snappish. And more painfully honest than he normally was with reporters. He tried to pull back. "Jemma's my best friend. She's already written a very successful profile of me. It made sense."

Nick smiled, but Colin was under the impression he wasn't very amused. "Yeah, it was a good profile. I mean, I *hired* her because of it. But a profile of a potential Heisman-winning quarterback that nobody knows at all because he won't really give interviews, and a life- and career-changing coming out interview of an NFL star? Yeah, those are two different beasts."

It wasn't so long ago that the pulse of anger Colin felt on Jemma's behalf would have been driven by very non-platonic feelings. He took it as a win that all he felt in that moment was loyalty towards his *friend*. It had been a really long year, but he didn't think he was in love with Jemma anymore.

"Doesn't mean she wouldn't have done a good job," Colin defended, because Nick got under his skin and made him a lot more expressly argumentative than he normally was. Normally he'd just give a vague smile and let the reporter's questions glide right over his placid surface.

Nick Wheeler churned up the water, and Colin didn't like it.

"She would have done the best she could, but it wouldn't have been what you needed. You and Jemma, you're too good of friends. She'd be more interested in protecting you," Nick said. "Those sensitive spots, she'd let you keep them hidden."

Colin opened his mouth, nearly on instinct, to argue.

"Don't sit there and tell me you don't have them," Nick said, his words precisely dismantling Colin's peace of mind. He reached into the bag under the table and tossed a glossy magazine between them.

Colin gazed down at the print version of himself, vapid-eyed and half-naked and no doubt photoshopped to hell. He didn't regret anything the way he regretted agreeing to pose for *Sports Illustrated*. And here it was again, rising Banquo-like just when he thought he'd left it behind for a *serious* sports career that had nothing to do with how hot his abs looked.

He wouldn't rise to the bait. He *wouldn't*.

"This," Nick said, jabbing a finger at the cover, apparently unconcerned at Colin's mutinous silence, "is what I'm talking about. You're like a cardboard cutout of a person on this."

"I'm pretty sure that's at least sixty percent excellent graphical manipulation," Colin said stiffly.

"Not just the picture," Nick corrected. "You never let anyone in. All anyone ever gets is this smooth, flawless persona. There's more to you than what meets the eye. And there's more to you than just football."

From a young age, Colin had prided himself on his self-control, but Nick was chipping away at it, one hefty chunk at a time.

"I'd think you might understand why I want to keep my personal life private."

Nick leaned forward. "Your personal life? That can stay private all you want it to. But you? Who you are? The essence of what makes Colin O'Connor tick? That's what I want."

Colin was speechless. He couldn't even form a sentence as fury raged through him.

"There," Nick concluded with a smirk in his direction. "Now you're pissed, and that's good. That's really good."

"Good?" Colin bit off.

Nick waved a lazy hand. "All that smooth, calm exterior, doesn't it get boring? Exhausting? Horribly tedious?"

"Not really, no." Colin fantasized about punching Nick in the face.

"Well it does for me," Nick retorted. "And that's really why I wanted to meet with you."

Colin leashed in his temper, *barely*. "So you could tell me I'm an emotionless, boring, cardboard puppet?"

Nick laughed, a startled, sudden sound. Like he hadn't expected the sarcasm to come from Colin's mouth. Which made sense because *Colin* hadn't expected it, either.

"No," Nick said, and now he *was* amused, "I'm not just going to need to be able to accompany you and meet with you a lot, I think we need to get a lot...closer than that. You'll block me out otherwise. I need to be with you."

Colin was pretty sure he was going to hate where this was going.

"I'm going to need to stay with you," Nick finally concluded, and yes, Colin really hated it. Big surprise.

"No," was all Colin said. With all the finality and certainty that he'd learned while dealing with slippery Mark.

"I don't have to tell you how important this is," Nick began, and Colin was way too familiar with this tactic, because Mark used it often. He shut it right down.

"Really?" he said, more sarcasm dripping from his words, *"you don't need to tell me that my coming out profile is important?"*

Nick laughed again, less surprise this time around. "What I mean to say is that this article is going to change people's lives. It would have changed my life."

Colin didn't know how he felt about Nick using his sexuality as a bargaining chip. He said so.

"It's the truth," Nick said, with very little guile. "I don't really want to burden you with my life history. That's not why we're here. But I guarantee an NFL quarterback, a Heisman-winning quarterback, admitting publicly he was queer, that would have changed the game for me."

"I'm not doing it for those reasons," Colin said. "I'm not doing it to be a pioneer or to change lives. I'm doing it for selfish reasons."

Colin took it back; Nick hadn't looked surprised before. Before he'd merely looked amused. Now he looked floored, but it still only took a moment for him to gather himself and cycle back to his point. Whatever Colin thought of him, Nick Wheeler was a formidable opponent if you decided to oppose him.

Colin didn't know if he should. Didn't know if he wanted to.

"Regardless of your reasons, I want to do the best job I can on this. I think you want that, too. Give me the chance to do that."

"You're asking?"

Nick had only demanded before, and now, he was asking. Colin told himself it didn't matter, but he knew he was lying.

Nick had the grace to look a tiny bit contrite. "It *is* your life," he said. "I can draw you a map, but you're in the driver's seat."

"And why can't you do what you need like this?" Colin asked, gesturing between them. "I'll answer anything within reason."

Nick grinned. "Is that a promise?" he retorted and then gave a sweeping gesture with his cardboard cup. "It's not about questions, it's about getting to know you in your natural habitat."

It didn't make sense, but Colin wanted to say yes anyway, even though the idea of this nosy reporter constantly digging made him queasy.

"Fine," Colin agreed. "But don't be irritated if I put you in the worst room of the house."

"Believe it or not, I think that might tell me a lot about you." He paused, his face growing softer, and there was a conspiratorial gleam in his gray eyes. They were even more hypnotic in person, and Colin had to force himself to look away. "Sort of like how you flirted with me during our first interview. That told me a lot about you, too. At least that you have good taste in flirting partners."

Colin gaped at him. "I didn't even *remember* you," he said, which might not have been the most tactful way to phrase the confession, but he was too surprised to do anything else.

"Wow…" Nick seemed equally surprised. "I…well, that does explain why you weren't as happy to see me as I thought you might be. I thought we'd had a really friendly chat the first time around."

It was obvious Nick was looking for an explanation, but Colin didn't feel obligated. So he just shrugged and said, "Sorry." He'd let Nick win a stay at his *house* for the profile. Let Nick dig a little harder and work up a sweat for this one.

It was the first time since he'd sat down that Nick looked uncomfortable. He shut his pad with a decisive click, and gathered it and the *Sports Illustrated* that Colin had spent the better part of their conversation attempting to ignore, and slid them into his leather satchel.

"I'll be in touch about when I'll be flying out," Nick said, clearly signaling that he was done. "If there's a better time for you, let me know, you have my email."

Colin remembered two-a-days in Alaska, where it was either cold or freeze-your-balls-off. He remembered the sickening pressure of his first college start at quarterback. He wasn't a stranger to dealing with unpleasant things if there was something bigger at stake. Even then, Colin nearly told Nick to forget it, that he couldn't let him in as deeply as he clearly wanted to go.

Nick was going to want the whole damn iceberg, and Colin had spent too long lurking underwater.

But then Nick paused, his hand on the table, his butt nearly out of his chair. He leaned over and caught Colin's gaze, those piercing gray eyes pinning Colin back to his seat. "I want you to know that you can trust me. With everything. But especially with this. I promise."

Then he was up and gone, leaving Colin with an indelible impression of a solemn sincerity that Colin hadn't even known Nick possessed, and a faint echo of butterfly wings in his stomach.

It turned out that a serious and engaged and *trustworthy* Nick Wheeler wasn't going to be someone that Colin could forget so easily.

"I thought you'd want to talk," Colin said again, barely holding back a whine, as he closed the car door behind him.

Jemma's head whipped around, her long, dark ponytail nearly decapitating him. "I can't believe you're pouting that I'm taking you to a sporting event," Jemma said darkly. "And a sporting event you can participate in. That's normally your jam."

The whole problem was that Colin wasn't *normal* right now. He was on edge and anxious over the upcoming profile and the publicity blitz of the next six months. He wanted to pour out all his fears and let Jemma laugh them off. He wanted Jemma to tell him that he wasn't being stupid or naïve or foolish to trust Nick to tell his story. He wanted Jemma to tell him that he wasn't any of those things for wanting to tell it at all.

Normal Colin would have been *thrilled* at the prospect of a team sporting event. He was an athletic nerd and he also really liked the challenge of winning something he'd never tried before. But today he wasn't himself, and admitting that was harder than he'd expected. Even to Jemma.

"You're gonna love it," Jemma said with finality. "Gabe and I play all the time, and I don't even hate it. So I can only imagine how you're gonna feel about it."

Jemma had asked him before he came to LA if he had a problem spending time with her and Gabe, her boyfriend of just over a year.

Colin hadn't prodded that particular wound in months, and to his surprise when he'd tested the scab, it had felt almost completely healed. He'd known he was getting over it. The very fact that he *wanted* to date again had been evidence enough, but when he'd pressed on it, imagining spending time with Jemma and Gabe, watching them be disgustingly in love, all he felt was a faint bit of regret at the loss of normalcy.

If Jemma had ever loved him instead of Gabe, he might not ever have to throw his closet doors wide open and let everyone see inside. It wasn't so much the idea of being honest that bothered him, but the painful loss of his privacy.

Colin could only imagine the amusement on Nick's face if he ever realized that the one woman Colin had ever remotely been interested in had never cared about him that way. It was a really good thing that he was almost certain that Nick, despite at one point being Jemma's boss and now her co-worker, had no clue.

"Isn't it sort of cheating to bring along a professional athlete to a pick-up game?"

Jemma shot him an evil smile. "Keep your hat on and don't take off your shirt and we'll be fine. You're my cousin, John Smith." She paused. "Besides, only half of this game is throwing. You're only a ringer for that half, really. I'm being downright generous to everyone else."

"Yes, I'm sure that everyone will be perfectly okay with that logic," Colin said with an eye roll as punctuation.

But Jemma had spotted Gabe, and it turned out that even after a year of dating, they were still really passionate greeters. The good news was, the longer and harder that wound got poked, the less it seemed to hurt.

"Yes, they're always like that."

Colin was almost a hundred percent sure he knew who had that deep, slightly sardonic voice. But he really didn't want to turn around to verify. Before he could, that voice spoke again.

"Let me guess, the hat is supposed to be a disguise, and Jemma thinks nobody will be pissed that she brought a Heisman-winning quarterback to a pick-up dodgeball game."

Colin turned around and tried really hard not to look sheepish.

Of course, Nick was standing there, dressed down in black basketball shorts and a ratty LA Clippers tank top. Colin tried not to check out his newly exposed and surprisingly toned arms and legs, and mostly failed. It was getting harder and harder not to notice how attractive Nick was, even as he continued to be a persistent pain in Colin's ass.

"It's not a good disguise?" he asked, even though he already knew the answer.

Nick shot him an incredulous look. "You're rather distinctive looking."

"I've never heard that before."

Nick smiled, and it was just as transformative as the first time Colin had witnessed it. It was becoming impossible to deny; Nick Wheeler was really, *really* hot. And Colin was afraid of what that might mean for him. "You should copyright that innocent expression. I know a lot of people who'd like to borrow it."

"Who said anything about borrowing?" Colin scoffed. "Mark would skin me alive for losing out on the revenue stream selling it could bring."

Every nerve ending on Colin's body pinged at Nick's slow, leisurely perusal. "I wouldn't blame him; it'd be worth a damn lot."

Colin might be able to claim he didn't remember them flirting before, but he wouldn't be able to do that again.

"You two done flirting yet?" Jemma piped up, and Colin experienced for the very first time what it might be like having her *only* as a friend. Apparently, she had passed right over supportive and landed right on annoying younger sister. She was a meddling pain, and he was going to accidentally send more than one ball her way tonight for that particular comment.

"Good to see you again," Colin said, extending a hand towards Gabe. He was still surprised that was the case. But Jemma was glowing and looked happier than he'd ever seen her.

Gabe could be scary intense and somewhat resembled a linebacker, but Colin had spent the last fifteen years of his life not being intimidated by men built like brick shithouses so it was easy enough to give his hand a firm shake and look him in the eye.

The type Colin seemed to have trouble with had a slimmer, rangier build, dark hair, and an unlimited supply of sarcastic retorts at his disposal.

"Let's get going," Jemma said, and led them all inside the facility.

Colin hung back, letting Jemma do the talking. Not surprisingly, Nick went up to the front desk with her, probably to make sure she didn't actually try to convince anyone that he was her cousin, John Smith.

"You realize you're about to get every ball in the place thrown at your head, right?" Gabe asked, his deep, rumbling voice threaded with amusement. "Most people never get a chance to hit an NFL quarterback."

Colin knew. He'd stopped going out for intramurals in college, and tried to stay away from the recreational sports leagues in Miami for this exact reason. Still, he was on edge today, and maybe a physical challenge, even with those gray eyes watching every move he made, might feel really good. Help him work through some of the jitters he couldn't shake.

"Maybe they'll all remember the last time I was here, when we played the Rams."

Gabe laughed. "You threw three touchdown passes. I don't think that's going to convince anyone to not throw a ball at your head."

"Oh, it might," Colin said with a shadow of Jemma's evil grin. "'Cause it definitely means I can hit them right back."

After a lot of hushed conversation at the check-in desk, Jemma and Nick finally returned with their marching orders.

"It's the local four on four tournament," Jemma said. "They're not thrilled that you're a professional athlete, Colin, but there aren't any rules against it, and this one," she nudged Nick with her shoulder, "threw a hissy fit. So, you're in. Just try to remember we're here to have fun." She rolled her eyes, which told Colin that last bit wasn't her contribution but management's.

When Colin glanced over at Nick in surprise, he shrugged. "We'd only have three without you, and we'd be disqualified."

"Well I'd better make sure to contribute, then." Colin might not have cornered the market on sarcastic remarks like Nick, but he could throw down if pushed.

"So how do we play?" Colin asked, as Jemma led them towards a big, open room. To his surprise, everyone seemed to be removing their...shoes?

"We play on a big trampoline," Gabe explained. "You've got to throw and hit the opposing players with the balls without being hit yourself. Last team standing wins. Best out of three moves on to the next round."

"Sounds simple enough."

Jemma laughed. "Simple doesn't always mean easy."

The first thing Colin had to figure out was how to most efficiently move on the trampoline. He hadn't been on a trampoline since he was a kid. Nick, Gabe, and even Jemma moved with the confidence of experience, while Colin constantly seemed to misjudge the elasticity of their playing surface.

Still, Colin thought he had enough raw athletic ability and learned skill to compensate for his lack of trampoline experience.

He didn't.

Before the first match started, Jemma kindly suggested since he was new at this, he might hang back as a second wave, and let Nick and Gabe move for the balls.

"Jemma," Colin told her seriously, "I won the Heisman Trophy. I'm not letting someone else take the lead here." He didn't usually bring up the award as a justification for anything, but Nick was smirking in the corner, and he'd already watched him nearly fall over about ten times just during their warm-up. Colin wasn't used to failing, and he wasn't going to give up. Especially now. He fully intended to wipe that infuriating smirk right off Nick's too-hand-some face.

"Fine," Jemma said.

It was never a good sign when Jemma whipped out the Fine Card. This was no exception.

When the whistle blew, Colin moved as quickly as he could, using the long, certain strides he'd practiced for so many years as a quarterback. And fell right on his ass, only to get drilled, with purpose, on the head by a big, red, bouncy ball.

The other team cheered, and he had to get up off the trampoline, not the easiest task, and hobble off with his dignity in shreds to the sidelines, the *first* person on their team knocked out. Even before *Jemma*, who refused to claim any athletic ability whatsoever.

On the sideline, Colin watched his other three teammates battle for their lives. Gabe, for all his size, was aggressive but surprisingly graceful. He also had excellent aim. As Colin had expected, Jemma wasn't the best athlete on the court, but she was smart and had the most beautiful pump-fake he'd ever seen, fooling every member of the opposing team at least once as the game progressed.

And Nick? Nick moved like he'd been *born* on a trampoline. If Gabe was graceful, then Nick was a dancer. A particularly good one. He snaked and jumped and slid around the balls, his body contorting and flexing around every ball thrown his direction.

Not surprisingly, he was the last one standing.

High fives all around and then Nick moved in his direction. "It's harder than it looks," he said, not even the tiniest bit winded, despite running around a trampoline for ten high-impact minutes.

"Right," Colin retorted.

Nick held up his hands. "I was trying to be nice. Would you like advice or would you prefer to salvage your ego in private?"

Colin wasn't stupid. He hadn't gotten where he was by not listening to people. "I'd love some advice."

"Keep it small. Every tiny movement," Nick said, holding up his fingers only an inch apart, "becomes *big*."

Colin chuckled. "Which is why my footwork didn't work."

"Forget about being a football player and you might be okay."

"He can't," Jemma piped in. "He actually just...*can't*."

Jemma wasn't wrong. It was hard to forget about so many ingrained habits and a thousand tiny details that assaulted him every time he stepped onto a field. They defined who he was. Without them, maybe he really was just a great pair of abs.

The next match, he listened and hung back. But like Gabe had predicted, he was a main target, even to the other team's detriment at points.

At least this round he lasted longer than ten seconds. He even lasted long enough to remind the other team that he'd won a National Championship with his throwing arm. The balls were bigger and squishier to throw than a football, but the same fundamentals applied.

Gabe tried to sacrifice himself to save Jemma, getting outed with a particularly well-thrown ball he couldn't evade.

That left just Colin and Nick. They exchanged a look, and Colin made a particularly showy move to try to dive for a ball out of range. Nick took advantage of the rest of the balls being aimed at Colin's head to finish off the rest of the other team.

"I like it," Nick said, smacking Colin's hand in a quick high five. "You're sneaky."

Nick's eyes were lit up with excitement for their win. He looked too good—a little flushed, hair mussed, those tan biceps sticking out of his tank. It really was an excellent look, and Colin couldn't remember the last time he'd felt so attracted to someone.

Colin saw a flash of Jemma's long, dark ponytail out of the corner of his eye and had a sudden, heart-stopping realization who it was exactly that he'd last been so attracted to.

Great.

Colin rolled his eyes. "Everyone forgets that quarterback is pretty much the sneakiest position on the field. I've got sneaky in my blood."

"Not just a pretty cover model, then." Nick gave him another one of those thoughtful perusals and the blood Colin had just been bragging about fizzed in his veins.

"I'm going to personally burn your *Sports Illustrated*," Colin said without heat. They were definitely flirting; the question was *why*. Was this just what Nick did? Or did it actually mean something? And what were they going to do together, living in the same house? Flirt until Colin wanted to bang his head against the wall?

"That," Nick said, taking a long sip of water, "implies that I only have one copy."

No, they were apparently going to flirt until Colin wanted to bang *Nick* against a wall.

Colin would have been lying if he'd claimed later he didn't try to impress Nick at least a little during their next few matches. And that every time he made a good move or threw another dart of a pass to eliminate an opposing player, that Nick's responsive grin didn't set him alight a little bit more.

They won the tournament and Colin pacified the dirty looks thrown their direction by promising to treat everyone to beers at the nearby bar—a suggestion that Jemma had whispered in his ear during their last break.

The truth was, he'd done more to hurt their team than help it, but he still felt good. *Alive.* The way he did after a good workout. Especially if that good workout had a cute boy to make eyes at.

"You're *not* subtle, by the way," Jemma hissed at him as they made their way to their car.

"I don't know what you mean," Colin protested.

"You flirt like a sledgehammer."

"There's nothing wrong with the obvious approach," Colin said. In any case, he preferred it, because then there was no question of misinterpreting someone's signals. And he'd never done enough flirting to be any good anyway.

Jemma shot him a reproachful look as she slid into the driver's seat.

"Who normally plays with you guys?" he asked, because anything was better than being lectured by Jemma about his flirting technique.

"Gabe's partner. But he was shot a few months ago, and he's still recovering."

"Oh, god," Colin said. Because what else could you say to that? He didn't miss the way Jemma's hands tightened on the wheel, knuckles going white, as they pulled out of the parking lot.

"You must worry about him a lot," Colin continued.

Jemma nodded.

And then it was her turn to change the subject. "Are *you* worried about anything?"

Colin nearly laughed over how poorly she executed the subject change. "If you want to ask if I'm nervous about coming out, then yeah, of course, a little. I think it'd be easier if I could just do it. Instead, there's like six months of preparation and laying groundwork and so many interminable steps in-between."

"Including Nick." Jemma's voice was sly.

"I really wanted it to be you, you know," Colin pointed out.

"Of course, you did. But I would have bungled it. We're too close. I love you too much. I'd have protected you, not exposed you."

Colin hated that he was beginning to see Nick was right. But he argued anyway, because he was still having trouble with the idea he'd lost his safety net. "Aren't I *supposed* to be protected from exposure?"

Jemma's glance over was painfully sympathetic. "Sort of the whole point of this article is exposure. So, no. And you're normally such a closed book. Too closed. Nick will be good for you. He'll pry you right open."

"That doesn't sound very appealing." Colin made a face.

Jemma pulled into a spot on the street and turned off the car. She turned to face him, her expression serious. "It won't be. It *isn't*. And you should remember how much you like him today in a few months when he's grilling you. Because you might not like him so much then."

"He's asked me to trust him."

"Is that a question?" Jemma asked quietly.

Colin nodded.

Jemma leaned back in the seat and held his gaze. "He's a great reporter. One of the best journalists I've ever met. I didn't like him very much at first, but he's grown on me. And he's been waiting for your story for a long time."

"My story?"

"Yeah," Jemma said, gathering her purse, and opening her door to get out of the car, "he's always wanted a chance to represent one of his own. Not a lot of you out in the open in the sports world."

Colin couldn't get Jemma's words out of his head. He'd felt alone for so long that it had never occurred to him that he was only one of many in a similar situation. At some point in his life, Nick would have had to make the decision to tell people that he wasn't straight. Just like Colin had. The thought shouldn't have been revolutionary, but it shifted his entire perspective enough that it was hard to distrust Nick on principle anymore.

He'd done this, too.

Colin thought back to that moment during the conference call when Nick had laid out his sexuality bluntly. He'd misunderstood and only thought it was a method to soften him up. But it was one man saying to another: *I understand.*

And he'd tried to tell Colin the day before, too, when they'd met for coffee. Nick had said, *"It would have changed my life,"* and asked him to trust him nearly in the same breath.

Of course, if he'd actually *said* these things, had said straightforwardly and clearly, *I know what you're feeling because I've felt it, too,* Colin might have understood sooner.

He'd been nursing a single beer the whole evening, spending more time in the corner alone than Mark would have been happy with—than even *Jemma* was happy with. But he glanced up now, and he was looking for only one person.

Nick was standing by Gabe, companionably sharing space and exchanging a few words. He looked relaxed, smiles coming easily, Gabe even getting a laugh out of him once.

Like the rest of the decisions he'd made about coming out, he made this one fast, too. Sliding out of the booth, Colin picked up his empty beer and approached Nick and Gabe.

Gabe didn't look particularly surprised to see him; Nick, on the other hand, looked astonished.

"I thought you'd grown into the table over there and by the end of the night, we'd have to chip you out with a dull steak knife," Nick said, and unlike the rest of his remarks, this one didn't bother Colin because he *got it.*

While Colin buried his personality behind walls of placid smiles and bland remarks, Nick fought with his smart mouth. And the smarter the remark, the more nervous he actually was.

It was like figuring out a particularly tricky defense; the brilliant flash of evading their clutches for the first time only to throw a long ball to his favorite receiver.

"Can I get either of you anything?"

Gabe smiled and shook his head. "I'm going to go find Jemma."

Colin caught the dark look Nick shot Gabe as he turned to go look for his girlfriend, but Gabe merely smirked and kept going.

Tipping his empty bottle towards Nick's equally empty glass, he asked, "What can I get for you?"

Nick stared at him for a long moment. "Vodka soda," he finally said.

Colin plucked the glass from his hand, trying to ignore the brush of their fingertips. One single touch and...a spark. As he approached the bar, Colin wasn't sure whether he was excited or terrified that all it took was one.

By the time he returned to Nick with their drinks, Nick had re-arranged his face into his typical, *I'm too cool for this* expression.

Colin hated that expression. He was pretty sure he knew why it existed now, but that didn't mean he liked it any more than he had before. In fact, discovering the reason for it made him all the more determined to chase it away.

"Tell me how you got into ultimate dodgeball," Colin said. Borrowing a page out of Nick's own book, he didn't phrase it as a question.

"I got stabbed in the stomach. My physical therapist recom-mended it as part of my therapy."

It turned out that understanding some of what made Nick tick didn't quite prepare Colin for his outrageously blunt deliv-ery.

"You were *stabbed?*"

Nick shrugged, like people got stabbed every day—which they *did,* but not people Colin knew. Not city boys like Nick, who wore skinny pants and probably had a pair of hipster, thick-framed glasses hidden away in his bedside table.

"You're going to have to explain," Colin continued. "I'm sorry, but you can't just say, *I was stabbed,* and expect me not to ask."

Nick glanced down, studying the liquid in his glass. He had long, dark eyelashes, and Colin hated how exquisite they were against his olive skin. He didn't want to be so attracted to Nick because that attraction made things infinitely complicated.

"To be honest, I thought you knew. I thought Jemma told you. It was why she ended up in Rio. I had to go home. I've always been...aggressively confident, let's say, and that finally caught up with me."

Jemma's trip to Rio for the Olympics Games. Well that *did* make sense, because that was when Jemma had severed their *will we or won't we* back and forth once and for all, and had sent him an email telling him she needed to take a break from their friendship.

He'd known he'd needed to get over her, but even being three thousand miles away in Miami hadn't been enough. It had taken Jemma being the bigger person and being painfully honest.

But they hadn't really been speaking during that time, and so he hadn't realized that Jemma's Rio trip had coincided with something happening to Nick.

"I didn't know, actually," Colin admitted softly. "She didn't tell me. We weren't really on speaking terms for a while."

"Ah, well, that explains a lot."

If Nick knew why that had changed; why by the time Colin was in LA to play the Rams in the preseason that things had changed yet again, he didn't say a word. Didn't give one hint that he knew that the reason Jemma had felt safer resuming her friendship with Colin was because she'd fallen in love with someone else.

All Colin remembered from that week was every minute of the football game. He could replay every down, perfectly, from memory. He couldn't remember anything else. Every ounce of what he'd had left after losing Jemma had gone into that game, and then he'd gone home to lick his wounds.

Maybe he'd flirted with Nick in the interview. If Nick looked even remotely as good then as he did now, he'd have noticed. Maybe he'd even been torn up enough to try to make himself feel better with a few flirty comments.

But he'd buried all the pain so deep that he wasn't even sure Jemma had noticed. Which had been the point.

"So you got Jemma and Gabe into ultimate dodgeball." Colin steered the conversation back to safer ground. He didn't want to revisit those horrible weeks, and he had a feeling, from the pained shadow in Nick's eyes, he didn't, either. "I'm surprised she agreed to play."

Nick shot him a long, pointed look. "When she doesn't worry about winning, she's got some great natural instincts."

Colin didn't need an explanation to know what Nick was really saying. Yes, he could be a competitive asshole. Get him on a field and he'd absolutely become a jerk about winning. That much was true. That was also why he had a Heisman Trophy and a National Championship and an NFL Rookie of the Year award.

"Jemma did warn you," Colin said, "I can't turn it off."

"Football or the need to win?"

"Your mistake is thinking they aren't the same."

Nick looked pensive as he took a long sip of his drink. "An entire life dedicated to succeeding at a single sport...I can see how the two might become intertwined."

"When you grow up with nothing, it's so easy for something to become everything."

"Can I quote you on that?" Nick's eyes gleamed.

Colin shrugged. He was trying to be more transparent. It wasn't easy, but he had made the decision to make an attempt every time they talked.

"Sure. You said you wanted to know about me."

"I did. I do." It was so hard to remember in that moment that Nick meant *for the article* and not because he just wanted to *know* Colin.

They'd swayed half a foot closer, which Colin kept telling himself was because of the noise in the bar, but he had a feeling it had nothing to do with that and everything to do with the flare of attraction between them.

"You asked me to trust you," Colin said softly.

Nick nodded.

"Was it easy for you?" he asked.

Nick's gaze sharpened. "Coming out? No, it was hard as hell and continues to be difficult at times, even today. But it does get easier. That much isn't a lie."

Colin let out his breath. "I misjudged you, I'm sorry."

"I wish...I wish I could make this easier on you, I do. But it's going to be fucking hard." Nick's voice grew rougher at the end, and for a split second, Colin thought he saw all the emotion he strived to bury, shining through in his eyes.

"I'm tough."

Nick shook his head. "Nobody is ever tough enough."

Colin wondered if Nick was trying to scare him. But that didn't make any sense. He was supposed to be preparing him and positioning him so it wasn't tough. So that he came out under the best possible circumstances. Colin pushed down the tendril of fear, and laughed.

"I'm the most stubborn person you'll probably ever meet. I can handle this."

The only thing Colin didn't feel certain about handling was Nick. How were they going to work so closely together and *live* together and not act on any of the tension that crackled between them? And if they *did*, what would that even mean? Colin's fingers tightened around the neck of his beer bottle.

"If only the legions of Colin O'Connor lovers knew how obnoxiously cocky you are, it might dull your Disney prince shine a bit."

"I think there might have been a compliment in there," Colin teased back.

Nick's responding grin was bright and real. "Only the best, from me to you."

Chapter Three

Even for a lifetime Californian, Miami was hot.

It was still only March, but Nick felt the skin under his collar grow damp with sweat as he waited under a miserly patch of shade for his pickup.

He'd emailed Colin last week with his flight info, and unsurprisingly, Colin had been stingy with his response. "Will pick you up," was all he'd said.

Nick wasn't stupid enough to expect heart-to-hearts or even an acknowledgement that the ice between them had begun to thaw in LA. He'd told himself not to expect it, even as he annoyingly couldn't stop thinking about the possibility of becoming friendly with Colin O'Connor.

For a long time, he'd waited inside near the baggage claim, expecting one of those blank-faced drivers to eventually hold up a sign with his name on it. But nobody had, and he'd finally texted the number he had for Colin in exasperation.

The text back had read: "Running late. Meet you outside in Arrivals."

It sounded like Colin had retreated back to the East Coast, spent the last two weeks overthinking those few electric moments that had passed between them, and had retrenched even further back. Nick gritted his teeth and tried not to imagine the worst.

He didn't even know what the worst was, but it probably entailed starting over from square one. The worst probably also meant that even the good word he'd begged for from Jemma would ultimately be meaningless.

Nick had just about given up and was about to track down an Uber, like he'd initially intended, when a sleek, black Audi R8 pulled up smoothly to the curb.

Even for a Californian used to excess, it was a fucking ridiculous car.

The driver's window rolled down, and Nick, caught gaping, was faced with Colin, *that asshole.*

"What are you doing?" Nick nearly yelled. "Don't you have people you can send? You're a millionaire!"

Colin just shrugged. "I like driving," he said unapologetically. "I'll pop the trunk. It's sort of small, though."

Nick stared as he rolled the window back up. He wasn't sure if he should be flattered or if this was the evidence he needed to confirm Colin was the most eccentric player in the National Football League.

He'd heard some weird shit about some of the linemen for Minnesota. But even those guys would have sent someone to the airport to pick up a reporter.

Nick rolled his suitcase around towards the back of the car and peered in the trunk. It was going to be a tight fit. Luckily, his laptop bag was small and he could carry that on his lap.

He shut the trunk lid a fraction harder than entirely necessary, and even though he lectured himself to stay calm as he approached the passenger side door, it didn't work very well.

He opened the door. The faint smell of expensive cologne and even more expensive leather floated out in a gust of cool air. Nick couldn't contain his glare as he slid into the seat.

"You're late, asshole," he grumbled.

"I told you, there was traffic," Colin said.

Nick knew he was in a bad place when the idea that Colin O'Connor was late and therefore human and not a robot made him gleeful.

"You," he finally ground out as Colin smoothly pulled out onto the freeway, "really are an asshole."

"You've called me that twice now," Colin said. He didn't sound particularly perturbed. In fact, he sounded rather gleeful himself. Nick's mood darkened. "I thought you'd be happier to see me." The smile Colin shot his way was just flirtatious enough to baffle Nick.

"It's official. You are definitely the most eccentric player in the NFL."

Colin's expression reflected zero surprise. "I think I'm supposed to be. I'm practically from another country, after all."

He drove well—fast but capably, shifting between lanes smoothly without the sort of aggressive *braggadocio* that Nick hated. He relaxed into the seat and the banter that came way too easily.

"You're from Alaska. It's not exactly another planet."

"Clearly, you've never been to Alaska," Colin retorted.

"Guilty as charged."

They drove in silence for a minute, and then another, Miami flashing by the tinted windows. "I live on an island on the edge of South Beach," Colin said. "Really private."

None of this was surprising; it had been an easy conclusion to come to that while most celebrities appreciated privacy and were willing to spend a lot of their money to obtain it, for Colin it was an obsession.

"Did you really not expect me to pick you up?" Colin asked.

Nick made a disbelieving noise. "Do you not have a PA? A hired car service?"

"Both." Colin had the nerve to blush under his tan. "But it always seemed so rude to me. You're not baggage to be collected. You're here to see me. You're going to stay with me. The least I can do is to pick you up from the airport."

"You hate reporters," Nick said slowly.

"And yet...you're still not baggage," Colin said. He paused. "And I don't *hate* them. I...their methods bother me sometimes. I don't usually trust them. But I don't hate them." Colin shot him a quick, pleading look, and Nick would have to be a hell of a lot dumber to not know what that look meant.

Or what it *could* mean, if Nick decided to forget all the rules he'd set for himself when he'd first started his career.

Don't sleep with the athletes. Don't like the athletes. Don't fall for the athletes.

It had never been particularly hard to keep them, but Nick had a feeling he was about to be tested.

Nick had known he was in trouble since Colin had first stepped off that elevator into the *Five Points* office looking even hotter than his *Sports Illustrated* cover. Since LA, Nick had been walking a very fine line between winning Colin's trust and giving his own away.

With a lot of sports stars he'd interviewed, Nick had been perfectly able to maintain a very professional distance, even while digging up all the dirt he could.

It was something he'd gotten very, very good at.

The problem was that Colin was smarter than that, and had assumed a position of *pay to play*. Colin wasn't going to give without something in return. The invaluable barrier he'd been hiding behind, constructed with all those sarcastic quips he loved, was never going to work with Colin. He knew this was personal for Nick, and he wanted a front row seat to all the bruises.

Nick wanted to tell Colin, *I hope you more than don't hate me.* But even if what crackled between them eventually flared into more, he needed to postpone the inevitable. Instead he said, "Hate the game, not the player."

Colin shook his head, a chagrined but hopelessly amused smile blooming on his face. "And people say I'm a dork."

"You *are* a dork," Nick said. He couldn't tell Colin that he had more integrity in his pinkie finger than most big shot NFL players had in their whole bodies.

Shaking everybody's hand as soon as he entered a room. Holding doors open for women. Once leaving a sideline interview to find an umbrella for Erin Andrews. Speaking about *everyone* with respect, and expecting respect in return or he would immediately cut the interview off. Insisting on picking up a reporter from the airport himself. All of this combined to make Colin O'Connor who he was in the public eye, and while many might claim he wasn't genuine, Nick thought they couldn't have actually met Colin and believed that. While closed off and intensely private, he still radiated sincerity.

He didn't want a rap career. He didn't want his own clothing line. He didn't want to get paid for attending any number of club openings. He didn't want a chain of groupies. He wanted to play football and go home to a simple life. And to so many who didn't understand, it looked old fashioned or dorky, but Nick had long believed it made him unique and authentic.

And that was the side of Colin O'Connor Nick was so desperate to show people.

"I wish more people were dorks," Nick added, and Colin laughed.

"If everyone was boring like me, you wouldn't have anything to write about."

Colin was wrong; if everyone was boring like him, Nick would have more opportunities to write about the things that actually mattered.

"You might not hate the media, but you don't like us, either," Nick pointed out. He was afraid if he started being honest, he wouldn't know where to draw the line. Everything out of his mouth felt dangerous, like he was creating that distant inevitability one word at a time.

Colin pulled off the freeway, and turned down a narrow street that ended in an even narrower bridge. At the entrance to the bridge, there was a gate, and a security kiosk. A guard stood in it, stoic and unsurprised at seeing the Audi pull up. But Colin still reached into the center console and pulled out a key card. He slid it into the slot and the gate began to rise.

"A guard *and* a security system?" Nick asked with a raised eyebrow as they began to cross the bridge. "I have to tell you, there aren't that many people in the world who look like you."

Colin shrugged. "I like my privacy." He paused. "Also, this is my island. I don't want anyone on it who doesn't belong."

Oh, god. They were going to be all alone on a whole tropical island and Nick was a few more soulful, heated looks from ripping Colin's shirt off. This wouldn't end badly *at all.*

Despite the excellent air conditioning, Nick felt himself begin to sweat again. "Are you saying I belong?"

It slipped out before Nick could stop it, a single question undoing everything he hadn't said up until this moment. Colin pulled around a long, circular driveway, and came to a stop in front of a small modern house tucked into the tropical foliage.

Key word: *small.* Nick was basically fucked.

"Yes," Colin said softly and with a ringing sincerity that made Nick want to jump out of the car and run back to the mainland.

It was the only way he'd be safe.

Colin got out of the car and Nick hesitated, slowly gathering up his laptop bag. He heard the trunk open and knew he had to get out of the car.

He'd made his career by not playing things safe. He'd always taken the harder road, the road that needed a path hacked through it with a machete and a shirtless Indiana Jones. But after Rio, he'd gotten scared and pulled his reckless tendencies in tight. It was a normal reaction, the therapist they'd made him see for PTSD had insisted, reminding him that he'd almost died.

Nick wasn't going to die here. But somehow, Colin O'Connor felt even more dangerous than that knife sticking out of his gut in that Rio *favela*.

"Get it together," Nick told himself quietly and firmly. He was being an overdramatic asshole.

He opened the door and plastered on a smirk.

"Your own island, O'Connor?"

Colin blushed. "I like the privacy."

"So you've said," Nick said as they climbed the wide steps that led to the front door.

Colin's house might have been small, but even if it hadn't been built on a private island, it still wouldn't have been affordable. The floor plan was almost completely open, with movable glass partitions dividing the rooms, and the inside from the outside. Nick followed Colin from the entry into a huge great room with the kitchen to the right. A single leather couch broke the expanse of the wide plank flooring. Nick opened his mouth to comment on the lack of furniture, but the view out the entirely open back expanse of the house shut him up.

Colin had managed to carve out a view of sky and sea. No people, no houses, not a single living being except for a seagull to break the impact.

You looked out this view and forgot that Miami, home to half a million people in its city limits, was only a few miles away.

Colin's voice was soft behind him. "It's something, isn't it?"

Nick had never questioned whether he'd been right to demand he stay at Colin's house. He'd been driven by a need to get *closer,* to know him enough that the profile became the single defining moment in Colin O'Connor's media history. But if he'd known this was how Colin wanted to live, he might have hesitated.

"We're not used to so many people in Alaska," Colin continued quietly. "I'm not used to walking out in my backyard and seeing three other houses. I…I didn't like it. It felt like everyone was always staring."

It was like he had no clue how he drew people's attention. How singularly attractive he was. "They probably were." Nick had a strong will, and he still had to fight the compulsion to look and *keep* looking.

"I'll show you the rest of the house," Colin said and Nick followed wordlessly.

The kitchen was ultra-simplistic, a single wall of cupboards, everything including the fridge hidden by a richly grained wood that Nick wanted to reach out and touch. A glass-fronted wine storage unit was the only punctuation, and it glowed softly.

Colin showed him a den, a single large desk with laptop computer on it. It also looked out onto the ocean, a single, glass sliding door opening it to the outside. "This is so cool," Colin said. "The door actually slides into the house." He demonstrated how the glass disappeared into wall, like the world's fanciest pocket door.

"You must have driven your contractor mad," Nick said as they walked up the stairs. "I bet you wanted him to add every fancy gadget you could get your hands on."

Colin paused and Nick had to draw up to avoid running right into him. Under different circumstances, he wouldn't have minded being plastered to Colin's back, but with every moment a growing temptation, he needed to keep his distance. "How did you know I built this house?" Colin asked, brows drawing together. Probably because this was supposed to be some sort of super-secret thing.

Nick shrugged. "It's obvious. It belongs to you."

The shadowed corner brought out the darkness in Colin's blue eyes. "You don't know me that well."

Nick considered lying for a split second. It wouldn't be hard; he was a good liar and he didn't think Colin was particularly adept at picking out truth from fiction. But something, maybe the loneliness and the distrust still lingering in his expression, kept Nick honest.

"I'm growing to. This house...it's like finally getting into the game after a long time on the sidelines."

"I thought maybe my contractor blabbed," Colin said, turning away before Nick could see his reaction. He felt an irrational need to reach out a hand and pull him back, let Nick see his face. One of Colin's outer walls had begun to crumble and Nick's need to see inside was growing even fiercer.

"Your secrets are safe with me," Nick said. Would the compulsion to convince Colin to trust him ever weaken?

"Except one," Colin retorted, like it was *Nick's* decision to share Colin's sexuality with the world. Nick inwardly grumbled and wondered how they were supposed to make it through the next three weeks without killing or fucking each other.

Colin perfunctorily shared the other two bedrooms, and told Nick that he could pick either one. "They're nearly the same," he said, though that was not entirely true.

One was a lot nearer the main bedroom that they were approaching now. The other was on the other end of the house.

The room was a vast swath of nearly empty space dominated by a huge raft of a bed. The entire fourth wall was open to the outside, with a folding glass door to protect it from the elements. A deck with a glass railing gave an unobstructed view of the ocean.

Nick shoved his hands in his pockets and avoided looking at the bed. He wandered out onto the balcony before he lost the fight with himself.

From this vantage point, he could see the lower patio and the pool. "It's an incredible house," he told Colin.

"I'm luckier than most," Colin agreed.

So many of the athletes Nick had interviewed over the years had people overflowing out of their houses. A constant barrage of needs and wants and never a moment where they could be alone.

Colin had set himself up on this island and had barricaded himself in a place where he was completely alone.

It was such a stark contrast, and Nick wasn't even sure Colin realized it.

Sometimes what you thought you wanted wasn't what you really needed.

Nick wasn't even sure that someone besides him had even been in this house. There was a complete lack of evidence that anybody else had even been here. "I thought you said you had a PA," Nick said because he realized he'd not seen any evidence of one.

"I do," Colin replied sheepishly. "Lindsay. She...I don't need her much. She mostly just arranges things for me. I don't really need her here."

Nick shook his head slowly. "You're the strangest celebrity athlete I've ever met."

"Right, well, probably because I don't think of myself as a celebrity. I'm just a football player."

Colin O'Connor wasn't ever going to be *just* a football player, but Nick let him keep that fairy tale. "Have you had Jemma out here?" He knew she hadn't been here, but it was worth asking to find out if Colin volunteered a reason.

"The house was just finished a few months ago," Colin said casually, like it wasn't a huge fat excuse. "And she's so busy."

"Right."

If Colin knew he'd given himself away, he wasn't obvious about it. Which didn't mean much, since he had a strong ability to batten down his emotions and refuse to give anything away.

"Well, I'll let you get settled in. What do you want to do for dinner?"

Nick had to remind himself that Colin wasn't *really* asking him, and that he wasn't really supposed to answer.

Forcing himself to shrug was tougher than it should have been. Definitely tougher than it had ever been before with all the other athletes he'd interviewed.

"Oh, that's right," Colin answered his own question. "I'm supposed to do *whatever I would normally do.*"

"So what would you normally do?"

Colin flushed. "It...it's boring. I like a routine."

Nick wished he found him a little more boring. "I spent a few weeks with Tom Brady once. Trust me, the routine's fine."

"Okay, well, I cook dinner and usually watch some TV."

"Then that's what we'll do."

"Okay, I'll let you know when dinner's ready."

And Colin just *left him* standing on the incredible terrace off his bedroom. Only when Nick was sure he heard Colin's steps on the stairs did he dare turn around and let the bed re-enter his field of vision.

"Yeah," he said out loud, "that's a big *nope.*"

He went back down the hallway and gave each guest bedroom a second glance.

It was just as he'd thought; the sheets and towels in both were clearly brand new, never used. They'd been washed once to take off the packaging smell, but that was it.

It shouldn't have mattered, but somehow that fact pushed Nick right over the edge and when he came back upstairs with his bags, he picked the room kitty-corner from the door to the main bedroom.

He unpacked. The dresser and closet weren't empty, but had a minimum of basic wardrobe requirements in a variety of sizes. Same for the bathroom; there was a fully stocked selection of toiletries in the cupboard under the sink. First evidence he'd come across that Colin's PA was more than a figment of his imagination.

There was a narrow desk in the bedroom, and Nick pulled his laptop from the bag and booted up. He opened the document he'd started when he'd first met Colin.

He liked to write down stream of consciousness observations and notes as they happened when he was working on a profile. He didn't usually write the article itself until much later, using the notes he'd already taken.

Nick ignored the words he'd already written and started a fresh paragraph with today's date as the heading.

He tried to be completely, bluntly honest in these observations. Never before had he worried about inserting himself into them. But he'd had trouble with the notes for Colin from day one.

Nick didn't have to look back to the beginning of the document to see the first thing he'd written about Colin O'Connor.

His eyes are too blue and his smile isn't honest enough.

Like it even mattered how blue his eyes were.

It shouldn't. *It didn't.*

Nick's fingers hovered over the keys and tried to marshal the timeline of events in his mind, remembering his personal observations but keeping it *impersonal.*

After three attempts, each worse than the last, Nick leaned back in the chair and stared at the ceiling.

It wasn't as if these notes were ever going to be seen by anybody but him. Did it really matter if he inserted himself into them? Forcing himself to do something that felt unnatural wouldn't change the way he was beginning to feel. Making writing his notes easier wouldn't change anything, except his frustration level.

It still felt wrong to break the rule; like a backslide into dangerous and unknown territory. But when he returned to the keyboard, restriction lifted, the words flowed easily and quickly, and he was able to type up today's observations in only a matter of minutes.

He didn't read through them, because *knowing* he was writing about both Colin and himself and how they intersected was one thing, and *reading it* were two different things.

The truth was, it was denial, but so far it was a method that was working, so he closed the document and then his laptop. He went back in the bathroom and checked his hair. It looked messy from the cross-country plane trip, but then the bedhead look was popular, right? He hesitated before forcing his hand down. He wasn't going to fuck with it, because he wasn't going to acknowledge he wanted to look good for Colin.

He didn't change his t-shirt, either, after a good minute debating in front of the dresser.

Colin could have him, travel smell and all.

After putting it off as long as possible, Nick wandered back down the stairs.

Dusk had fallen, and Colin had the living room doors wide open into the balmy evening. The muted, recessed lighting on the terrace shone on his hair, dipping the edges into gold. Music played lowly over hidden speakers. At the center of it stood Colin at a grill built into the side of the patio, flipping their dinner.

Nick's throat went a little dry. Maybe this was what he did for himself every night, but all the scene needed was a partner to walk into it, move behind Colin and press their lips to the strong, tanned curve of his neck.

Tasting salt, Nick swallowed hard.

Colin turned, spatula in one hand glinting off the lights. "Hope you like chicken," he said, with a wider, freer smile than Nick remembered. Like being here in his sanctuary unwound him, pared him back to the essentials.

"Uh, yeah, chicken's great."

"I realized when I was at the store today, I forgot to ask you if you had any dietary restrictions."

"You went to the store?"

Colin shot him a funny look. "Yeah, it's this great place, where you can buy all sorts of food to eat."

"No, I mean, *you* went to the store." Nick paused. "Like you, yourself. And not your PA."

"It seems really stupid to have Lindsay do all these things for me when I'm perfectly capable of doing them myself." Still, it seemed Colin was aware of how different that attitude was, because he suddenly looked a little uncomfortable and Nick felt bad he'd pointed it out. He hadn't meant to, it'd just sort of popped out because in all his years of interacting with athletes, every single one with a profile similar to Colin's used the hell out of their PA.

They didn't go grocery shopping. Not on a regular basis. Definitely not just because they *could*.

"Well, you cook, so I'm impressed right off." Nick changed the subject and tried to ignore the pulse of guilt that he'd spent nearly his whole time here telling Colin how weird he was.

"It's just grilled chicken. Simple marinade. I had to learn to feed myself in college. It was either that or starve."

Nick leaned against a patio table. "I'm sure you could've found some alternatives."

"Probably." Colin didn't need to add that neither forcibly conscripting underclassmen into feeding him or begging football groupies to bring him meals were something he'd have done. That much went without saying, considering he had an employee who he was *paying* to run errands for him, and he still did all them himself.

"Not your style, I know," Nick responded dryly. "I'm beginning to discover that."

Colin loaded the chicken onto a platter and turned off the grill.

"Is that so wrong?" he demanded as they walked into the house. "Do people really want some sort of ego-maniac caveman? Because, it's not just you, every time I turn around, that's what people not only expect, but what they're looking for."

Colin marched over to the coffee table in front of the sofa and that's when Nick noticed that he'd set two places there. Clearly taking Nick's stricture to do whatever he normally did to heart. Dumping chicken onto each plate, he stalked back to the kitchen and yanked open the fridge. Nick had seen him annoyed before this moment, simmering away inside, but now he seemed pissed. Nick half-expected to see the tips of his hair catch fire and his eyes to raze a path in their wake.

Nick stayed wisely silent and settled down on the deep leather couch. There was a salad on each plate, full of neatly chopped vegetables, and the chicken, which smelled really good. Colin flopped down on the couch and handed Nick a beer. Nick pretended not to notice when their thighs brushed together. It was a comfortable couch and *big*, but Colin was big, too.

The truth was, it didn't seem quite big enough.

"You can tell me to shut the hell up," he said wryly, his anger already cooling to a simmer.

"Considering why I'm here, that seems a counter-intuitive choice," Nick pointed out.

They ate in silence for awhile. The food was delicious, but then Nick wasn't surprised. Colin wanted to be good at everything and Nick imagined that not much stopped him from achieving that goal.

"What do you think?" Colin asked.

"It's all really good," Nick said, gesturing to his nearly empty plate. "You're also a grill master, apparently."

"No, I mean, why do you think people want me to be different?"

Nick had never had an interview where his interviewee was so interested in *him*.

"You're assuming I have an opinion."

Colin shot him a frank look. "You're full of them. Your eyes never stop. They're constantly calculating and analyzing and *judging*."

Nick practically choked on his mouthful of chicken. He chewed slowly and swallowed, taking a long sip of beer. Whatever Colin had put in the marinade, it had a bite. Or maybe that was the conversation. Talking with Colin was deceptive. You thought he was all mild-mannered, until he weaseled under your shields and skewered you with a pointed question.

"I don't *judge*."

"Don't dodge the question," Colin persisted. "I asked you why because I know you have an opinion."

"Maybe I don't want to share it." Nick felt uneasy and off-balance. This wasn't how his interviews usually felt: like *he* was the one being interrogated. He dared to glance up, only to see those blue eyes pin him right to the couch. It was hazardous to underestimate Colin O'Connor, even if you weren't a defensive coordinator in the NFL.

"That's usually how it goes, isn't it?" Colin asked, but it clearly wasn't a real question because he kept going, his eyes narrowing in on the flaw they'd discovered in Nick's defense. "You ask the questions. You analyze the subject. Nothing back. Well, I'm going to tell you," he drawled. "That isn't how this is going to go."

It was only force of habit that prevented Nick's jaw from dropping to the floor. "And how do you think this is going to go?"

"I think this is a two-way street."

Nick shook his head emphatically. "It's not. And even if it was, I'm not very interesting. I promise."

Colin's expression turned both unbearably fond and unbearably sly. "I find you pretty fascinating. I promise."

Nick was so, so, *so* fucked. "You're flirting with me." Maybe if he'd been a little less shocked he could've kept the words in. But as it was, Colin had decimated his brain to mouth filter.

Colin didn't look surprised or dismayed or even the tiniest bit shocked. He looked fucking *delighted*. "Yes, I am," he said. "Am I any good at it?" He seemed genuinely curious, as if he didn't really know.

Nick's head fell into his hands. "Better than you realize," he mumbled through his fingertips.

"Great," Colin said, and changing subjects like Nick's entire foundation of *you can't possibly be attracted to the athlete* wasn't crumbling around him, continued with, "you want some ice cream? I've got some great frozen yogurt. And we can put on Netflix."

"Yeah, sure," was all Nick could mumble in return. What did Colin even mean? Was he just practicing? Playing a game? Serious as fuck? It was impossible to know, unless Nick asked, and Nick wasn't nearly stupid enough to ask. Colin might actually tell him the truth.

Nick slept like shit in the room that was just a *little* too close to Colin's.

Would it be weird for him to switch rooms now? He'd probably have to make up some lie, a bullshit excuse that Colin would see through in half a second. He'd give Nick that wide-eyed bright smile with the sly edge that promised he wasn't nearly as naïve as he seemed. Nick couldn't risk that smile, so he stayed. He wasn't sure which was worse.

By the time he wandered downstairs, the sun was bright in the sky and the house was quiet.

Nick went through the cupboards one at a time, finding an obscene amount of protein shakes and powder, and a lot of basic staples that proved Colin probably did know how to cook. That hadn't been an act, though he was beginning to wonder how much of the Colin O'Connor he'd seen wasn't. Probably almost none of it, and that was terrifying.

He had just poured milk into his Cheerios when Colin jogged up to the patio and into the house, wearing a pair of loose-fitting athletic shorts, a thin layer of sweat, and nothing else.

Nick choked on air. So much for his peaceful breakfast.

"Good morning," Colin said with that annoying smile. All innocence with just the tiniest edge of something more. Like he knew exactly what he was doing and how effective it was.

"Morning," Nick mumbled into his cereal.

"I was going to wake you up for my jog, well *our* jog, but you seemed to be sleeping pretty soundly."

Nick tried not to think about what sort of picture that made. Or that Colin had looked into his room and had seen him sleeping.

"Do you jog every morning?" Nick asked, even though he already knew the answer. Anything to abort that line of thinking.

"Usually about ten miles or so. Went fourteen this morning, felt really good." Colin reached for his forgotten t-shirt hanging over a barstool and shrugged it on. It stuck to his skin in sweaty patches, which shouldn't have been attractive, but apparently, Colin O'Connor defied logic.

"Bullshit," Nick mumbled.

"Tomorrow you want to join?" Colin asked like he hadn't heard as he grabbed a water bottle out of the fridge.

"Not for a fourteen-mile jog," Nick said.

"Not even for ten?" Colin wheedled.

"Not even for ten. You could probably convince me to do about half that."

"Then you're on. I've got to take a shower, and then we'll go into town. I have a meeting with Mark."

"Your agent, right?" Nick asked.

Colin rolled his eyes. "If that's what we're calling him, sure, yeah. My agent."

They were in the car heading to Mark's office when Colin brought it up again. "I keep expecting you to ask me tougher questions. Instead you ask me why I drink protein shakes and about my house and how many miles I like to jog in the mornings."

Nick saw Colin's gaze cut over to him once, then twice, as if he could barely contain his curiosity.

"What did you expect? Me to interrogate you over your morning Wheaties?" Nick snarked.

"You saw my pantry. I don't have Wheaties. Too much sugar."

"No Cocoa Puffs or Lucky Charms?"

"This is what I'm talking about," Colin said in exasperation. "This couldn't possibly be going into my profile."

"How do you know? I think the American public deserves to know that Colin O'Connor has an unfair prejudice against break-fast cereals that actually taste good."

Colin laughed, the sound shocked right out of him.

"It does seem like false advertising, I'm on the Wheaties box and I don't even eat them."

"This is what I'm saying," Nick said, grinning back. It all felt so easy, like they'd been doing this a lot longer than the few weeks they'd known each other.

"Gonna have to bring that up to Mark. He needs to find me some better promotions."

Nick imagined that he was trying. He was beginning to appreciate what Mark went through with his client, who seemed like the most laid-back, most affable athlete on the planet, but who was actually incredibly intelligent with a sneaky and penetrating insight.

"Don't tell him I said anything."

"Your secret's safe with me." Colin shot a side-eyed, amused look in Nick's direction. He caught it and felt hot all over. He couldn't believe he'd flown in yesterday and thought that he could keep his distance. It hadn't even been twenty-four hours, and distance was a laughable thing of the past.

It killed Nick to leave the room while Colin was deep in discussion with his agent, but the name on his phone's screen was someone he couldn't ignore.

Scratch that. He'd ignored her plenty—but before he'd flown to Miami, Duncan had pulled him aside and insisted that he keep his regular appointments with Mary, his therapist.

"I don't need a therapist anymore. I'm *fine*," Nick had told his boss, who was as inflexible on this point as he was notoriously rumored to be.

"Humor me," Duncan hadn't asked, he'd demanded. "Fifteen minutes, once a week. Or else I put someone else on the Colin O'Connor story."

Nick knew Duncan wouldn't, but Nick wasn't willing to take the risk by calling his bluff.

He answered the call, tucking his phone against his head as he slunk into an empty hallway, with only closed doors to overhear him. "Mary," he said testily.

"A joy to talk to you again, Nick," she said and it would have been impossible to miss that she didn't sound happy to hear his voice either. Of course, he was probably just as unpleasant an obligation as she was to him. *Five Points* had hired her to make sure their star journalist wasn't emotionally traumatized by his attack, and she was contractually obligated to see it through.

"Apparently Duncan's threats are as effective as rumored," she continued. "I was surprised you answered."

"This is a waste of time. Both yours and mine. And I have something considerably more important to do with mine."

"What?" she asked.

Anything seemed better than discussing his nightmares or the attack. He reminded himself of her very airtight contract, which supplemented the normal rules about doctor-client privilege. "I'm doing a big story. An athlete coming out of the closet."

"That *is* an important story," she said. He hated her annoyingly bland platitudes and the way she encouraged him to talk by saying nothing of substance herself. His habit of unloading on her in a normally uncharacteristic manner was one of the biggest reasons he'd stopped answering her calls.

He leaned against the wall and tipped his head back. "An understatement."

"Important for you personally, I'd imagine."

The most important. Important enough that he needed to stay focused on the end game. Important enough that he should be in the room with Colin and Mark, watching the former fight the latter every step of the way.

"You've not got me to lay bare my sad teenage years yet, and it's not going to happen now," he reminded her testily. "But yes."

"The last time you had a big assignment, you were attacked. It's understandable you'd be anxious about this trip," she said, even though he'd said nothing about anxiety.

It was just another reason he mistrusted her. She seemed to read him even better than he read his own subjects, and that made him endlessly uneasy.

"Are you having nightmares still?" she asked.

"Haven't had one in a month," he said, which was almost true.

"That's good, especially with this story starting up," she said. "I want you to call me if you start getting them again."

They both knew he was completely capable of promising and lying about it—or promising now and never following through. He'd done both in the past, which was why Duncan had become involved this time.

"How about this," she suggested, breaking the tense silence, "how about you call me if you feel like there's nobody else you can talk to about them?"

Mary had not proved to be particularly flexible up 'til this point, continually insisting on follow-through and the traditional counseling methods. Obviously, she had discovered that he wasn't a traditional sort of patient.

"Fine," Nick said.

"I know you're thinking you won't ever reach that point. You very well might not. But trauma has a habit of creeping up on us when we least expect it, even after we believe we've conquered it. Even when we believe we're stronger than the memory. I want you to know I'm here for you, if you ever need someone to talk to about it."

"No more required phone calls?" he asked hopefully.

She laughed, and it humanized her, shaped the outline of her in his mind, even though she'd always just been a disconnected voice to him. "We both know that you'll never agree to them without Duncan's threats. I'd rather you know you can come to me, on your own."

"I'm really fine. Nearly all the time." Nick shoved a hand through his hair, hating the thread of guilt in his voice. He'd sort of treated her like shit, and he didn't usually do that. He'd learned very early in his career that you trapped more bees with honey than with vinegar.

"It's the rest of the time that worries me. But we'll cross that bridge when we come to it. Go back to whatever's got you preoccupied. We'll talk if you need to."

Chapter Four

"You're gonna kill me," Nick panted as they rounded the corner towards the house.

Colin glanced back, even though he was fairly certain that Nick was in no danger of dying any time soon. Like he'd expected, Nick's gait was smooth and his face was slightly flushed, but he was clearly in no danger of collapsing.

The sound Nick made when Colin turned back was somewhere between a groan and a grunt. "You're unfeeling. I'm gonna put *that* in your profile," Nick said.

In the last twenty-four hours, Nick had threatened to put all sorts of things in the article, and Colin was even more certain that he was making up all of them. Also certain: the way his heart raced when he realized that Nick was creating inside jokes with him.

"I'm going to tell everyone America's favorite quarterback leaves dirty dishes in the sink."

"If you don't use a turn signal, every football fan who works at the DMV is going to conspire to suspend your driver's license."

"If you don't stop stealing all the popcorn, I'm going to tell the world that Colin O'Connor likes to binge-watch Gossip Girl*."*

Nick thought he was pretty funny, that much was obvious. The problem was that Colin found him pretty funny, too.

No doubt that was also appallingly obvious.

That might be the only even slightly embarrassing thing that Nick hadn't threatened to expose to a wider audience. Colin was taking this as a good sign that maybe Nick wasn't completely immune to his terrible attempts at flirtation.

Colin felt like a tool jogging without a shirt, but he'd seen Nick's gaze skate over his bare, sweaty chest yesterday and had chalked that up as a win, which meant he was going to be jogging shirtless for the near future.

He pulled up short on the terrace, and gave his back a quick stretch. He knew he was playing dirty, using his physical attributes as a way to attract Nick, but *god*, he couldn't remember the last time he'd felt this way and it had felt *good*.

Falling in love with Jemma had been confusing and at points, both scary and exhilarating. But after it had become clear that she didn't feel the same way, so much of that feeling had soured into guilt and regret.

It felt good to flirt and be flirted with back. Like cliff diving, the wind whistling past your ears, that first startling cold submersion.

"I know what you're doing," Nick huffed in annoyance.

"Stretching?" Colin asked innocently, even though there was absolutely nothing innocent about the way he was bending over in these ridiculous shorts or the way Nick's eyes were mentally peeling them off—at least Colin hoped that was the case. The possibility was the only reason he was even wearing them.

Nick huffed again. "I'm going to write that you're an exhibitionist. Which would explain the *Sports Illustrated* cover."

Colin laughed. He'd done a lot of that in the last two days. Having Nick around wasn't anything like he'd expected or even dreamed it might be. He was full of those snarky comments still, but they didn't feel impersonal anymore. Each one seemed to glide right over Colin's skin, like they were calibrated just to bring a smile to his face.

"You and that cover. I'm going to go out and get a life-size version for your room."

Colin, still stretching with his back to Nick, fully expected another verbal volley in their game, but Nick went uncharacteristically silent. Colin turned around to see Nick, redder in the face than he should have been from their run and staring at the ground as he stretched his quads. *Really* nice quads, if Colin was looking, which he absolutely was not.

"Gonna go grab some water and a shower," Nick said, letting go of his leg. "Have a lot of emails to answer this morning."

Colin watched his back disappear into the house and wondered what he'd said that was wrong.

Was Nick, who brought up that stupid *Sports Illustrated* cover as often as humanly possible, *embarrassed* about being called out on his obsession?

With Nick doing work, Colin took a shower and settled down at his desk in the office to do the same. He opened his email and couldn't hide the grimace as his inbox rapidly filled.

His email was only a mess because he didn't let Lindsay deal with it like every other PA would have.

That had been only one of the lectures that Mark had prepared the day before.

"We need to start lining up bigger and better sponsorships," Mark had said. "I want to see you out more. I know Boomer and the other guys invite you. You should go out with them. People need to *see* you."

The problem was that Colin didn't want to be seen. He wanted to stay hidden on his private island, in his beautiful house, and if he was being painfully honest with himself, keep laughing with Nick.

He still loved the perfect stillness of this house, but it had never seemed lonely until Nick showed up.

"I don't get how people seeing me in a club is going to bring in sponsorships." Colin rarely let Mark just do his job, and he wasn't going to pull any punches just because his stupid crush was sitting in the corner, scribbling words Colin desperately wanted to read. His fingers itched to grab the notebook out of Nick's hand and greedily devour every word on the page.

Mark had leaned forward across his desk, dark eyes intense and the early afternoon sunshine sparkling off that goddamned rose gold Rolex. "People are beginning to talk. You're becoming a recluse. Nobody picks a recluse to sell their shit."

Colin had burned with the injustice of that accusation—and the embarrassment that Mark had said it in front of Nick. He could still feel the echoes of it now, which was why he'd worked so hard to keep Nick's attention during their morning jog and its aftermath.

It was hard to say whether he would have cared about Mark's directive if Nick hadn't been here. Colin deliberately didn't think about it. Instead, he pulled his phone out of his pocket and started texting.

Teddy. Boomer. Ricky. Oliver. He sent a variation of the same message to all of them, plus most of his O-line, and then dialed a number that Mark had given him ages ago that he'd never bothered to use.

"Yeah, this is Colin O'Connor," he said when a woman answered.

The drawn-out beat before she remembered who he was definitely didn't help to convince him that Mark was wrong.

He was the most exciting quarterback in the National Football League and even if he hadn't been, he was still the *only* professional quarterback in Miami. The Hibiscus concierge's silence was humbling, even when he didn't care if she didn't know who he was.

He reasonably reminded himself that she had no reason to know his name. He'd never been to Hibiscus, which claimed to be the hottest club in Miami.

"Oh, yes, Mr. O'Connor. Mark said you might be calling."

Colin ground his teeth and ignored that she'd played him into thinking she didn't know who he was.

She must have realized she'd taken it a step too far, as she continued with a smooth apologetic tone. "What can I do for you?"

"I'd like to bring some friends to your club tonight." Okay, he didn't *want* to; he'd essentially been ordered to. But after Mark's admonitions, Colin didn't think he could offer Nick another night of homecooked meals and *Gossip Girl* binge-watching with a straight face.

She asked all the important questions. How many. Who. What would they like, specifically. Colin was stumped at the last question, but she smoothed that over too, promising them a unique experience.

Colin told himself when he hung up, guilt twinging because he'd promised himself he'd never stoop to calling that particular number, that this was easier. This way, Nick could meet his friends in Miami all at once. Because unsurprisingly, his inbox was full of acceptances and excited emojis, everyone thrilled that he'd finally gotten the stick out of his ass.

That last bit was his own embellishment, but Colin wondered just how true it might be.

"You starving me tonight?" Nick asked as he wandered down-stairs after a long afternoon of work upstairs.

Colin had spent the afternoon trying to distract himself with emails, then paperwork and then TV so he wouldn't go out of his skin at the thought of going to the club. He fumbled for the remote and the mute button at Nick's words. "Uh, no, not exactly. We're going out."

"Out?" Nick raised an eyebrow and Colin wanted to keep him forever, a little like Rapunzel in her tower. Unfortunately, he found himself sympathizing with Mother Gothel and her need for Rapunzel's constant attention.

He flushed. "You heard yesterday. Mark wants to raise my profile. He's been suggesting I try this new club for a while. Hibiscus. I thought we'd meet some guys from the team there tonight."

Nick's expression was horrifyingly emphatic. "If that's what you want to do, then that's what we'll do."

Colin knew Nick knew the truth—that he didn't want to go at all--but he couldn't admit it. Maybe it was the way Mark's lip had curled when he'd called him a recluse.

He was killing two birds with one stone; he was finally doing Mark's bidding, and he was banishing the idea in Nick's mind that he never wanted to leave the house.

"The car will be here in an hour," Colin said awkwardly into the silence that had descended between them.

Those gray eyes seemed to be cataloging every miniscule reaction of Colin's and he had a sudden horrible thought that Nick might understand him better than even he understood himself. "I'll be ready," Nick said.

Colin didn't think he was going to be ready at all.

Still, he dutifully trooped upstairs to his bedroom, and even contemplated the shower, even though he'd taken one a few hours ago and hadn't done anything more strenuous than sitting on the couch since. He settled for dampening his hair and doing his best to style it, even though all the cowlicks he had made it difficult.

Staring at his reflection, Colin tried to see in the mirror what so many others claimed: that he was *hot*, that he was gorgeous. He was one of the few that didn't, that much was indisputable, considering how many copies of that stupid *Sports Illustrated* issue had been sold.

It was hard to forget what Nick had said about that cover. *You're a cardboard cutout.*

Colin glanced back in the mirror. He knew sometimes he was distant. He knew he hid himself away. But the last thing he wanted was for Nick to think that about him, the *real* him. He didn't want to be a cardboard cutout; he wanted to be a flesh-and-blood man. Living and breathing and feeling.

Shaking off his melancholy, Colin approached his walk-in closet more carefully than he had in months. Since ever, probably.

Lindsay the PA bought a lot of clothes he didn't wear. He bought the rest, the ones he actually did. Typically, he avoided *that* side of the closet, but tonight he was supposed to be trying.

Of course, he wasn't trying hard enough to pick something ridiculous, and so he settled for probably the simplest item she'd purchased for him: a bright turquoise shirt with sinfully soft fabric. Colin briefly contemplated a pair of skinny jeans that rivaled even the ones Nick wore and decided he wasn't feeling that dutiful. His regular jeans would do just fine.

Colin was just about to slide his wallet and phone into his pockets when he remembered Nick's wandering eyes this morning. How much he'd appreciated those tiny running shorts. Maybe he wasn't acquiescing to the demands of his position as much as making moves to gain something entirely different.

The skinny jeans were true to their title, and Colin hoped he wouldn't end up doing any physical activity because his movement was greatly restricted, but gazing at the full-length mirror at himself, he definitely saw the benefits.

He walked out of the bedroom just as Nick closed the door to his.

Colin had been trying very hard not to look into the fact that out of the two nearly identical bedrooms, Nick had selected the one nearest his, and not the one all the way at the end of the hall.

It was getting harder and harder not to think that Nick had an ulterior motive in being so close, especially with the way he was looking at him right now, all heat and nothing held back. Nothing like he'd been earlier downstairs.

Colin gave himself a pat on the back for taking a fashion risk with the skinny jeans and made a mental note to give Lindsay a raise. And maybe to give the clothes she picked more than a cursory glance going forward.

Nick's perusal was a nearly unbearable slow burn. "Glad to see you've decided to discover twenty-first century fashion, O'Connor," he teased, the tone low and intimate.

Colin was stone-cold sober, but the way Nick was looking at him kept his blood simmering. "I figured they looked so good on you, why not?"

Nick smiled. "I'm *very* happy to take personal responsibility for the way you look in those."

The doorbell rang, and Colin eyed the stairs. He wasn't quite shameless enough to troop down the staircase first, letting Nick ogle him the whole time. "I forgot my phone, can you grab the door?" It was a blatant lie, but it also let him get a split-second view of the way Nick's ass looked in *his* dark gray skinny jeans. And yes, there was a god, and he was blessing Colin right now.

Nick was already in the car when Colin slid inside.

Directions dispensed with, Nick turned to Colin. He'd done something swoopy with his hair, and it looked almost exactly like it did in Colin's imagination when he'd managed to seduce Nick to his bed. That was going to be incredibly distracting. "Tell me more about who's coming tonight?" Nick asked, as if Colin needed a reminder of his main capacity. It wasn't to create cute inside jokes and stare at his butt in skinny jeans, and it wasn't to be his date when he didn't want to go out.

Colin took a deep breath. "You know Teddy. He was traded to the Piranhas the year before I was drafted. He's sort of my...mentor, I guess."

Nick's expression was speculative in the dim lighting of the car. His eyes glowed unearthly, nearly the turquoise shade of Colin's shirt, something he hadn't considered when picking it. "Does Colin O'Connor need a mentor?"

"Colin O'Connor isn't perfect," Colin retorted. *That* was easy. "I'm the last person on earth to tell you that he is."

Nick made an impatient gesture like, *tell me more.*

"You know how it is. Even coming from an elite collegiate program, the NFL is a different universe. The rookie programs they've put in place the last few years help, but they don't nearly make up the difference. Teddy sort of self-appointed as a bridge." Colin paused. It shouldn't have felt like a big deal confessing this. *Normal* people probably didn't feel so constrained when discussing their personal lives. "He's my best friend in Miami, basically."

"I'm assuming he knows about what you're planning," Nick said.

"He was the first...no, the second. The first was Mark. The second person I told in Miami about my sexuality. Teddy's always been cool about it."

"What about the others?"

Colin frowned. "The others?"

"The others on the team that know? I'm assuming everyone who's coming tonight knows."

"Uh…not exactly."

Nick did a double take and Colin continued before he could freak out. "I mean, I know I need to tell them. The whole team. We've been talking about the best way to go about it. Helen and I."

"Right." Nick did not seem convinced.

Colin shifted uncomfortably in his seat. "That means we can't be honest about why you're here. We can just say you're doing an article."

Nick's gaze was unapologetically frank. "I'm okay with that. But you do know waiting isn't going to make it easier."

"Helen wanted me to talk to the players when OTAs start."

"But that's—"

"Right before the article comes out? I know. I've been trying to convince her that I need to do it earlier."

"She's trying to make sure nobody blabs," Nick huffed. "I get it, but it's *stupid.*"

"Well," Colin said, grinning over at Nick, "maybe you wouldn't mind dropping a line to her about your feelings."

"Count on it," Nick retorted. "Now, who are the others coming tonight? Besides Teddy?"

Colin described Boomer, the younger tight end he'd befriended, and the other two rookies from his draft year who were still on the team, Ricky and Oliver. "Also," he added, "probably most of my O-line. I try to invite them to a bunch of stuff."

"Makes sense. They protect your ass. Might as well show some gratitude." Nick's mouth quirked up. "It's definitely an ass worth protecting."

"The way you tell it, *Sports Illustrated* should've gotten a rear shot and not the front," Colin teased.

Caught up in the rhythm of their banter returning, Colin totally forgot that his crack about Nick's *Sports Illustrated* obsession hadn't gone over well earlier. He froze for a split second, dreading Nick's reaction. But Nick just laughed this time, completely unbothered by the comment. Even *amused* by it.

"If *Sports Illustrated* was a softcore gay porn mag, maybe," Nick said wryly.

Colin, who'd at some point been terrified to even *look* at gay porn because of what it might mean, yearned for the sort of comfort Nick had with his sexuality that let him make jokes about it.

Still, the words came out of his mouth before he could stuff them back in. "Are you saying that I've got gay pornstar potential?"

Nick laughed incredulously. "I can't believe you don't realize how hot you are."

Colin didn't quite have the nerve to tell him that he didn't care how hot he was; he only wanted Nick to tell him how hot Nick thought he was.

Hibiscus was everything Colin had assumed it would be.

Personally, he didn't see anything particularly special about it; nothing to give it the sort of *caché* that led to Miami begging to be let inside. If Mark was to be believed, anyway.

Yeah, it looked neat, with all the different exotic floral arrangements tastefully backlit against the dim interior. The hostesses were beautiful, the men and women displayed like the flowers. But Colin remained cold, immune to the seductively pumping music and the shadowy corners.

"Welcome, Mr. O'Connor," the hostess purred. She was brunette, and there was something about the tilt of her lips that reminded him of Jemma. But Jemma had never had a reason to rehearse a smile, and the hostess' was entirely practiced. "Your party is already seated in your private cabana."

He barely held back the eye roll as he nodded in the affirmative. Colin thought he could see Nick staring at him out of the corner of his eye, but then the hostess was leading them down a spacious hallway, and he was distracted by the suites that opened up on either side.

They passed another set of open doorways and Colin realized that this wasn't set up like a normal club. It was all small suites of rooms, separate and intimate, leading to the idea that you weren't just here with the rest of Miami's party scene, you were *special*.

Colin was too familiar with the concept of *special*. He'd seen it ruin people, up close and personal. There was an immensely talented wide receiver in college who was projected to draft in the high rounds who got caught with coke and ended up going to jail instead of the combine.

They hadn't been close, but the sheer waste had devastated Colin and remained a haunting reminder to never depend on being "special."

That was all this club was selling; the chance for its patrons to feel exclusive. Colin, who'd never particularly enjoyed Miami nightlife, hated it.

The hostess turned into a side room, and Colin went through the motions, greeting his friends, his co-workers. Nick's presence was written off with a simple, "He's with me, doing a focus profile."

Only Teddy's gaze lingered on the reporter, and that was almost certainly because he already knew why Nick was there. The rest of the guys didn't care. Reporters faded into the woodwork, especially when they'd signed NDAs.

The hostess listed off the activities available to them. Food and drinks in the cabana, which opened onto a private lanai and hot tub. The main dance floor was in the center, circled by the private lanais. They were free to venture out into the crowd or to stay closer to their private cabana.

She left with a last word to Colin that *whatever* he wanted was available, he just needed to ask. Her exit was closely followed by the arrival of food and a VIP bottle service setup. Colin settled uncomfortably on one of the low couches and was relieved to see Nick sit down next to him.

"This is sort of wild, and I spent most of my early twenties in clubs," Nick murmured, ducking his head in close to nearly whisper in Colin's ear.

Colin shrugged. Sure, it was nice, but it didn't really entertain him. Teddy was pouring drinks, and handed him something that was probably heavy on liquor and light on mixer. Which, considering how long this evening was going to be, was probably better.

"Vodka soda, with a lime," Nick told Teddy when he asked what he wanted. Teddy's eyes slid from Nick to Colin, who was currently sipping his own vodka soda with lime.

Nick leaned back on the couch, cradling his drink. Colin resolutely tried to ignore the arm he'd slung over the back, the fingers of which could have brushed his own collar.

Normally he would've eaten it up, maybe even sunk into the embrace, but ninety percent of this room didn't even know he was interested in men and he wasn't really sure flirting with a reporter was the best way to tell them.

"Are you sure you're not secretly a gay pornstar?" Nick's voice slid over his ear again, just for the two of them to hear. He gestured with his glass. "I've been drinking these since I started going out in WeHo."

"Weho?"

Nick laughed. "West Hollywood. Gay clubs, O'Connor."

"Oh. Right." Colin couldn't help the pulse of shame that he'd needed to ask. And a pulse of envy, too, because while Colin had been slaving away at practices, afraid to look above the floor in the locker room, Nick had been embracing and exploring his sexuality.

"Give me a few more of these, and I'll show you some of my moves."

Colin's default answer to dancing was universally "no." But the idea of dancing with Nick was irresistible, even though everyone with the exception of Teddy wouldn't get it.

Though, Colin observed as he watched them all drink like their glasses were bottomless, maybe they'd be all too drunk to care.

He was on his second drink before the food arrived and feeling it in the pit of his stomach. Or maybe that was the heat of Nick's thigh nearly pressed to his and his hand *so close* to his neck. Colin craved and dreaded the moment his fingers might slip and graze the skin at the top of his spine.

The food was ridiculous, tiny, beautifully plated bits of nothing that did nothing to soak up the alcohol pooling in his stomach. Which, he realized as he poured them new drinks, and Nick and Teddy chattered away with Boomer about his new charity, was probably the whole point. Hibiscus' whole premise was designed to smooth away the real world under an exotic layer of exclusivity, sex, and alcohol.

Ricky and Oliver had stripped down to the swimming trunks the club provided, and were dancing in the hot tub, drifting closer to the music. Colin, sipping his drink, stared out in the seductively dark mass of dancers, the anonymity they might provide, and felt his resolve slipping.

He wandered over to where Nick, Boomer, and Teddy were standing, and tried to not look like he was collecting his date for the evening.

Because as much as he might *know* differently, that was how this felt. How, deep down, Colin *wanted* it to feel.

Boomer, a glass of scotch in his hand, didn't seem to pick up on the subtext, but Teddy did. And Nick glanced up as Colin approached, his eyes growing warm and soft, the palest pearl gray. A smile glimmered at the corner of his lips, like he could read Colin's mind and knew why he was here and what he really wanted.

"I keep telling O'Connor he needs to start his own foundation," Nick said, even though they'd never even talked about it. If they had, Colin would have told him that he was waiting until he could found something with extensive LGBTA+ ties. "He'd do so much more good."

"The kids," Boomer raved, "the kids love it so much. They need more positive role models. O'Connor is a great one, but we need more."

Colin morosely had to wonder if Boomer would still be saying that if he knew he wanted to drag Nick off by his hair and shove him up against the nearest, most convenient wall and finally find a way to shut up his smart mouth.

Nick's glance over in Colin's direction was sly. Colin shouldn't have found it as hot as he did. "He sure is something. Practically a modern-day Captain America. America's quarterback."

"I told you," Colin inserted, because apparently tonight the vodka was making him chatty, "I'm from Alaska."

Teddy threw his head back and laughed. "Another world, right?"

"They shouldn't have put you in those damn stars and stripes flag shorts on the *Sports Illustrated* cover then," Nick added. His eyes glowed with amusement. Flirting with Nick right under Boomer's nose was a lot more fun than he thought it might be. His fingers still itched to *touch* but he was patient; he could wait until the right time. *Maybe.*

"Oh, he *hates* that cover," Teddy said, laughing again. "I made photocopies and posted it on every locker in the practice facility. We called him Doctor Model for a week."

It had been horrifically embarrassing at the time. The incident was one of the reasons why Colin hated the cover so much.

Nick tilted his head and his eyes sparkled. "Doctor Model. I'm gonna use that."

"Teddy," Colin groaned, but somehow the humiliation in the memory had faded. He could only assume that Nick's obvious appreciation of the visuals had helped remove much of the sting.

"You," Boomer said, pointing to Nick, smooth and suave in a way that Colin envied, "and I are gonna make something happen."

"I'm going to write an article on his foundation," Nick explained.

Colin knew how worthwhile Boomer's foundation for disadvantaged kids was—he'd personally spent time volunteering for it in the last year—but he was stupidly envious of anyone else gaining Nick's attention.

"Oh, don't pout, I'm sure that the article Nick's writing on you will be a hell of a lot more high profile." Boomer grinned like he had no idea how true his statement was. Which he didn't. He couldn't possibly.

"I'm gonna write in that you're high maintenance to boot," Nick said, then gestured with his empty glass before heading over to where the bar was set up.

Boomer turned to Colin, a suddenly serious expression on his face that Colin would have guessed was an impossibility considering how many glasses of scotch he'd downed tonight. "Are you going to tell me what's going on, O'Connor?"

"Uhhhh," Colin stammered. He was a bad liar under the best of circumstances. Vodka did not create ideal circumstances.

"I know you don't do features. And it's the wrong time of year for a football profile. What are you planning on telling the world?"

Colin took a long, deep drink and prayed he wasn't making a huge mistake. Prayed that tomorrow Boomer still wanted to talk to him. "I'm coming out as bisexual."

Colin had always believed he was good at hiding his biggest secret. The complete lack of surprise on Boomer's face told him that maybe he wasn't as good as he'd thought he was.

Instead, he smiled brightly and slapped him on the back, hand lingering long enough to telegraph loud and clear that Boomer didn't give two shits about touching him. Same as Teddy hadn't. Colin exhaled in silent relief. Boomer didn't hate him. Teddy didn't hate him. That was two down, about a million to go. "Good for you," Boomer said. "It won't be easy. Any time you need me for anything, you just say the word."

"Thank you" seemed insufficient, but they were the only words Colin seemed to be able to dredge up.

"And Nick, I've heard he swings your way, too." Teddy grinned. "Why don't you go ask him to dance? He looks like he'd show you a good time."

Colin spluttered into his drink. "I guess expecting the match-making to end was too much to ask," he said ruefully.

Teddy shot him a frank look. "I say this as an almost completely straight man, O'Connor, but you are *too hot* to stay at home watching Netflix all the damn time. Go have a good time. However you want to."

Colin glanced over towards the bar station. Nick was pouring his drink, his hips unconsciously moving to the beat of the music outside.

"Don't mind if I do," he said, downing his drink in one motion and steeling his courage to walk over to Nick.

It's just dancing, he told himself. But he'd never been able to do things by halves, and Nick didn't seem to be any different. Colin knew he wouldn't be able to settle for just a dance before Nick went back to LA.

"Hey, come dance with me," he said because he couldn't say something crazy like, *come kiss me until we can't breathe* or *come stay with me until you don't want to leave.*

Nick looked up in surprise. He smiled. "I thought you'd never ask, O'Connor."

As they skirted the hot tub and headed towards the dance floor, if Colin let his fingers brush the small of Nick's back, it was dark enough that it stayed between the two of them.

Besides, Teddy, and now Boomer, knew. The rest of the team and then the world would know soon enough. He needed to learn what not hiding felt like.

They made their way to the dance floor, and Colin realized it had only been a month since the last time he'd danced with someone. He couldn't even remember that man's name, though at the time, losing even the tiny bit of normalcy he'd found that night had been the push he needed to reveal himself.

But tonight, all Colin could think about was Nick.

His dark hair shone under the stars, his smile soft and genuine as they turned towards each other. They were surrounded by hundreds of people, but with Nick's eyes gazing at him, the rest of the real world seemed to fall away.

The music was a drumming pulse in his blood, the rhythm seducing him into movement, his feet inching closer to Nick. Swallowing hard, Colin reached out a hesitant hand and giving Nick plenty of warning and time to back away, slid his palm against the curve of his waist.

He was shockingly real and solid, the damp cotton against his skin, and Colin wanted to feel more, touch more, but he didn't know how much he dared.

Then he felt the hesitant brush of fingers on his own hip, exploring the tight denim of his jeans carefully, hesitantly, but even that touch exploded in Colin's brain. *Nick is touching me. This is not a drill. Nick is touching me. He wants to touch me. This is definitely not a drill.*

They moved closer, dancing leading to swaying to the seductive beat, and Colin let his hand drift, feeling the taut muscles of Nick's back, the same muscles he'd been trying to pretend he hadn't seen that day playing dodgeball. But he had, and he hadn't been able to forget. And it turned out that even these cautious sweeps of his palm were enough to send him into a pulse-pounding, damp-necked fever.

But even the risk of the rising heat in his blood couldn't stop him, especially not when Nick's eyes seemed to only encourage him on, the pupils expanding into the bluish-gray. Then Colin's thumb swiped over the bottom edge of Nick's t-shirt collar, the edge just barely grazing the soft, damp exposed skin of his neck. And they both shuddered.

Just the feel of Nick's skin under his thumb had Colin weak-kneed and swamped with the need to lean down and see if his bottom lip was as delectable as it looked.

He squeezed his eyes shut. He couldn't kiss Nick for the first time on a crowded dance floor, not with both of them most of the way to drunk, with the possibility of Colin's teammates witnessing it all.

"Are you okay?" Nick asked, and Colin wondered how he had even managed to ask the question. His own throat felt swollen and uncooperative.

He nodded, but still moved back half an inch. Just for now, he told himself. There was no way this would ever be enough. All touching Nick had done was unleash a fundamental need for *more*.

Colin told himself it was better like this anyway, because not even thirty seconds later, Ricky appeared at Nick's side, drunk and happy and dancing around like he'd just scored a touchdown in the Super Bowl.

"Yo," he yelled at both of them, clearly having no comprehension what he'd nearly almost interrupted. Nick took a half a step back as Colin shot his friend a friendly smile.

The rest of the guys meandered out to the dance floor, until Teddy was giving his own twerking demonstration. Colin laughed like he was supposed to, but deep down, he was still trying to bury how disappointed he was that Nick had stayed a good few feet away the rest of the evening, even though he'd been the one to move away first.

Later, they rode home in an exhausted, semi-drunken stupor and Colin wanted to fill the silence with explanations and entreaties, but nothing he composed made sense.

Probably the vodka talking.

Maybe that had been the vodka talking earlier, for Nick. Colin hoped not, because the man seemed to enjoy his company plenty sober. But then, he'd never touched Colin sober.

What Colin wanted more than anything else was to touch and be touched again in return, but he had no real idea of how to go about doing it. His lack of practical experience had never seemed like such a wide gap before, but now it felt insurmountable.

His head fell back against the seat, and he wished the vodka was smart enough to do his talking for him.

Chapter Five

Nick woke up panting for the completely wrong reasons.

Normally, with his proximity to Colin O'Connor and all the flirting tossed in for good measure, he might have had some X-rated dreams that woke him in damp sheets with a hard dick he'd have to take care of himself. But after Rio, those much more pleasant dreams had been entirely supplanted by terrifying nightmares that almost always ended with a knife stuck in his body, blood dripping down the handle.

Not so unlike what had happened to him a little over a year ago.

With shaky fingers, he reached over to the nightstand and grabbed his phone. Squinting at the screen, he let out an inward groan. It was only 3 am.

He wished the dreams would at least come with some sort of reliable frequency, but they were impossible to predict. With the alcohol he'd imbibed tonight, Nick had been almost certain he'd avoid the dream entirely, but instead it had come after him with vicious claws, the violence enough to curdle his blood and leave his skin damp with fear.

Throwing on a t-shirt over his bare chest, he padded down the stairs as quietly as he could. The last thing he wanted to do was wake Colin. He didn't want to explain the dreams or his sleeplessness in their wake. If he couldn't be honest with his therapist about them, how could he ever tell Colin?

He shouldn't have lied to Mary about the dreams stopping, because in the last few days, they'd come back with sharper claws than ever.

Nick grabbed a bottle of water from the fridge and without turning the lights on, pulled open one of the sliding glass doors and stepped onto the terrace.

He stood for a long time staring at the inky outline of the ocean, trying to calm his breathing and his nerves, trying to convince himself he was as far removed as he could be from the Rio *favela* he continued to dream about.

Mary had suggested the dreams were his subconscious' way of telling him that he hadn't resolved his own guilt over the entire incident.

Frankly, Nick thought that was bullshit. He'd resolved his guilt; he *was* guilty for what had happened. No, he hadn't shoved the knife into his own stomach, but he'd gone against every scrap of advice. *When you get held up, give them whatever they want,* Jemma had told him over and over again as he'd prepared to travel to the Brazilian capital. Instead, he'd stupidly argued, offering the robbers some money, but not his phone. It had been monumentally stupid to risk his life over a few interview snippets he hadn't been able to back up to his cloud account, but he hadn't been thinking about his own safety. He'd been gallingly arrogant, certain of his own triumph, unable to process the concept that he might be fallible.

The truth was, he might be standing in Florida, on Colin O'Connor's private island, but a part of him was still bleeding out on that Rio street.

That was probably why he missed the obvious sound of the footsteps behind him.

"Hey, Nick, are you okay?" Colin's voice asked softly from behind him.

Nick jumped and swore under his breath, the plastic water bottle slipping from his hands and bouncing on the concrete of the terrace.

He turned to see the outline of Colin, standing by the door, shirtless and clad only in a pair of low-hanging athletic shorts.

Nick tried to focus on the sight in front of him. Colin O'Connor *was* unfairly and certifiably gorgeous. Especially in the moonlight. *Especially* wearing practically no clothes. But the echoes of the dream still thrummed in his blood, and it would take more than the sight of Colin's spectacular pecs to dismiss them.

Unfortunately.

He sighed. "I guess."

It was a total cop-out answer, and Colin must have known it, because he ventured further onto the terrace, stooping down to pick up the fallen water bottle and pressing it into Nick's hands.

"Why don't you tell me what's up?" Colin asked, his own gaze staying securely glued to the horizon.

Nick hesitated. Confessing the truth seemed impossible, but a lie felt worse, bitter and ugly at the back of his throat.

"Bad dream," he finally said, because it was as much of the truth as he could share.

He half-expected Colin to call him out on it. In Colin's place, he absolutely would have. Would have pushed for the real truth, digging and prying, using every tool at his not-inconsiderable disposal. It was what made him an excellent reporter and also an asshole.

"It's peaceful out here. Helps me too, sometimes," Colin said, accepting with that innate *goodness* he seemed to emanate Nick's cop-out answer and making him feel like utter shit in the bargain.

Colin settled down on a lounge chair and drew his knees up under his chin. "I come out here whenever I can't sleep," he continued.

The question was right on the tip of Nick's tongue. He was *dying* to ask why sometimes Colin couldn't sleep, and not just because he was here in a capacity to discover everything he could about Colin O'Connor. Nick *wished* it was only professional interest that was driving his curiosity now.

It was impossible *not* to ask a question, the habit was too ingrained in him, but at the last second, he swerved. "You didn't really like it tonight at the club," Nick stated.

In the dim light, he watched as Colin shrugged. He hadn't taken his eyes off the horizon, but ever since he'd walked outside, Nick couldn't take his off Colin. "It's not my type of thing."

"Why do you let Mark push you?"

Colin glanced over, the shadows obscuring the details of his face, but Nick imagined he saw frustration in the hardening curve of his jaw and in the depths of those blue eyes. "I usually don't," he admitted. "But sometimes it's easier to meet people's expectations than to constantly flout them."

Nick pondered this, and while his sleepy brain was still trying to process Colin's words, he continued on. "And," he said, his voice growing wry, "I didn't want you to think I was some sort of recluse."

It shouldn't have, but it heated Nick right up that Colin apparently cared what he thought of him. He was *trying* to work with the assumption that his feelings were still one-sided enough that nothing would happen. But that assumption was rapidly falling to shreds.

"I don't think you're a recluse. But we don't have to do things you don't want to do, either. What would you rather have done if we didn't go to Hibiscus? I'm assuming you have places you *do* like to go?"

"Of course. They're just not..." Colin trailed off and then shrugged again.

Nick walked over to where Colin was sitting on the lounger. Every molecule was screaming at him to *stay away* if he wanted to keep things platonic between them, but he needed to have enough self-control for this. Because somewhere along the line, someone had convinced Colin that he wasn't the "right" kind of person to be who he was, and he needed to understand that was just plain bullshit.

Nick gingerly sat at the end of the lounger and when Colin lifted his eyes to look at him, his face was finally out of the shadow. Perfect. If he could only ignore the way Colin looked and sounded and even *smelled*. How did he smell so clean after a night of dancing and drinking? Nick was sure he smelled like a locker room full of flop sweat and too much booze.

"Listen, you don't have to do what everyone expects. Even if it's easier. Especially if it's easier." Nick inched closer and tried to ignore the desperate pounding of his heart at Colin's nearness. If he moved half a foot closer, he'd be close enough to kiss.

Kissing was definitely not what Nick needed to be thinking about right now, especially when Colin's expression was still skeptical.

Nick changed tactics. "Do you know what they call weird people if they're rich? They don't call them weird. They call them eccentric. Money and success buys you the ability to break the mold. You can do whatever you want. You're about to change your whole life. Embrace that you're different. Stop apologizing for it."

It was slow, but the doubt on Colin's face had begun to melt a little. Nick prayed a little and threw his Hail Mary. "The first time we met, you told me that your personal role model wasn't Tom Brady. It was Nelson Mandela. That's *you*, that's not the cardboard cutout the media wants you to be. *Be you*. Trust me, you're a hell of a lot more interesting than the cardboard cutout Colin O'Connor."

"But you've always been easy to win over," Colin smirked, echoing that first interview. Nick had to swallow down the lump that had grown in his throat, because Colin had insisted he hadn't remembered that interview. But maybe some of it had come back.

"True," Nick said. Anything else was a complete lie. He'd been easy to win over from the first moment. The *easiest*, probably.

Dawn was beginning to creep over the sky, and Colin looked contemplative. But instead of continuing their conversation, Colin changed the subject. "I've got to go to the practice facility for a workout this morning. Do you want to come?"

"Will I miss anything?"

"Me doing a hundred reps?"

Nick laughed. "I meant for the *story*."

Colin looked very amused. "Then, no."

"Okay, I've got some research I promised to put together for a co-worker. So, I'll let you sweat your brains out alone this time."

"Trying to avoid our morning jog?" Colin asked archly.

"Absolutely."

"Then tonight," Colin said casually, "I'll take you out."

Nick's brain short-circuited before he remembered that he'd *asked* Colin to take him somewhere he liked. It was absolutely, definitely, not a date, no matter what it sounded like.

"Sure," he said, trying to keep it casual and his own hopes buried somewhere in *this is a very bad idea* land. He got up off the lounger and started to make his way into the house.

But before he made it inside, Colin's voice rang out across the terrace.

"You're wrong, actually. I didn't have a terrible time tonight."

Nick knew he should go into the house and shut the door. He shouldn't listen to the rest of this, because the walls between them were crumbling fast enough without Colin pulling them down. But somehow his feet rooted in place and he couldn't move. "Oh?" he said, because he was a fool who apparently couldn't keep his mouth shut.

"I liked dancing with you." Nick watched, words shocked out of his own mouth as Colin swaggered by into the house, smug smile plastered on his face.

Nick's shock and awe expression stayed with Colin through the forty-five-minute drive to the Piranhas' practice facility in Coral Springs.

He'd been so close to just leaning over and kissing him. He'd hesitated at the last second, and shot him the cockiest grin instead, but it was hard to ignore the feeling that he'd just lost a second opportunity.

Colin had literally made a career out of going after what he wanted with determination and focus. He'd played it closer to the chest with Jemma, never pushing too hard and letting her set the tone of their friendship. He wasn't sure anything would have made her love him the way he'd wanted to be loved, but Colin had already decided that he wasn't going to sit back and make the same mistake with Nick.

He was trying to be blatantly obvious that he *liked* Nick, and while he was somewhat certain the feeling was mutual, Colin was having trouble with that final step.

Inexperience was definitely a contributing factor to his hesitation.

It might have been a mistake, but he was a little desperate for advice, so as they lifted weights, he asked Teddy.

"What did you...um...well...how did you convince Maria to go out with you? You know, *date* you?"

Teddy had been married to his college sweetheart, Maria, for almost ten years now, and they had three beautiful children. So the double take he shot Colin after he finished his reps was to be expected.

"You're really tellin' me you need *romance* advice," Teddy said with disbelief. "*You?*"

Colin would have thrown up his hands but he was currently pushing through his own set of reps, the burn setting in deep in his muscles. But his hands didn't waver on the bar. Very unlike how he'd shied away from the perfect opportunity this morning.

It had been undeniably romantic. Them sitting together on the lounger. The sun beginning to creep over the Atlantic Ocean. Nick's sleepy eyes, more gray than blue in the pre-dawn light. Nick encouraging him to go after what he wanted. The perfect move would have been to lean over and make it unequivocally clear what he wanted.

Just reliving it convinced Colin even more that he did in fact need—desperately—some romance advice. "Yes," he told Teddy seriously.

Teddy just laughed. "I promise you, it'll be easy for you. Just say the word, and they'll fall all over you. They usually do."

Teddy wasn't wrong, which had been the bitterest pill to swallow when it came to Jemma. He'd turned down women right and left, while the woman he wanted had friend-zoned him.

Colin made a frustrated noise, which had nothing to do with the sweat dripping into his eyes or the way his barbell was balanced at the very edge of his reach and his endurance.

With a smooth motion, he set it back on the rack and sat up, wiping his face with the hem of his t-shirt. "I'm serious. What did you say to Maria?"

"Sometimes it's not about words." Teddy's expression grew sly.

"Fine," Colin said. "Then what did you *do*."

Teddy's voice dropped. "This about that reporter?"

Colin shot Teddy a reprimanding look. "Does it matter who it's about?"

Teddy threw up his hands. "I really, really don't care, man. Man or woman or alien. As long as you're happy, it don't matter. *But* I'm not sure it's the same."

"I'm pretty sure it's the same," Colin bit off.

Teddy's dark brown eyes grew more serious, with a gleam of understanding. "Okay, okay. What did I do? I made sure she knew how I felt, not by what I said, but what I did. I sought her out. I touched her—not like groping. Like, held her hand. Put my arm around her shoulders. Any reason to give her a reassuring touch. To let her know I wasn't going anywhere. People want to believe it's real. So, if it's real, show them it's real."

Colin was pretty certain he understood. In their line of work, you ran into a lot of people who weren't real. It wasn't always easy sorting out the few who were. Colin had been burned more than once. Nick, who'd spent his career with athletes, would want to make sure Colin wasn't just playing around.

Nick needed to know Colin was serious.

"I can do that," Colin said, feeling for the first time since Nick had arrived in Miami like he finally had a solid plan.

Teddy grinned and clasped him, sweaty back and all, into a tight hug. He slapped him on the shoulder. "Man, you are the realest. If anyone can do it, it's you."

Like she had a sixth sense, Jemma called him almost as soon as he got into the car to drive back home.

"Good timing," he said, "I'm on my way home from the practice facility."

"I know," she said.

So she'd called Nick first, to make sure Colin was alone. He'd just taken a quick shower at the practice facility, but he nearly started sweating again. "Am I about to be interrogated?" he only half-joked.

"Very funny," Jemma snarked back. "Maybe I wanted to ask how it was going since you have neglected to tell me *anything*."

"Obviously fine, otherwise you probably would have gotten a text."

"*Obviously*," Jemma imitated him right back. "Maybe I was more interested in hearing how *well* it's going."

Colin sighed. "What do you want me to tell you, Jem? That I like him? You already know that."

She was quiet for a long moment. "Do you think I'm angry about that and that's why I called? I'm fucking *thrilled* you like him. I want you to be happy."

"Yes, well, it's not that easy." He hated the way he sounded so wounded and defensive, like he *wanted* her to be angry that he'd moved on. And that hadn't been true for a while now. He'd not wanted nor expected her jealousy.

"You're kidding, right?" Jemma laughed all of a sudden, lightening the mood. "You actually *must* be joking."

"Why does everyone say this is so easy?" Colin grumbled. "Romance is difficult."

"Yeah, maybe for people that aren't *Sports Illustrated* cover models who are attempting to win over men who are *already crazy about them*."

"We don't know that's true."

"Actually, maybe *we* don't know it's true, but I certainly do. Nick has been absolutely fascinated by you from day one. Why do you think he hired me?"

Colin felt his insides jellify. "Seriously?" he demanded.

He could feel Jemma's eye roll over the phone. It was *that* powerful. "The only one who doesn't seem to know how crazy Nick is about you is *you*, dumbass."

"I really hope you abuse Gabriel this viciously," Colin retorted.

"A sign of my true love and affection," Jemma sing-songed back at him.

"*Still* not easy," Colin complained, "though definitely getting easier."

"You've owned him hook, line, and sinker since Nelson Mandela. Though god knows why."

"You're just jealous he got to reveal that tidbit to the world."

Jemma huffed. "That's assuming I *wanted* to tell people that you rank Nelson Mandela over Tom Brady."

"I hate to tell you, but your big fat crush on Tom Brady is showing."

"And so is yours. Except it's not on Tom Brady."

Colin was silent for a moment. "Do you really think I should make a move? Like a *real* move?"

Jemma was rarely serious, but because she was his best friend, she knew the exact moment he needed her to be. "Yes. If a real move is asking him to be your boyfriend and then your husband and to white picket fence your stupid private island, then *yes*. Make a real move. He's a great guy. He tries to hide it, but it's there."

"I know," Colin said softly. "I see it."

"I thought you would," Jemma said, and she was being a good enough friend that he valiantly ignored her smug tone. Which told him exactly what she'd been doing, inviting him as their fourth to that stupid ultimate dodgeball tournament. Jemma was a lot of things, but subtle was rarely one of them.

"Text me updates," Jemma demanded. "If the real move happens, I want to hear about it."

"Really?" Colin asked dubiously.

"Gabe and I might have a bet going," Jemma admitted a little sheepishly. "*And* again, I want to know because I want you to be happy. This is a big thing."

"Don't say that," Colin begged, trying to ignore the fluttering of nerves at the base of his stomach. He knew some people called them butterflies, but they just made him nauseous. "Keep telling me it's gonna be easy."

"You won the Heisman, O'Connor," she teased him. "You've got this in the bag."

Colin came home to a quiet house. He grabbed a water from the fridge, and climbed upstairs, pausing at the landing to debate whether he should go to his room as planned for a quick nap or if he should look in on Nick. The door was open and he could hear music playing and the rhythmic tapping of Nick's fingers on his laptop keyboard.

He didn't let himself think about it, and instead forced his legs to carry him (despite the rolling of his stomach) towards the doorway of the bedroom Nick had claimed.

Nick glanced up, hair mussed like he'd been running his hands through it, eyes crystalline blue, and a smile playing on his lips. Colin felt his heart stutter. "Hey," Nick said, sounding pleased to see him. "Have a good workout?" "Yeah." Colin couldn't find words but he could still grin foolishly, which was all he was doing. A long morning away and he grinned like an idiot when he was back with Nick. He was in *bad* shape.

Nick wiggled his fingers on the keyboard. "I've been getting a workout of my own."

Colin tried to act casual by leaning against the doorjamb. "I'm gonna take a nap, but we'll go out in a few hours, if you're cool with that?"

"Sure, I'm down with whatever." Nick grinned. "Did you think of someplace?"

"Oh, I know exactly where I'm taking you," Colin said. "I hope you're ready for a re-match."

"A re-match?" Nick looked very intrigued, his eyes gleaming with curiosity. It was a really good look on him. Colin was about five seconds away from leaning over and showing him just how much he liked it.

"Yeah," he said, his voice going low and smoky. Nick's eyes widened, like he knew exactly what Colin was thinking when he sounded that way. And he didn't look like he hated it. At all.

Maybe Jemma was right. Maybe this was going to be easier than he'd thought.

Colin took Nick to his favorite hole-in-the-wall pizza place, at the far end of a run-down strip mall, where the pizza was hot and greasy and the owner had a collection of old school video games and pinball machines in a back room.

When they walked into the unassuming entrance, Nick shot Colin a delighted look.

"I'm so glad you approve," Colin retorted as they sat down in a far booth, even as he couldn't stop grinning.

"I knew this was in you *somewhere*, Mr. Private Island," Nick crowed.

Colin laughed. "I'm from Alaska. It was always there."

"But now," Nick said, his expression growing sly and knowing, "you're letting me see it."

Colin traced the carved graffiti on the scarred wooden tabletop with a finger. "You were right," he said. "I've been hiding who I am for too long."

Nick leaned forward, eyes sparkling with enthusiasm, and Colin could only hope that at least some of Nick's excitement wasn't professional. As he leaned forward, his hands shifted closer towards Colin's and he had a sudden, intense, throat-drying desire to reach out and grab Nick's hands and hold them. After all, that had really been Teddy's advice, hadn't it? *Touch him*, Teddy had practically said.

Colin steeled his nerves—the same place he dug from every time he faced down a blitzing defense, and threw a touchdown pass against all odds—and reached out, merely brushing his fingers across the back of Nick's hand. It was a tiny touch, miniscule and maybe inconsequential to the rest of the world.

To Colin, it felt like everything.

Nick's eyes met Colin's, an irresistible smoky blue. "Not anymore, you aren't," Nick said softly.

"Not anymore," Colin confirmed, letting his fingers trail more firmly over Nick's skin—his knuckles, his wrist, his palm, until he was loosely cradling his hand. "This is who I am."

Maybe if he'd been a tiny bit braver, he could have added, *and you're who I want*, but Colin figured the hand-holding was fairly self-explanatory. And he intended to become even clearer as the night progressed.

He might not always be able to say what he felt, but he could show Nick, and Colin hoped that would be enough.

The waiter appeared at their table, a young teenager with blue hair and a nose ring. "What can I get you?" he asked, his eyes skating over where their skin was touching. It wasn't an intimate touch, but it was enough. The kid's eyes widened a little, but he kept his mouth shut.

Colin, too, found he couldn't find the words. "We're going to need a minute," Nick said dryly, shooting Colin an amused glance.

"First time?" Nick teased after the waiter moved on.

"You know it is," Colin said.

"Right, well, let me guess. You like lots of meat on your pizza."

"Half-right," Colin retorted. "I'm an equal opportunist. Personally, I like the Panhandle Classic."

Nick flipped open the menu, consulted the description and gave a sharp nod. Glancing over at the whiteboard that had the day's draft beers listed, he picked out a microbrew that Colin knew was smooth and easy to drink.

When the blue-haired waiter returned, Colin was feeling even more confident and had made a pointed show of tucking his fingers between Nick's.

They ordered, and after the waiter left, Nick looked up at him. "Aren't you worried that he'll tell someone? He must have recognized you."

"I'm not hiding," Colin said simply. "Besides, I sort of thought the plan was to tell everyone."

Nick shot him a look.

"I mean, *obviously* in your article, but something like this doesn't gain much traction if it isn't official, right? It's just someone's word, if he even chooses to tell anyone."

Nick's expression grew troubled. "Yeah, of course, but it's one thing to come out as bisexual and it's another to actually publicly demonstrate interest in men."

"I mean...*that's the point?*" Colin was confused and couldn't pretend otherwise.

"I guarantee," Nick said, a trifle bitterly, "you'll come out and say you like both men and women, and some people will only hear half of that sentence."

"Then they're morons," Colin said.

Nick just shrugged. "I'm just telling you what's likely to happen."

"That's not right."

Nick's expression was wan. "So much of the world isn't, especially about this."

The waiter arrived back with their pitcher of beer, and Nick gracefully untangled their hands to pour them each a glass.

"I think a man's favorite pizza says a lot about him," Nick observed, clearly wanting to steer their conversation away from less potentially charged topics. "What's this pizza going to tell me about you?"

"Nuh-uh," Colin said, wagging a finger at him. "It's definitely your turn. Tell me about *your* favorite pizza. I told you that you had to pay to play."

Nick leaned back in the booth, crossing his arms over his chest in mock protest. "Never mind that I'm here to learn about *you*," he huffed.

"Don't care," Colin insisted.

"Fine," Nick said. "It's a place that's pretty similar to this one actually. Strip mall in LA. Ugly as hell. Ratty upholstery and broken booths. But the pizza is fucking heaven. My favorite is actually this white pizza they make—homemade mozzarella and garlic and basil. It's the simplest thing on earth and incredible."

Colin grinned at him. "You're saying you're simple?"

Nick grinned right back. "I'm saying I'm delicious."

Colin was stunned into momentary speechlessness. Or maybe that was the tsunami wave of *want* that was suddenly crashing over him. He already knew Nick was going to be delicious, he *wanted* to taste so much he felt lightheaded with it.

His fingers tightened on his beer glass. "This place doesn't only have pizza, actually," Colin said, because he couldn't keep talking about kissing and stay on his side of the booth. "There's a pretty big arcade in the back."

"You challenging me to a game?" Nick's eyes had gotten impossibly smokier as they regarded Colin over the rim of his glass.

"Absolutely."

"I'm sure you'll be a worthy opponent."

The pizza came and they dug into the pie enthusiastically. As Nick chewed through his second piece, he glanced over at Colin. "I think I figured it out," he said. "What this says about you."

"Oh?" Colin finished his third piece and reached for another.

"I think," Nick said thoughtfully, "that it's deceptive. On the surface level, it's just another pizza from another neighborhood place. The kind that gives out trophies for the little league teams, and hosts the annual kids' soccer parties, and it's the place where they know your order when you tell them your name. But it's way more than the sum of its parts. The crust is good, the sauce is solid, the toppings are fresh. But together, they work in harmony. You can't judge them by themselves. You gotta take it all together."

Colin raised an eyebrow. "And that's like me?"

"I mean," Nick gestured with his pizza slice. "Heisman Trophy winner. National Championship team. First pick in the NFL draft. Rookie of the year. Private island owner. People try to judge you by all of those things, but the truth is, you're bigger than all of them. You're *more.*"

"That's awfully philosophical for pizza night."

Nick set down his pizza and his expression grew serious. "I'm just tryin' to figure you out, O'Connor."

"Got anywhere yet?" he asked, forcing his tone to stay light in comparison.

"Maybe," Nick said.

"So what you're telling me is you come here, eat pizza, play some games, and try to win this popcorn machine?" Nick gestured at the displayed full-size popcorn cart that had a big, red sign that proclaimed it could be won for 100,000 tickets.

"That's right," Colin said, refusing to feel an ounce of shame. Nick had claimed, in good faith, to want to know the real him. This was a big part of who Colin O'Connor was.

Nick stared at the popcorn machine, then looked over at Colin with the dopiest expression on his face. "That's the fucking cutest thing I've ever heard. You know, you could buy about a hundred of those, *easily*."

"Probably about a thousand. Or more," Colin admitted. "But that's not the point. The point is to win 100,000 tickets."

"How many do you have so far?"

Colin thought of the tickets he had piled in a plastic storage bin in his hall closet. Did a quick calculation. "Probably about 40,000."

Nick shot him a challenging look. "Then we have some ground to make up. You got some quarters?"

Shoving his hand in his pocket, Colin brought out four rolls of quarters. "Stopped by the bank today just for this," he said, handing two of them to Nick. "I've got more in the car."

"Of course you do," Nick said with an eye roll as punctuation, but his voice was very fond.

It probably would have made the most practical, logical sense to split up. But Colin had no intention of not following through on his plans to show Nick how much he liked him. So he trailed behind him, suggesting the best pinball machines and being supportive when Nick proceeded to lose painfully at Space Invaders.

"I used to be better at this," Nick said ruefully. "I held the high score at my local arcade for almost six months."

"Wow, six months, really?"

Nick smacked Colin's arm. "You're not as funny as you think you are."

Colin smirked. "You seem to think I'm pretty amusing."

Nick rolled his eyes, but his eyes were glowing with affection as they headed to the Gauntlet console. "As long as you let me be the Sorceress, you're the funniest guy on earth."

"Done," Colin said, and let his hand drift down from Nick's shoulder to the curve of his waist. He'd used every opportunity he could to touch Nick casually, and Nick had not only seemed to like it, he'd done it back, until Colin was about to go out of his skin.

When they got into the car, a few thousand tickets richer, Colin felt his nerves wrenching even tighter with anticipation. He just hoped that it wasn't only him, and that Nick, too, had felt the heat growing between them, each casual brush of their hands, every lingering touch, raising the temperature a few degrees.

For someone who used words for a living, Nick seemed to go quiet when these moments came, and they drove home in almost total silence. Colin had to force himself not to fill the unnerving quiet with stupid babbling chatter. He wasn't about to risk how well this evening had gone by putting his foot in his mouth at the very last moment.

Still, he felt his palms begin to sweat as he pulled into the driveway. They'd made it home, to the island where only they would know what happened between them.

Colin took a short, unsteady breath and opened the car door to get out. Nick had already made it to the front steps. He paused at the top of them, waiting for Colin to come unlock the door.

It felt like a thousand first dates that Colin had never been on. He'd never been able to climb the steps to a house, his heart thumping wildly, desire and fear warring inside of his stomach. Maybe this was the chance to set all those should'ves to rest.

Nick turned towards him as he approached the top of the steps. "I had a really nice time," he said, and then flushed bright red, like he'd just realized what he'd said.

Colin, who was renowned for making the most of every opportunity that came his way, grabbed on to this one with both hands. He sidled a little closer, letting his keys jangle in his hands. If they'd been a teenage boy and a teenage girl, this would have been every cliché mid-1990s teen romantic comedy.

"You know I did too," Colin said softly.

Nick raised his eyes towards Colin's. He swore he saw the moment Nick decided to stop fighting the chemistry between them. Colin hadn't been sure *why* he was, but all he cared about in that moment was that he'd stopped. Colin took a step closer. Nick tilted his head and Colin's hand gently cupped his waist.

The air was cool for Florida, but it felt thick and muggy between them, like Colin was trying to paddle through it. He moved slowly, making sure Nick was a hundred percent with him. He closed his eyes at the last moment, and leaned the last bit of distance. Their lips brushed, softly, chastely.

"I've wanted to do that since the first time I saw you," Nick confessed when they broke apart. Colin's lips felt swollen and sensitive, like they'd been stung by a bee. He wanted more—as much as Nick would give him.

"For me, it was the conference call. You looked so annoyed that I'd forgotten who you were," Colin admitted. "And so hot."

Nick looked smug. "Do I still need to remind you who I am?"

Colin's arms tightened around Nick's waist and back, his fingers tracing the supple strength of his muscles. "No," he said simply, and leaned in again, kissing him more firmly and with a lot more confidence. Nick's fingers circled his collar and swept into his hair, digging into his scalp, pulling him tighter against him.

They kissed for a long, drawn-out minute. It was softer and sweeter than Colin had imagined it might be, more achingly vulnerable than he'd dreamt. There were glimmers of heat, tiny nibbles on Colin's bottom lip, Colin's tongue teasing Nick's lips.

Colin could have deepened the kiss, but Nick seemed okay with how it was, and Colin, who'd never felt his lack of experience so keenly, didn't push any harder or faster.

"God, you're gorgeous," Colin said when they finally broke apart and Nick's eyes fluttered open. He'd thought it so many times since they'd met, and he'd stifled it every single time. Suddenly it seemed very important to finally say out loud.

Nick laughed, and he sounded happier and freer than Colin could remember. "Okay, Dr. Model."

Chapter Six

Nick woke again with a pounding heart, a damp hairline, and that all-too-familiar, dank, foreboding sweeping through his whole body in nauseating waves.

Rolling over, he stared up at the dark ceiling and tried to catch his breath. He rarely had the nightmares two nights in a row, but since coming to Florida, he'd had them several times in a week. So much for the object of his affection magically curing him.

He could stay in bed, or he could venture downstairs again and risk having Colin discover that the nightmares were more serious than he'd let on.

Reaching over for his phone, he held it in his hand, debating for a long moment. He could call Mary. But she'd said, *if you don't feel like you have anyone else to talk to.* And he still had people he could reach out to. Calling Mary felt like admitting he was out of options, that he had let the nightmares own him, instead of the other way around.

Nick unlocked his phone and quickly typed out a text to Jemma. It was still fairly early on the West Coast; she might still be awake. And *bonus*, she was the only one at *Five Points* who knew he was still dreaming about Rio.

He lay there for a few minutes, anticipating her answer, and trying to decide what he could do to distract himself if she didn't respond. He could still theoretically go downstairs. He'd just have to be extra quiet. He was trying to decide when there was a soft tap on his door.

Nick glanced over at his dark phone in betrayal. "She didn't, she *wouldn't*," he muttered, as he swung his feet out of bed and threw a shirt on. He pulled the door open and wasn't surprised at all to see Colin standing there, looking sheepish.

"Sorry," he said. "But Jemma said..."

Nick was really going to want to know what Jemma said *at some point*, but right now there were more important things to discuss. Like reassuring Colin that he wasn't a complete fucking mess who needed his hand held through the night.

"I'm fine," Nick snapped.

Colin reached out and brushed his hand hesitantly over his brow, no doubt feeling the sweat along his hairline. "You don't have to be fine."

He shouldn't have, but he sort of sagged into Colin's touch. Colin must have expected it, because he didn't shift at all, just took his weight and held him up, firm and unmovable. Colin's other hand smoothed down his back in reassuring strokes.

"I'm sorry," Nick huffed out breathlessly, stuck between extreme embarrassment that Colin was seeing him like this, and intense relief that he wouldn't have to figure out how to tell him. Because at some point, it was sort of inevitable that they'd end up sharing a bed and Nick already had Colin pegged as a cuddler.

Colin pulled back a fraction but didn't move his hands, one cradling his back, the other his cheek. "Don't be," he insisted.

But they couldn't stay in this doorway forever, and Nick refused to invite Colin to his bed for the first time when he was a fucking wreck over a nightmare, so he said, "Can we go downstairs? Being outside, that helped."

Nick could feel Colin's smile, even in the darkness. Somehow, he'd become so attuned to him, he could picture every miniscule adjustment to his expressions. The days of the cardboard cutout felt very far away.

"I've got something even better that I think you'll like," Colin said, and proceeded to pull him even tighter against him, supporting nearly all of his weight. Nick nearly argued that he wasn't an invalid, thank you very much, but then as he put up a hand to Colin's back to steady himself, he realized that Colin wasn't wearing a shirt. And the truth was, he was absolutely willing to look a little weaker if he could keep touching all this gorgeous skin.

It wasn't something to be proud of, but Nick couldn't work up even a smidgen of shame.

Colin took them down the hall to his own room, and Nick was just about to protest when they passed the bed right by. Lifting his hand off Nick's back, he pulled open one of the large sliding doors that led to the upstairs terrace and ushered them outside.

The edge of the terrace was glassed in, and Nick gently pulled away and grasped the glass railing. One breath, then another, and his lungs were nearly working normally.

"I feel stupid asking this," Colin said, "but I feel like I have to. Are you really sure you're okay?"

Nick glanced over wryly to where Colin had come to stand next to him. "If I said yes, would you believe me?"

"Probably not."

"But you're still asking."

Colin huffed in frustration. Nick wanted to reach up and smooth out the wrinkle between his brows. He didn't, because he was still a little afraid of what might happen if they kept touching. His foundations had rocked at their kiss earlier tonight, and they still hadn't settled. Nick wasn't sure they ever would –or if he really wanted them to.

"All right," Colin finally said, plopping down on a chair, and swinging his feet over the side. Nick glanced back and saw he was staring at him steadily, a determined look on his face. "If what it takes for you to share is for me to share first, I'd be happy to tell you everything you want to know."

Nick couldn't help the tension that suddenly ratcheted through him. He wasn't doing this to get a good story out of Colin. Not even to get the truth out of Colin. He opened his mouth to protest, but Colin started talking anyway and didn't seem particularly interested in stopping.

"When I was thirteen, one of my friend's older brothers came home from college, and liked to walk around without a shirt on, probably stupidly trying to get a tan in Alaska. In *Alaska*. But that was enough to finally make me acknowledge what I'd tried to ignore for years—that I probably wasn't normal. I didn't really like girls. I felt drawn to boys instead. And then the next year, the little brother hit a growth spurt and I decided he was just as cute. Maybe cuter."

"Colin..." Nick interrupted, pained and struggling.

"Shut up," Colin insisted calmly. "I want to tell you this. I should have told you this probably a long-ass time ago, I just didn't. Which was dumb. So, I'm going to tell you now. And when I'm done you can either tell me about Rio, or not. It's your choice."

Nick gripped the edge of the glass, but the smooth finish refused to bite harder into his palms. He might have even welcomed the pain; that thought scared him. "Okay."

"Anyway, the little brother. His name was Dylan. He played football with me, and it didn't take very long for me to figure out that he was staring at the floor, too, when we were in the locker room." Colin paused, and Nick could *feel* the bitterness in the air. It scorched his tongue as he breathed it in, remembering his own years growing up gay and terrified. "Dylan," Colin finally continued softly, "he *knew* but he...well...he hadn't quite come to grips with it yet. I think, I do think he liked me. The way I liked him. We kissed a few times. Enough for me to know, a hundred percent for sure. But by our sophomore year, I was being recruited by colleges, and so was he, and he told me we had to quit. Nobody could find out."

Nick wanted to cry at the crack in Colin's voice, but he swallowed hard. If Colin could tell him this story, then he could listen.

"So for the next two years, I focused on football. I decided to go to Oregon. I couldn't bring myself to go so far from home, even though everyone thought I should go to an SEC school."

Nick remembered those conversations. He'd already been on the sports journalism track in school, and a lot of people had been surprised by where Colin O'Connor had declared. But Nick really hadn't been. Why would a born and raised Alaska boy want to go to Alabama or Florida or Texas? He'd want somewhere familiar.

"I went to college believing with as much certainty that you ever have about these things that I was gay. I'd never really been attracted to a woman before. Then my first college class, I walked in, and Jemma smiled at me. And suddenly, that wasn't true anymore."

He'd known. Nick told himself he'd guessed and that he'd practically *known,* but it still felt like a shock to hear Colin confess that he'd been in love with Jemma.

"Of course," Colin said wryly, "she wasn't interested in me that way. Ironic, that. We became friends instead. But that was when I really began to understand what being bisexual meant. It's mostly theoretical, but I'm pretty sure I'm mostly into men. Occasionally into women." He took a deep breath. "And now you know everything. Though I'm sure some of it you already knew."

"I suspected about Jemma," Nick confessed. "Not at first. But when she came back from Rio, after meeting Gabe, a lot of things made sense."

"You don't...I don't know...think less of me for loving her?"

Nick's head snapped towards Colin. "No, *never*. I don't care if you like women, too. That doesn't bother me. If I liked women, I'd probably be into Jemma, too, and then we'd both be fucked, because she's in love with Gabriel."

Colin laughed, a painfully dry chuckle. "I'm not in love with Jemma anymore. In case you were wondering."

"I wasn't." Nick walked over and leaned over where Colin was sitting. He brushed a kiss on the crown of his head.

"Good." Colin tipped his head back and their lips met again, soft and gentle. Innocent almost, even though Nick knew his own feelings didn't really strike him as particularly innocent.

Though with Colin's story of his romantic relationships, maybe that made a little more sense.

Nick pulled back and knew it was his turn to share, even if his own story was more embarrassing than anything else.

"I would tell you about Rio, but there honestly isn't much to tell. I was dumb. I did something people told me not to do—repeatedly. Jemma, especially, will probably tell you that if you ever bring it up. But I thought I was bigger and stronger and invincible, I guess. I never thought something bad might happen. Not to me. I remember the flash of the knife. I remember a lot of blood. I remember Gabe's face over mine in the hospital. I don't remember much else. I don't like telling the story because it's not very special or heroic. Some stupid white person being stupid. That's all. My therapist tells me the dreams will fade in time, and they have, sort of."

"Doesn't seem that way," Colin said reproachfully.

Nick shrugged. "For some reason, you mess me up. And maybe all that..." Nick flapped his arms, "churning, I guess, brings it back up. I hadn't had one in months before I came here."

"I'm sorry." Colin sounded so perfectly apologetic, Nick wanted to slap him.

"Don't be sorry. It's a good sort of churning, the dreams notwithstanding."

Colin gazed up at him with a bright grin. "For me, too."

Nick leaned in and kissed him again, a little hotter, a little firmer this time, slipping his tongue against Colin's bottom lip with more insistent determination.

It wasn't until he sensed Colin's hesitation that what had been flirting around the edges of his brain hit Nick straight on in the face.

Colin had mentioned only *two* romantic interests: Dylan, who practically nothing had happened with, and then Jemma, who *nothing* had happened with.

"Wait," Nick gasped, breath suddenly uneven. "I mean, there *were* others, right? You went and experimented and you didn't... *wait* did you? For Jemma?"

Of course, Colin had waited for Jemma. As soon as the question was out of his mouth, Nick was embarrassed at how stupid it was. Like he hadn't been paying attention at all. When he *had*, just not to the right things.

Colin sighed. "One of the first lessons I learned was people *talk* about athletes. Everyone wants to share every tiny thing they know. It makes *them* feel special, to know someone they think is special. It's why I stopped telling people things. But to answer your question, no...I didn't experiment. And I was in love with Jemma, of course I waited for her. Even after I knew she wouldn't...I loved her. I didn't want anyone else."

"Oh, god," Nick exhaled unsteadily, suddenly and inexplicably turned on by this new realization. "You're a virgin."

"Don't say it like it's a curse," Colin said, embarrassment rife in his tone. "I have a little bit of experience."

It wasn't a curse, of course it wasn't a curse. It was just...insanely, stupidly hot. Nick could barely wrap his exploding brain around the concept that he could be the first in every way it counted. Colin O'Connor, who everyone tried to get a piece of, but nobody ever had. And Colin wanted *him*, that much was clear, he just wasn't sure how to go about it.

Nick knew exactly how to, in a lot of variations. He could teach Colin everything. It would probably ruin Nick for everyone else, but he wasn't sure that hadn't already happened.

Reaching down, he tangled his fingers in Colin's. It was dark outside, the barest light illuminating Colin's face, but there was a hopeful shine in his eyes, even in the shadow. "Would you like some more?"

Colin's voice was soft like velvet. "With you?"

"Yes."

Nick could barely breathe as Colin's fingers shook a little against his. It took everything he had, but he didn't open his mouth again, and instead let the silence spin out. He didn't try to whip out a laundry list of reasons why he would be great at initiating Colin into the realm of sexual experience. He knew how aware Colin was of their chemistry together. They'd be good together, even if he didn't know a thing. Which was probably one of the reasons why Colin had been flirting so diligently with him.

He'd wanted this, but he'd not known how to ask.

"I..." Colin stumbled, and it was one of the few times since Nick had met him that he seemed genuinely uncertain. "I...do...I just..."

"It's okay," Nick said, wrapping his arms around Colin's broad shoulders and squeezing tight. "We can take it slow, I promise. There's nothing to be nervous about."

"Really?" Colin seemed surprised and Nick rolled his eyes.

"Really. As slow as you want. But I draw the line at kissing. I'd like to kiss you. A lot more, if I'm being honest."

Nick felt Colin's smile bloom against his chest. "I'd like that," he said, his voice muffled by the cotton of Nick's t-shirt.

"We can even Netflix and chill, if you want," Nick teased.

Colin let out a sound that sounded suspiciously like a giggle. It was endearing and adorable and Nick was *gone* on this man. Like possibly never recover from, shout to the heavens, dance down Main Street, *gone*.

"You realize I'm going to have to thank Jemma now," Colin pointed out. "She told me to come find you."

Nick had a feeling that Jemma's motives were not as altruistic as Colin supposed. After all, it seemed she and Gabe had a bet going. He wondered if she'd won, and then realized that he didn't give a shit. He was the real winner.

If Nick had expected things to change that night, they didn't.

He and Colin continued to orbit each other, the circles getting smaller with the kiss and then Nick's offer, but not merging completely.

They'd watched the sun rise, cuddled together on the lounger, but then Colin had gotten up and with only a lingering brush of his fingers on Nick's shoulder, went to go work out. Nick wasn't a masochist or a professional football player, and so he went back to bed. Alone.

Even though he was bone tired from two nights of interrupted sleep, he'd had trouble falling asleep. The offer he'd proposed to Colin had run through his head in all its variations, and finally he'd drifted off, but his sleep was unsettled.

He'd not woken 'til noon, and stumbled downstairs to find Colin gone. "Meetings," the note on the fridge read, "there's food in me."

Opening the fridge, Nick had foregone the sandwich fixings and had reheated leftover pizza instead. After a quick shower, he took his laptop outside, telling himself it was too nice of a day to stay inside.

"Working" quickly segued into dangling his feet in the water and listening to one of his favorite weekly podcasts as he worked on his tan. The good news was that nobody was around to see him play hooky and ignore his inbox.

He was in a perfect zone of water, sun, and sports commentary when he heard footsteps behind him. Assuming it was Colin, he merely rolled his head lazily and said, "Oh good, you're home. You can rub some sunscreen on the back of my neck. It's feeling a little crispy."

"Uh," came the female voice behind him, which got Nick up in a hurry, water droplets sprinkling over his bare chest.

The girl standing on Colin's terrace was mid-twenties, and looked shocked to see Nick sitting in Colin's pool. Nick would've guessed that the girl, definitely cute, was a friend or *more*, but then he'd personally heard Colin's recitation of his practically non-existent love life the night before, and he'd not mentioned any women currently on that list.

Therefore, this had to be the personal assistant that he paid but didn't let do her job.

"Hi, I'm Nick Wheeler," he said, extending a hand. "Sorry, I wasn't expecting anyone."

She shook his hand and then shoved her sunglasses onto the top of her head. Her eyes narrowed. "*You* weren't expecting anyone? How do I even know you're supposed to be here?"

Nick couldn't believe it; Colin hadn't even told his *PA* that he was coming to stay with him. He began to wonder if she even knew he was on the cusp of coming out.

"I'm the journalist doing the feature on Colin for *Five Points*." Nick didn't think he should mention the subject matter, just in case she *didn't* know. Which, if that was true, he and Colin were going to have a really serious chat. He *had* to start telling people.

"Oh," she said flatly. "Then why aren't you with Colin?"

Nick didn't particularly feel like confessing the truth. But then she must already have had a clue they were *friendly* because of the way he'd greeted her when he'd thought she was Colin. How many football players in the NFL rubbed sunscreen on reporters' necks?

"Because I had work to do," Nick said.

She tossed her hair. "Yeah, really looks like you were working."

It was almost fair, because he had been sitting in the pool. *Still.* Nick was beginning to understand why Colin rarely used his PA and preferred to do things for himself. She seemed to act like she had some sort of claim over him.

"Sort of how like Colin buys his own groceries, I'd imagine," Nick retorted dryly. The PA didn't know she didn't want to get into a verbal war with him, but she'd soon find out.

Her eyes shot venomous sparks his direction, and she went stomping back inside the house, which was all Nick had really been after—to get her out of his hair.

Regardless, he wasn't particularly looking forward to discussing this encounter with Colin tonight.

Five minutes later, his mind still wouldn't shut up about the whole thing, which pretty much blew his whole peace and relaxation thing out the window. He got up and went inside the house. The PA was leaning over the kitchen counter, typing on a laptop.

She looked up when he walked in. He ignored her and went to the fridge for a bottle of water.

"I looked you up," she said, the faintest hint of guilt laced through her voice.

He leaned back against the opposite counter. "And?"

She shot him a stony glare, and shrugged. "You are who you say you are. I'm just surprised that Colin didn't tell me you were coming."

Nick wondered what she'd say if she discovered he'd already been here for a week. Probably nothing good. So he didn't, because he'd already dug a deep enough hole for himself to climb out of.

He adopted a commiserating expression. "It must be frustrating that he won't share. Especially with someone who's supposed to be helping him."

Nick wasn't considered a crack interview reporter for nothing. Her face crumpled and he saw all the discontent and uselessness she hid behind the bitchy attitude. "He'll only let me keep his schedule. And sometimes deal with email. Basically, he uses me to keep the world out."

That sounded *very much* like the Colin who Nick had discovered since coming to Florida.

"And you want to do more," he said.

"Of course, I want to do more! I was *hired* to do more," she shot back with exasperation. "And I've told him that, but he just gets that blank look on his face and gives me an answer that doesn't really mean anything."

The cardboard cutout strikes again.

"I'll talk to him," Nick said, even though it was the last thing he wanted to do. He'd come to Florida to interview Colin, and somehow in the last week, their lives were becoming increasingly intertwined. And the part that alarmed him the most was that he wasn't really alarmed at all.

"Would you really?" She looked genuinely relieved. "Mark has been trying to talk to him about me, but he never gets anywhere. But then I'm not sure he really trusts Mark or takes much of what he says seriously."

Nick wasn't sure Colin trusted Mark, either. He had a reputation as a shark, and Nick had a feeling that Colin had his hands full making sure that Mark didn't go off the rails.

"I'll see what I can do…" He paused, realizing that even though Colin had told him his PA's name, he'd completely forgotten it. Which was unlike him. Probably Colin had said it shirtless and he'd been too busy trying to keep the drool off his chin.

"Lindsay," she supplied with a small smile. "And I'm sorry about earlier. I should know better than to think Colin would tell me he'd have a reporter over."

"Ah, well," Nick said before he could really stop himself, "we're friends, too. So maybe that's why he didn't mention it."

"Friends. Right." Lindsay didn't seem convinced at all, and Nick realized that if she hadn't suspected Colin wasn't straight before now, she definitely did now.

Whoops.

After Lindsay left, Nick returned to the pool and to make up for his complete lack of productivity, swam a couple dozen leisurely laps and told himself it was exercise. He was just finishing up when Colin walked out onto the terrace.

He swam to the edge of the pool and slicked his hair back. "Hey, you're back."

Colin smiled, the sun reflecting off his aviator sunglasses. "Yeah. Sorry it took so long. I ended up reviewing some film with the receivers and Teddy."

"Not a problem. I was lazy today."

"I have days like those," Colin said, which Nick doubted very much, if his off-season schedule was always like this.

Nick lifted himself out of the water, and knew that Colin was watching him as he walked over and grabbed his towel, quickly drying off. He knew he was attractive, but not as attractive as Colin made him feel.

Colin looked at him like he never wanted to look anywhere else, and Nick would be lying if he said he didn't really, *deeply* enjoy it.

"I stopped by the store on my way home and grabbed some steaks," Colin said, plopping down on one of the loungers. "I figured it might be nice to stay in, and maybe catch a few more episodes of *Gossip Girl.*

Nick's fingers on the towel froze as he rubbed his hair. "Sounds great." He was proud of how casual that sounded and not at all like, *oh yes, please, let's make out on your couch while pretending to watch* Gossip Girl.

Nick dragged his nearly-sunburned ass back upstairs and showered. After, he had a lengthy debate in front of his suitcase about what he should wear. Should he slip jeans on or should he essentially acknowledge what they'd probably be doing and just wear a pair of loose sweatpants?

Who was he kidding?

He put the sweatpants on and tried not to blush when he came downstairs and saw that Colin had changed into a very similar pair.

Okay, so they both had sex on the brain. Of course, Nick thought that was sort of inevitable when there was a man in front of him who looked like *that* and had already professed an interest in fooling around. That was like asking the sky not to be blue.

"I'm gonna grill the steaks," Colin said, stealing a handful of not-very-subtle glances at Nick's choice of attire.

Nick followed him out to the grill, determined that it wouldn't get weird. He wasn't going to let it. He let his hand settle on the curve of Colin's waist as he stood at the grill. "Lindsay came by today," he said, combining the new touch with the routine observation.

"Oh god, I forgot she usually comes on Tuesdays," he said. "I'm sorry."

"Nothing to be sorry about," Nick insisted. "Though she was a little taken aback to see me here. I guess she didn't know I was coming."

Colin flushed and turned away, shifting the steaks around with a pair of tongs. "She didn't need to know."

"I think she might have liked to. She wants to help. There's more she could do. There's more she *wants* to do." Nick paused, letting his thumb slip under the hem of Colin's loose t-shirt and brush the skin above the waistband of his sweatpants. "Of course, I'm just a reporter. Alternatively, you can keep everything the same and tell me to go to hell."

Colin set the tongs down with a decisive click and turned to face him. He was still blushing but there was determination there, too. "I'll think about it. I know I haven't been very fair to Lindsay. I let myself get carried away with the privacy thing. There's probably a lot more balanced solution. And...you're more than just a reporter, you know that."

"Do I?" Nick waggled his eyebrows and grinned.

"You do," Colin insisted, and leaned down to kiss him. It was more than the hesitant kiss from the night before, certain and sure in ways that kiss hadn't been. It set Nick's blood racing and his fingers sliding up Colin's back.

Colin broke the kiss and rested his forehead for a moment against Nick's. "I wanted to do that since I walked in the door, and you were in my pool, looking like you belonged there," he confessed in a murmur.

Nick didn't answer; instead, he reached up and grabbed Colin's collar and pulled him down again, kissing him thoroughly and completely as an answer.

The steaks came out a little burned. Nick finally had to walk away to get the TV set up, because they were never going to eat dinner with Colin reaching for him every ten seconds. Normally

Nick might not have complained, but all he'd eaten today was a few pieces of leftover pizza and he was starving.

They sat at the couch, steak and corn and a handful of beers between them as the next episode played. "This Nate guy is no good for Blair," Colin observed, his forehead wrinkling, "but I'm not sure Chuck is any better."

"They're both assholes," Nick pointed out, relaxed and full as he gestured at the TV. "But I think Chuck loves her. She's just a convenience to Nate, and she's worth more than that."

"Blair terrifies me," Colin confessed, very seriously.

Nick tried to stifle a giggle and failed.

"What? She's terrifyingly competent at being...well, whatever she is. A high school girl, I guess. Though I didn't know any high school girls like her."

Nick shot Colin a look he *knew* was incredibly fond. He should've made even a token attempt at censorship, but he was still feeling warm and fuzzy from Colin's *looking like you belonged there* and he didn't feel like fighting it. "She's the Queen B, O'Connor."

Colin sighed with exasperation. "I've never been happier to be from Alaska. We don't have those there."

By the time the next episode started playing, they'd moved from distinctly upright positions to Nick's head half-leaning on Colin's broad shoulder. By mid-episode, they were full-on cuddling. Nick wanted to kiss him again, but also didn't want to make the first move. The choice needed to be Colin's. This had the potential to be a lot more than a few long kisses like while he'd been cooking the steaks, and Colin needed to be okay with that before anything else happened.

Colin's arm slid around his shoulders and when Nick glanced up at him, he was staring intently, not at Blair and Chuck on the screen, but at Nick's face. "You're gorgeous," he said softly and Nick tried, unsuccessfully, to tamp down the ballooning infatuation he was feeling. It had been growing since that first interview, and right now it was at an increasingly terrifying rate.

Colin leaned down and kissed him, their lips moving together soft and sure, more at ease since they'd begun to learn each other. As one kiss moved into another, they grew hotter and deeper, Nick's hands shifting to reach behind Colin's head, fingers tangling in his hair. Colin pulled Nick over further and further with each kiss, until a few minutes in, he just wrapped his arms around him and dragged him fully onto his lap.

"Colin," Nick gasped as he straddled him. Colin was flushed, his breathing coming in shallow pants, and Nick could absolutely feel how hard he was, poking right into his thigh. It was a struggle not to bear down and rub his own hard dick against Colin's. But Colin needed to know what they were edging towards; the last thing Nick wanted was to end up in a place where Colin wasn't comfortable with the outcome.

Colin answered the unspoken question by bucking his hips up and meeting Nick's halfway. They both groaned, and Nick grasped Colin's head more firmly, angling it exactly like he wanted before diving in again, his tongue brushing against Colin's as they kissed.

Every sweep of Colin's hands under Nick's shirt left his nerves tingling, and Nick knew he probably had wet through his sweatpants with pre-cum. He pulled back, and tried not to get distracted by how incredibly kissable Colin's mouth looked right now, lips red and swollen. "What do you want?" he managed to ask, praying that they at least wanted the same thing, which was hopefully no clothes and some form of orgasm. Nick wasn't feeling particularly picky at this point.

Colin's hand moved downwards and Nick gasped, high and breathy, as his fingers delved under the waistband of his pants and trailed over his hard cock. It twitched as Colin continued to explore, cradling the length of it in one big hand. "This," he said, his voice sounding a little more awestruck than Nick could understand. "Can I?"

Nick couldn't imagine a world in which he'd say no, so he nodded and helped Colin push down his sweatpants past his knees. He settled back in Colin's lap and felt his brain melt as Colin licked his hand slow and sure and reached down again to touch his dick.

"Tell me what you like," Colin said, his voice gravelly and thick. His thumb swept over the head of Nick's cock and his back bowed with the sudden jolt of pleasure.

"That," Nick barely got out, then fell forward, pressing his lips recklessly to Colin's, trusting everything he was doing. "*Definitely that.*"

Nick felt his body overloading on pleasure as Colin continued to work his dick with slow, steady pulls, his hand a perfect pressure around him, Colin's tongue stroking against his own.

"Yeah, yeah," Nick panted into Colin's mouth, the pressure building higher and sweeter. "I'm gonna—"

"Yeah, baby, come," Colin said, in that deep, incredibly sexual rasp, and Nick was gone, unable to hold off a moment longer once Colin had told him to.

His knees were unsteady as he sank down into Colin's arms, fuzzy and sated, as Colin whipped his shirt off and wiped his hand. Apparently, all it took for everything to refocus was for all that skin to be displayed, because Nick was suddenly very interested in returning the favor. As soon as possible.

He wiggled out of Colin's grasp and when his knees hit the floor, Colin let out a deep groan. His head fell back and Nick pulled his sweatpants off. Colin's cock was beautiful, Nick thought in a daze. Thick and long and *so* hard, the tip beading with pre-cum.

It looked delicious, and Nick had dreamed about tasting this cock for over a year now. He leaned forward and curled his tongue around the head, sucking it into his mouth.

Colin's body reacted like it had been electrocuted, jerking, his hands mashing into the piles of pillows, knuckles white against the dark navy blue fabric.

Nick let a little more dick slide into his mouth, loving the heaviness on his tongue, the way it filled him up completely. He normally enjoyed blowjobs, but this, giving Colin his very first, felt like a privilege.

His hand curled around the base and he took Colin as deep as he dared, stroking off everything he couldn't fit into his mouth, using his tongue to hit all the hot spots, trying to make it as good as he could for Colin.

Colin's thighs flexed under his other hand. Nick felt his cock twitch in his mouth and knew he was close. He pulled off, glancing up at Colin. Colin's eyes were all pupil, his mouth slack and his expression dazed with pleasure. Nick twisted his hand, letting the excess spit smooth the way, and leaned forward to suck on the head. That was all he needed, Colin's body spasmed and his cock pumped cum into Nick's waiting mouth. Swallowing as best he could, Nick let Colin's cock slide slowly out of his mouth, prolonging his orgasm as long as possible.

Colin trembled as he came down. Nick wiped his mouth and didn't move back to the couch, just kneeled and waited for Colin to come back to himself.

When Colin's eyes opened and his gaze drifted down, it was worth it. There was something in his expression that Nick hadn't ever seen directed his way. Like he was something special to be treated gingerly and carefully.

"Wow," Colin said unsteadily, reaching down to grasp Nick's arm, and to pull him up to the couch.

Nick wouldn't have blamed Colin for not kissing him, but he didn't hesitate at all. He leaned over and kissed Nick deeply and thoroughly, the kiss the equivalent of the look in his eyes.

They settled back on the couch, Nick's hands gravitating to Colin's skin. "Should we rewind?" he asked drowsily.

Colin made a scoffing noise. "I gotta find out if Blair invites Chuck to her birthday party."

"I thought she terrified you," he said, reaching for the remote.

"She does," Colin insisted with indignation. "Doesn't mean I don't want her to fall in love."

"You're a grade A sap, O'Connor," Nick said.

Colin pulled him even closer. "Yes. Make sure you don't forget it, either."

CHAPTER SEVEN

THE NEXT MORNING, COLIN texted Jemma while Nick was in the shower. **Advice much appreciated. But I'm good now.**

Her response back was immediate and insistent. **Well? Did you make a big move? THE big move?**

Colin blushed, as an array of images flashed through his memory.

Kissing Nick.

Touching Nick.

Nick's lips around his cock.

But it wasn't necessarily just the sex that Colin focused on when he thought about last night, even as fucking incredible as it had felt. He'd loved hanging out with Nick, each offering snippy comments about *Gossip Girl* and growing sleepy, cuddling together on the couch. And then heading upstairs, and the awkwardness Colin had feared never becoming an issue. Wordlessly, Nick had grabbed his cell phone charger and had slid into the opposite side of Colin's bed.

They hadn't exactly cuddled all night, but Colin couldn't deny that waking up to see Nick's dark hair against the pillow next to his had been a life-changing moment.

The sex had been *awesome*. But there was something deeper about waking up the morning after, both trying to hide their morning breath, all while not being able to take their hands or eyes off each other.

When Nick had finally slid out of bed, claiming he desperately needed a shower, Colin hadn't been able to help the giddy smile that now seemed permanently plastered to his face.

He couldn't express all of this to Jemma in words, and frankly he didn't really want to. So he just sent her a blushing emoji and hoped she would leave it be. He should have known better.

Her next text came in even quicker. **Really, O'Connor? Gonna make me drag it out of you? Or should I have Gabe text Nick?**

Colin typed out his reply, his smile still giddy despite Jemma being a pest. **Gabe loves you a lot. But probably not that much.**

He put the phone down and decided that this morning he could forgo his normal run and maybe share a romantic breakfast with Nick. He could *make* Nick breakfast, Colin realized as he scrubbed down in the shower. He had eggs and some frozen sausage in the freezer, and he could even go out and grab some pastries and fresh orange juice.

Throwing on shorts and a t-shirt, he ran a haphazard hand through his hair and called it good. After all, Nick hadn't seemed to mind this morning.

"Hey, O'Connor," Nick's voice echoed through the bathroom. Colin looked up and Nick was leaning in the doorway, looking like a model in jeans and a t-shirt. "I'm starved."

"I was about to go out and grab some groceries and make breakfast."

"Or..." Nick said slowly, "we could grab breakfast together?"

Colin didn't need Nick to explain the expression on his face. He was concerned that Colin's first instinct was to stay on his island and avoid the world.

"Right, that makes more sense," Colin said, like it wasn't a big deal. And it wasn't. Or at least, it shouldn't have been. It was just breakfast.

He grabbed his keys and they climbed into the car. When they were driving over the bridge, Colin glanced over at Nick. He didn't want to bring it up, but the thought of leaving it unsaid was even worse. "I'm not a recluse. I swear to god, I'm not agoraphobic, not that there would be anything wrong if I was. But I'm not. I just...it's easier sometimes. Actually, it's *always* easier."

"I didn't think you were," Nick said, and his voice sounded as open and honest as it usually did. But then he continued, and he had, as Colin liked to think of it, his reporter voice on. "But it does surprise me that *you* would choose the easiest way out. I thought you lived to prove the world wrong. To fight injustices, etcetera, etcetera."

"I think that's Captain America," Colin said wryly.

Nick's smile was smug and impudent. "Easy mistake. You sorta look alike. You know, blond hair, blue eyes, ridiculously tall, built like an eighteen-wheeler."

Colin pulled into the diner parking lot that he used to frequent a lot more often. He *had* been staying home an awful lot, more than he'd realized. Something to think about.

"You are not the first person to say that," Colin said, secretly very glad they could switch so easily from serious conversation to teasing with so little awkwardness. But he also knew Nick, and he had a feeling that this subject wasn't one that Nick was going to let go of so easily.

"And yet," Nick said, hand on the steering wheel, his eyes sparkling and impudent in the sunlight, "the first to truly enjoy it." He got out of the car, and Colin knew he had the smuggest expression on his face. Because how was *he* supposed to walk inside with a hard-on in his shorts? These loose athletic shorts didn't hide much, and with Nick's comment, it was suddenly very hard to think about anything else, even with his stomach grumbling.

He got out of the car, thinking of his great aunt Beatrice and her smelly pug, and jogged up next to Nick. "You," he said lowly right before they approached the door, "are a *menace.*"

"Really?" Colin said as he jabbed a finger at the top of the written agenda Helen had just distributed to everyone at the conference table. "The Rainbow Clause meeting? And you even managed to find the time for a rainbow graphic?"

Helen shrugged. "That *is* what we've always called it, isn't it? Seems as appropriate now as it did then. And I didn't do the graphic, I have a new assistant and he's basically useless, so I have to give him really simple tasks."

"You should be happy; you practically have a catchphrase," Mark said.

Colin grimaced. This meeting was frankly ridiculous even without the silly rainbow graphic hovering next to the meeting title. How many meetings did one need to come out of the closet, anyway? Before the last two months, he would have said exactly *one.*

The one where he told Helen and the Piranhas organization what he'd decided to do.

Instead, it turned out there was always yet another meeting needed to hash out more interminable details. At the last one, Helen had brought in a rack of clothing, and, with her assistant, proceeded to suggest that Colin wear more pink and purple.

Now that he thought about it, his incredulous reaction might be why Helen had a brand-new assistant.

At least he was able to bring Nick to this meeting. Colin glanced next to him, trying to keep it cool, because he was not ready to reveal to Mark and *especially* Helen that he had discovered the man he very much wanted to be his first public boyfriend.

Nick was doodling what looked like penises on his Rainbow Clause agenda. Flushing, Colin hastily looked away, wondering if he'd discovered what Nick really felt about these endless, infuriatingly-circular meetings.

"I'm not using the Rainbow Clause as a catch phrase," Colin said, because he suddenly realized that both Helen and Mark might actually consider this a legitimate idea.

"Of course, you're not," Helen said briskly, shooting a daggered glare in Mark's direction.

"Actually," Nick piped up, because he'd seemingly run out of paper to draw hairy-looking dicks on, "I'm going to use it."

Colin gaped at him. "What?"

Nick shrugged. "I think it'd be a great title for the article."

"You...uh...*what,*" Colin repeated, no longer caring if he was intently staring at the man in front of Helen or Mark. He was terrible at non-verbal communication, but Colin hoped his sour lemon expression of *we're definitely going to be discussing this later* was clear enough.

"It's cute, it's catchy. It's self-explanatory. It doesn't need to be a catch phrase to be effective."

Apparently, Nick hadn't gotten the memo.

Colin exhaled and leaned back in his chair. Helen and Mark both made approving noises, and this meeting, designed in the pits of hell, moved on.

"I've finalized the interview schedule," Helen said, passing out more sheets of paper, also adorned with rainbows.

Colin focused all his frustration on the undeserving rainbow, glaring at it so hard he was a little surprised it didn't spontaneously combust.

"I really think he needs to be with Anderson Cooper first," Nick piped up.

Colin did a double take, and then realized that he'd exclusively focused on the stupid rainbow instead of actually *reading* the list of interviews. As he skimmed the list of names and filming dates, he broke out in a cold sweat.

"I can't do all of these," he said, his voice wavering embarrassingly at the end of his sentence. "I thought…I thought I'd do the article, and then maybe one or two, like, *small* shows. I don't want to make it too big of a deal."

He really, *really* should have known better. He should have known when they'd had to hold countless meetings discussing every single annoying detail. He should have known when they tried to micro-manage his behavior. He should have known when they'd nicknamed the stupid *clause* that had been written into his contract.

But somehow, he'd remained oblivious—almost certainly on purpose, he realized now—because if he'd known the extent to which this would be publicized, he might not have gone through with it, no matter how much he wanted to be free.

Helen leaned over the gleaming expanse of conference table between them. He wasn't sure what kind of wood it was—something expensive and rare. Something bought with the profits of the PR machine that ran this team. Colin stared at it, trying to focus on the grain of the wood but couldn't.

"Mr. O'Connor," Helen said in a voice which she only used when she had reached a new level of frustration with his reticence, "tell me, do you know how many athletes currently playing in the National Football League have announced their sexuality as something other than heterosexual?"

Colin felt Nick's hand brush his leg, his fingers dig into the material of his jeans. The sensation seemed to ground him for a split second, but not enough, not *nearly* enough.

"Michael Sam—" Nick started to say. He couldn't even get the rest of the words out before Helen cut him off.

"Doesn't count," Helen said. "He was barely drafted, barely made it off the practice squad, ended up in Canada and then retired. *And*, I didn't ask you."

Abruptly she stood, and started pacing back and forth in front of the floor-to-ceiling windows that overlooked the practice fields. "There's a reason we wrote the Rainbow Clause instead of encouraging Mr. O'Connor to come out before or right after we drafted him. We thought, with a little more experience in the NFL under his belt, and with some more playing time to adjust both the fanbase and the other players to him as a person, his revelation would be far more accepted than Michael Sam's was."

Nick's voice was just as harsh. "Michael Sam is an American hero, and I don't like the way you're talking about him."

Colin watched as Helen swiveled around to face Nick. "I appreciate that you're partially here for sentimental reasons, Mr. Wheeler," she said, "but I'm not. I'm here to sell game tickets and season tickets and jerseys. I want just as much support for Mr. O'Connor as you do, but you've *got* to let me do my job."

Colin knew exactly what doing her job would probably mean for him—a complete inability to stay under any radar at all, going forward.

"The marketing opportunity here is endless," Mark inserted, because of course he never knew when to shut the hell up. "You're going to be the most recognized man in America."

Colin jerked up, his chair screeching on the floor as it flew backwards.

Nick was up half a second later. He'd kept his distance, despite sitting next to him, since they'd walked in the room. But now Colin felt him place a reassuring hand on his shoulder as Colin faced down Helen and Mark.

"Listen," Nick said soothingly, his voice low and calm, "I know it sounds crazy. I know it sounds *awful*, but you're pretty recognizable now. And there isn't a way to do this that *doesn't* end up with you becoming more well known. It's big news. You're not technically the first, but Helen's right, they set things up so that you might have a little more success in the end. That's a *good* thing."

Helen seemed to have caught on when she spoke up next. Colin wanted to ignore her, but he'd gotten himself into this thing, and panicking now when he was already sure this was the course he needed to take wouldn't get him anywhere.

"These are all *very* sympathetic and easy interviews," Helen said. "We'll practice. You'll see all the questions ahead of time. There won't be a single surprise. All you'll have to do is tell the truth."

Like telling *this* truth was easy. Colin already knew it wouldn't be. Nick had warned him that this would be hard. Colin wished he had listened more. Had asked more questions. Had not just stuck his head in the sand and hoped it would all turn out okay because he had the goddamned Rainbow Clause.

He looked back down at the list of interviewers.

Anderson Cooper.

Ellen.

Jimmy Fallon.

Ryan Seacrest.

"What about the sports networks?" he asked.

"We'll do some call-in stuff with them," Helen said. "But most of the sports side is going to be covered by the article Nick is writing. And good news, I just got confirmation that *Five Points* has worked out a deal with *Sports Illustrated*. Looks like you've just booked your second cover."

Colin sat down and tried to process. Couldn't, really. He landed somewhere around *laugh so you don't cry*. "Maybe they'll put me in rainbow swimming trunks this time around."

Mark actually started to nod his approval of this idea when Colin shot him a withering look.

"It'll be classy. The whole thing will be, I promise. I want this to work just as much as you do," Helen said. Sadly, Colin believed her, because she wouldn't shoot herself in the foot. She still needed to sell the tickets, get butts in the seats, and sell his jersey.

"Fine," he said softly.

Colin was terrifyingly quiet as they reached the car.

"Are you okay?" Nick finally had to ask, because he was afraid he'd overstepped his bounds in the conference room, given both Helen and Mark a clear indication of what was going on between them, and that Colin was panicking over the entire coming-out process.

Both were bad news. The real problem was that one was fixable, while the other was not.

Nobody—not Nick, not Helen, not Mark, *nobody*—could make this process easier on Colin. It would be hard every time he was faced with a new person he needed to tell. And while Nick had struggled at points with even telling one person, they were expecting Colin to get on national television and tell millions.

"Not really," Colin said.

Nick's heart ached for him.

"And don't say it gets better," Colin added with a wry tone.

"Even if it does?"

"Especially if it does. I just want to not think about it. To not worry about it. To just face it when it comes and let it happen."

"Well," Nick said hesitantly, "you're also about to become rather more recognizable. Is there someplace you'd like to go before that happens? We've got time and nowhere else to be."

"Like the pizza parlor?" Colin asked, his brow wrinkling in confusion.

Nick laughed. "No, like…someplace other than here. Somewhere other than Miami."

He wasn't quite ready to tell Colin that after winning the National Championship and the Heisman and then being drafted first in the NFL, topped off by *that* cover on *Sports Illustrated*, that he was *already* recognizable. Coming out wouldn't necessarily change that as much as Helen or Mark might expect it would. People already knew who Colin was. But it was a good excuse to get out of town, get Colin off his island, and distract him for the week Nick had remaining in Miami.

"The guys are always telling me how great the Keys are," Colin said slowly. "But I've never been."

Of course, with a nearly unlimited bank account and resources, Colin would pick something within easy driving distance. Nick didn't even know why he was surprised anymore.

"You want to go to the Keys?" he asked.

"Yeah," Colin said, more decisively this time. "Yeah, I think I do." He glanced over and even if Nick had wanted to, he couldn't have missed or mistaken the look in those baby blue eyes. "With you, definitely."

It was such a heady thought; frittering away their time even more lazily than before, but after the events of the last few days, with a closeness that Nick had only dreamed could be possible.

"Then," he said, reaching over and weaving his fingers with Colin's, "let's go to the Keys."

It was hard for Nick to conceptualize, even after years of being around professional athletes and their notoriously flexible schedules, that Colin could decide to go to the Keys, get on the phone with his assistant as they drove towards the house, and have the next week cleared in ten minutes.

"You're in charge while I'm gone," Colin told Lindsay, and Nick had to hide his smile behind his water bottle at her shocked silence. She'd wanted more responsibility, but she'd not really expected him to hand it to her.

"Of course," she stammered.

"What I mean is," Colin clarified, "I'm not taking my laptop. I'm not going to look at email. I'll answer Mark's calls, but they'd better be important. Text me if you need anything."

"What about Helen?" Lindsay asked, which went a long way in explaining to Nick how much Lindsay knew. And who she was probably *really* reporting to.

"What about her?" Colin huffed, clearly still bothered by the earlier meeting.

"You have a really big thing coming up, and I know Helen's gonna want to talk to you."

Yeah, Nick decided, there was no "probably" about it. Lindsay might work for Colin, but she was definitely reporting to Helen.

Truthfully, he wasn't sure how he felt about it. He knew how Colin would feel about it, if Nick ever decided to tell him, but Nick knew Helen was eminently capable at her job and part of that was keeping a whole team of professional athletes from doing stupid shit.

A wild card like Colin who she already knew was in the closet? If Nick had been in Helen's position, he'd have sent someone to watch him, too. Of course, Helen couldn't have known at the beginning that Colin would reject nearly all the trappings of his position, including his personal assistant, leaving her flying blind.

Colin turned onto the bridge that led them to the island. "What can't wait, you can text me about. But this is a vacation for me. Away from any coming-out talk, if I can help it. Okay?"

"Yeah, of course. I'll do what I can to take care of it."

Colin parked in the front of the house and when they got out, Nick said to him, "You realize that everyone thinks we're sleeping together, right?"

He typed in the front door code, then glanced over at Nick. "Yep." He smiled, big and goofy, and it wasn't that Nick hadn't realized he was in profound trouble before this moment, but *he was in deep shit.* How was he going to spend the next week with this fluffy asshole who looked like a model and who had the soul of a golden retriever and then fly home like nothing inside him had fundamentally changed?

Nick really didn't know how to answer that, so he pushed the thought from his head.

"Right." He grinned back. "I suppose I should be very flattered."

"That's what I keep telling myself," Colin said, reaching out and grasping Nick's shoulders with his hands. Pushing backwards gently, Nick's back hit the closed door. Colin grinned like a puppy and then proceeded to lean in, hold him down, and kiss him with every ounce of filthy skill he'd gathered. Hot, wet, messy kisses, his tongue nimbly searching Nick's mouth. Pleasure spiked through Nick's body and he tried to rock up against the hard body holding him against the door, but Colin was just far enough back and just strong enough that he thrust up against empty air.

Nick's breath was a damp gasp against Colin's neck when the kiss ended.

"Wanted to do that all day, *especially* in that hell-spawn meeting," Colin murmured into his hair.

Nick's hips finally connected with Colin's and the pressure left them both groaning. "Then," Nick said, "you should've just thrown me down on the conference table and had your way with me. Everyone already thinks we're hooking up."

Colin chuckled, a low, diabolical sound that sent the rest of Nick's blood straight to his dick. "Now I know what you've been fantasizing about with your *Sports Illustrated* for reference."

Nick flushed brighter than he wanted Colin to see. He wasn't ashamed exactly, because desire was a healthy thing, but Colin had ended a little too close to the truth for comfort.

"Does it bother you, that they might know?" Colin asked quietly, like that was the source of Nick's embarrassment. Which, it wasn't, at all. In fact, he'd sort of never been prouder that of all the men and women in the world, Colin wanted to be with *him*.

Pulling back, Nick made sure Colin was looking him straight in the eye. Nick didn't like the sudden furrow between his brows, didn't like the way he'd shifted backwards the tiniest bit. Like this *was* something to be ashamed of. "No," he told Colin with certainty. Another moment, he might have scoffed like it was silly—which it *was*—but the serious expression on Colin's face told him it wasn't the right time to joke about this. "Not in a million years would it bother me. We could hook up on the table in front of them, and I wouldn't care."

Colin's short exhale of relief told Nick that he'd gone the right route. They might not have defined exactly what was happening between them—at least *out loud*, because Nick had a terrifying thought he knew exactly what was happening, at least on his side—but that didn't mean it was just casual between them.

Colin pressed a quick kiss on Nick's hair and stepped away, heading towards the stairs. Nick looked mournfully down at his partially erect dick as he realized that Colin had every intention of teasing the hell out of them both before they got to the Keys.

He should be unhappier about it, but he realized as he climbed the stairs towards his room that he enjoyed seeing a more playful side of Colin emerge. Not many people had probably ever been privileged enough to witness it.

"I made a call and we're gonna borrow one of my teammates' getaway cottages," Colin said as they headed down the highway towards the Keys. Yet another sign advertising an alligator petting zoo flashed behind Colin's head. "It's on Marathon."

"Which teammate?" Nick asked, because he was curious which of Colin's teammates he was on close enough terms with to call up last minute and borrow their vacation home.

Colin shot him a quick slant of a look that made him wonder if he'd figured out what Nick was thinking. "Teddy, actually."

"Then *cottage* is probably not the right term," Nick said. Teddy had been playing in the NFL for years and was one of the highest paid defensive ends in the game.

"Probably not," Colin admitted, and it was his turn to flush. "I could've called up a hotel, I guess, but I wanted privacy, and I know Teddy's place will be nice."

Nice was likely an understatement. Luxurious and palatial was probably closer to reality.

"You trying to impress me, O'Connor?" Nick asked, trying his best to ignore the frisson of pleasure he felt at the thought.

Colin's laugh was bright and infectious. "I can't believe it's taken you so long to figure that out."

It was a little too close to all the thoughts that Nick had been having lately. Thoughts like *always* and *forever* and *boyfriend*. And that little four-letter word that had never terrified him before, but now with Colin, was throwing him for a loop.

He changed the subject. Picking up the phone Colin had carelessly tossed into the center console of the car, he noted it was hooked up into the car's sound system. "What's your password?" he asked. "It's a long drive, we should put some music on."

Colin flushed again, hotter this time and a whole lot redder, the color creeping up his neck and settling bright on his ears.

"Is it something really embarrassing?" Nick demanded with a teasing edge to his voice. This was a lot safer ground than admitting that Colin had never needed to win him over. He'd been fairly won in those first five minutes, when Colin's eyes had matched his polo shirt, and he'd smiled shyly, like everyone didn't end up speechless and awestruck when they met him for the first time.

Colin shook his head, but his ears grew brighter. "It totally is," Nick said. "Is it like *sexy bottom cum slut* or something?"

"Oh god," Colin said between gasps of hysterical laughter. "*No.*"

"Then what is it? If you don't tell me, I'll just keep assuming it's something completely deviant."

"It's *not*, it's just...well, it's embarrassing, just not embarrassing like that."

"And?"

"It's *password*, okay?"

Nick was more surprised than if the password *had* been *sexy bottom cum slut*. "Seriously?"

If Colin's ears got any redder, they might spontaneously combust. Nick thought it was fucking adorable.

"Lindsay needs to use it sometimes," he said, a touch defensively. "So I wanted to keep it generic."

"You're cute," Nick said as he typed it in. "My *grandmother* uses that as her password."

Opening the music app, Nick scrolled through his albums. "You've got decent taste in music, though."

"Imagine my relief that there's something you can't tease me about," Colin said dryly, though when Nick glanced up, he was still smiling.

"Sorry, I know my asshole tendencies get annoying," Nick said, wishing he'd listened when Jemma had told him once that everyone didn't enjoy being teased.

"Don't apologize," Colin said. "I like it."

"If you're sure—"

Colin cut him off before Nick could even finish his sentence. He settled a big, warm hand on his thigh and gave him a bit of a squeeze. "I'm *sure*. Stop worrying."

It took over two hours to get down to Marathon, and then another fifteen minutes to navigate through the island to find Teddy's (naturally) beachfront property.

When Colin pulled up to the gate and punched in the code Teddy had texted him, Nick couldn't help but roll his eyes. "Of course, there's a gate and a code."

The house itself was shielded by the fence and a thick barrier made of tropical vegetation and palm trees, but as it came into view, Nick made a shocked noise.

"Just when you think Teddy can't surprise you..." Colin said in an awed voice.

The cottage that they'd both expected to have more in common with a mansion, was in fact, a *cottage*. An unassuming, simple, white-sided building, square and squat, and undeniably small.

"He surprises you," Nick finished.

"Are you okay with this?" Colin asked as he pulled into the driveway and stopped the car. "I can still call a hotel."

Nick opened the door and realized as he stepped out that other than the rudimentary driveway, everything else was sand. The house was literally *on* the beach.

"Hell no," Nick said. "This'll be fine." He grabbed his bag from the back and instead of waiting for Colin to find the code to the front door on his phone, walked around the side.

"I think I found out the reason for the gate," Nick called out to Colin.

Spread out before them was a gorgeous expanse of pristine, private, white sand beach. The house had a long veranda across the back, with steps right down to the sand. Floor-to-ceiling windows on the entire back of the house meant that the view would be incomparable.

A single dock stretched out from one side of the beach, and a sleek speedboat was housed under a simple wooden structure at the end of it.

"Wow," Colin said, walking up behind him. He slung a casual arm around Nick's shoulders, and even that simple touch made him want to sink into it.

"Wow is right," Nick echoed. "This is pretty incredible."

"The house is pretty simple," Colin said, and Nick glanced back, realizing one of the sliding glass doors off the veranda was open and that Colin had come from inside the house. "But of course, because it's Teddy, it's still perfect."

"I wouldn't expect anything less."

"Honestly," Colin said softly, "I think this is where he and Maria come to get away. Without the kids or anyone else. There's basically a bedroom with an enormous bed, a bathroom and a tiny kitchen. That's it."

Nick had no compunction in dropping his bag to the ground so he could slide his hands around Colin's neck. "That's all you need, when it's right." He tugged Colin closer and kissed him deeply. It was the perfect moment, the sea breeze winding around them, the smell of the salt water in the air, standing on a private beach. He didn't even care if he'd given everything away with his words.

Reality didn't intrude until they were exploring the tiny bungalow together and they discovered a basket full of condoms and lube placed very prominently in the middle of the bathroom counter.

"Uh," Colin stammered, his face bright red. Nick, fighting down his own embarrassment at how obvious they'd probably been, reached over and flipped open the card sitting in the basket.

"*Have fun and be safe, love Teddy*," Nick read out loud. "Well tha t's...something."

Colin rubbed his neck and shot him a rueful glance. "One way of putting it."

Nick had forced any twinges of embarrassment aside and was examining the contents of the basket. He was pretty sure Teddy was straight, as he'd been married to Maria for over ten years—an eternity in the world of professional sports—but the items he'd selected definitely had some thought behind them.

The kitchen was more of the same. Not actual lube and condoms, but a case of expensive champagne, lots of fresh fruit, and stuff to make simple breakfasts. Eggs, bacon, bread. And a large tray you'd use to serve breakfast in bed if you were so inclined, resting so helpfully on the tiny kitchenette table.

"He is *not* subtle," Colin said, pointing out the obvious.

There was another note posted to the fridge. *Some groceries to get you started,* it read, *and don't forget a romantic breakfast in bed, Maria loves those. Also, I know you know your way around a boat, but be careful with my baby. Teddy.*

Nick was more the kind of man who took what he wanted, and asked questions later. But he broke his usual rules and asked first because not asking suddenly didn't feel acceptable. "Are you okay with all of this?"

They'd originally come to the Keys, if there'd really been any intention at all, as a quick getaway to distract Colin from the pressures of coming out. It hadn't been designed as a romantic getaway, necessarily, even though they'd begun to explore the possibility of sex.

Teddy, whether explicitly instructed or not, had morphed the purpose on his own.

Colin looked surprised at the question. Probably as surprised, Nick realized, as he himself had looked when Colin had asked him if he'd rather stay in a hotel.

"Of course, I am. Teddy, well, Teddy has a pretty good idea about how I feel," Colin said. "Are *you?*"

Nick felt like he was seventeen again, and he'd caught the cute boy on the track team looking at his legs. He desperately wanted to ask what *Teddy has a pretty good idea about how I feel* meant, but he wasn't quite ready to answer on his own yet, so he couldn't really demand it of Colin.

Instead he answered, "Yeah, of course. This place is amazing. And I'm happy to be here with you." Nick figured that should make his own feelings obvious enough without stating them absolutely.

"Great," Colin said, leaning in to kiss him again, his hands reaching up to bracket Nick's face, his fingertips brushing the contours of his features. It was soft and slow and sweet, but Nick couldn't tear his mind from the enormous bed with its wrought iron headboard and miles of fluffy white sheets, or the basket sitting in the bathroom.

He wanted Colin stretched out on the bed, all golden skin against the stark white of the sheets, face blissed from pleasure.

"Let's go to bed," he murmured against Colin's lips. "I want to see you."

Colin didn't say a word but nodded, letting himself be easily tugged towards the big bed. Nick pulled off his shirt and his fingers made quick work of the button and fly on Colin's cargo shorts. Colin's hands echoed his movements, pulling Nick's clothes off with clumsy but effective movements.

Naked, Colin fell onto the bed and Nick stood in the space between of his legs. "Come here," Colin said, no doubt trying to use his seductive voice.

Nick almost told him that seduction was unnecessary. Having him spread out on the bed this way, gloriously and gorgeously naked, that was all the seduction he needed.

"What do you want?" Nick asked. He knew what he wanted, but he wanted to make absolutely sure Colin was on the same page.

"Anything you'll give me," Colin said, honesty glowing out of his face.

"Okay," Nick said unsteadily. "Don't move." He walked the few steps to the bathroom and grabbed the basket of supplies.

He saw Colin go a little white at the sight of them in his hands, and he laid a reassuring hand on his leg. "Don't worry," he said, "we'll go slow. Nothing you don't want to do."

Depositing the basket on the nightstand, he climbed on top of Colin, and couldn't help but moan shamelessly as their mouths met and their hard cocks brushed together for the first time.

"So good," Colin gasped as they moved together, skin to skin, their kisses intense and slick.

Kissing Colin was so good it was hard to stop, but Nick knew he couldn't wait forever. His lips cruised downward, and he relished the taste and the scent and the feel of Colin's skin under his mouth, the tremble of his muscles, and the quiet moans that kept escaping.

Sucking Colin's cock was just as good the second time. He let his hand drift lower, and then lower still, brushing his balls and then searching with one spit-damp finger.

When he found it, Colin moaned shamelessly, pushing back against Nick's finger as it traced the furled edges of his hole. "You want this?" Nick asked, breathless and on fire.

Colin's eyes were impossibly blue as their gazes met. "Anything," he panted.

"We'll go slow," Nick said quietly, reaching over for the lube.

They definitely went slow, not just because it was Colin's first time, but because he was so sensitive, so incredibly responsive, Nick had to keep stopping. His lips poised at the crown of his cock, his fingers buried inside of him, as Colin fought off orgasm. He'd re-center himself, and then Nick would continue, the way his body flexed tightly around his fingers painfully pleasurable. He was so turned on it would be a miracle if he actually got inside before coming.

Three fingers in, Colin flushed and panting, sweat slicking up his chest, Nick let his instincts take over. He slid Colin's cock back in his mouth, instead of merely teasing the tip, and sucked hard, sending Colin's body into a tense arch. He pressed in with his fingers, searching for the spot that would send Colin off the cliff, and barely had any warning when it happened, Colin letting out a fierce yell as he spilled onto Nick's tongue.

His own skin was almost unbearably sensitive, Nick realized, as he reached up to smooth a shaky hand along Colin's torso.

"God," Colin said, his voice wrenched. "Now come here and let me return the favor."

Nick made a token protest. Colin overruled him by literally picking him up and settling on top of him.

"Done arguing?" Colin asked smugly.

"Maybe you could use something to shut your mouth up," Nick teased.

"Don't mind if I do," Colin said, taking it seriously and carefully and deliberately slipping the head of Nick's cock into his mouth.

It was clearly his first blowjob. There might have been awkwardness or hesitation, but Nick was out of his mind with want and didn't care. He only cared that it was Colin and Colin's mouth, and that what he might not have in skill, he easily made up for in enthusiasm.

Wiping his mouth, Colin stretched out beside Nick and pulled him close against him. "Already, best vacation ever. Hands down," he murmured into Nick's shoulder.

"I would like to propose never leaving this bed again," Nick sighed.

"I'll make it happen."

Once, it might have felt like a silly joke to Nick, careless words exchanged back and forth in the glowing aftermath of some very good sex. But he could hear the ring of truth in Colin's words, and suddenly, he terribly wanted to know what Colin had told Teddy.

Wanted to know so that he wouldn't have to be the one to say it first. Knew he wasn't alone in these thoughts, but still wanted the reassurance of Colin's feelings.

Nick was still trying to figure out how to ask when he fell asleep.

CHAPTER EIGHT

Colin's house, bright and open and overlooking the ocean, was nothing compared to the view that greeted the two of them the next morning.

"Wow," Colin breathed out, the sheet shifting down his torso as he propped himself up with an elbow. "What a view."

Even though the ocean and sky and sand were hazy with the golden light of the rising sun, Nick still had trouble taking his eyes off the man next to him.

"Yeah," Nick said, still staring at Colin. "Fucking fabulous view."

Colin glanced over and flushed. He rolled over and slid out of bed, bare feet padding on the tile floor as he headed towards the bathroom. "When you look at me that way," he said, his voice carrying back into the bedroom, "it's easy to believe I really look as good as you say."

"You should believe it," Nick said as Colin returned to bed. Nick knew he needed to use the bathroom, too, at least to brush away his surely horrible morning breath so he could kiss this beautiful man next to him.

Just one problem. Nick glanced at the tile floor with dismay. "Is that as cold as it looks?"

Colin shot him a playful smile and gave him a little shove to the edge of the bed. "Your turn to find out," he said, and Nick gave a half-hearted smile, expecting to freeze his balls off as he tiptoed to the bathroom. Instead, he found the floor to be shockingly warm against his bare feet.

"Teddy, that rich bastard," Nick exclaimed as he walked to the bathroom. "Heated floors."

Nick brushed his teeth and took a piss, returning to bed with warm feet and cold hands, which he proceeded to place right on Colin's rib cage. But Colin didn't flinch, only tugged Nick closer, until their limbs were tangled together. Nick shifted up a fraction and hesitated, their eyes locked together and their lips only an inch apart.

"You keep talking about me," Colin murmured dreamily, his hand smoothing down a wayward tuft of Nick's hair. "But you're gorgeous. I stare at you all the damn time."

It was hard not to notice and impossible not to feel smug that Colin O'Connor spent at least half his waking hours staring at his ass.

A large hand slid around his hip and cupped that ass—but not with the sort of tacky possession that sometimes gave Nick a bad taste in his mouth, but with reverence and a playful affection that made his heart ache.

"I know you notice," Colin continued, the edge of his lips quirking into a smile. "You're too nice to call me out on it."

"What, and make you stop?" Nick asked.

Colin chuckled, slow and low in the back of his throat, just rough enough to send shivers down Nick's spine. Sometimes it was easy to forget Colin was still technically a virgin because he could be painfully sexy. And part of the mystery of that, Nick thought, was that Colin wasn't really trying. He just *was*.

Colin's way of just *being* was pushing around Nick's good intentions like they weighed nothing.

"You like it?" Colin asked back.

What Nick desperately wanted to say was that he didn't just like it, but the other *L* word was looming dangerously in his mind, and so instead of answering with words, he leaned in the last half an inch and pressed his lips to Colin's.

They made out for long, slow minutes, their lips catching together again and again, tongues lazily stroking into each other's mouths, hands wandering and caressing every inch of bare skin.

Colin let out a low, uncontrolled moan as Nick's hand trailed up his inner thigh, creeping towards his already hard cock. It twitched, clearly wanting the attention it hadn't been receiving. "I want you," Colin said, breathless and intent.

"How do you want me?" Nick asked.

Nick watched as he took a steadying breath, fighting the flush that came to his cheeks. "Do you... um...would it be okay?"

"Yes," Nick interrupted, because he knew what Colin was asking, and the answer was always going to be *yes* if it was Colin asking.

"Would you like to do it, or should I?" Nick asked, reaching over Colin's torso and grabbing the lube they'd used the night before.

"Uhhh," Colin stammered again. Someone else might get impatient with Colin's hesitation, but Nick found he enjoyed it; it was a reminder that he was the only one who'd ever made Colin flush so red.

Nick flicked open the lid and wet two fingers. "How about I show you?"

Colin's face was puce, but the hungry look in his eyes was pushing Nick closer and closer to the precipice of losing control. It prickled all across his skin as he shifted backwards, to his knees, and reached up, slowly pushing a finger into his hole.

He let gravity take over, pushing in and sinking down, relaxing more muscles as he felt the familiar stretch.

"Let me see," Colin begged, his eyes wide and blown, only a tiny ring of blue around his pupils. Nick moved, and tried to remember the compliments Colin had said about him as he opened himself up to Colin's gaze.

"God," Colin exhaled in a low growl. "You are so fucking hot, I can barely stand it."

That was all the motivation Nick needed to push a second finger alongside the first, and Colin swore.

"You're fucking incredible," Colin continued, awe dripping from his words.

Nick was nearly adjusted to the stretch when he felt Colin's hand grasp his hip and then another cautious but intent touch where his fingers were buried in his body. Arousal was burning through him, his cock leaking steadily onto the sheets, but the idea of Colin touching him rocketed through him like a tsunami.

Colin carefully pushed in his finger alongside Nick's two. "Is this okay?" he asked, sounding even more turned on than Nick felt, which was insane because they'd barely touched each other yet.

"More...more..." Nick stammered as Colin's finger pushed his and he accidentally bumped his prostate, sending electricity through his veins. "More than okay."

"Good." Colin made a satisfied humming noise as his finger settled all the way into Nick's body, and Nick nearly cried with how good it felt, and how hot it made him for Colin to be watching *and* helping.

"Need you," Nick said, and he felt Colin's finger drag alongside his own as he pulled out.

"Right here," Colin said smugly, and Nick looked over his shoulder to see Colin laid out like the best present he'd ever received, cock hard and red, Colin's hand smoothing lube over it, shiny and wet.

"*Fuck*," Nick said, his fingers slipping out of him as he tried to get his legs to work, to carry him over to where he needed to be, more than he needed oxygen or water or even his morning coffee.

His knees were unsteady as he climbed over Colin, hands braced on his bare chest. He shook even more as he lined up Colin's cock and started to sink down slowly onto it.

Colin's eyes rolled backwards and he arched up, mouth open in a soundless yell as Nick bottomed out. His fists clenched at the bunched up sheets, knuckles white and mouth a determined line of control as Nick shifted around, adjusting to the length inside of him.

It was almost too much to see all of this beautiful man, undone by pleasure, as he felt the answering surge begin to crest through him. Nick closed his eyes and tried to regain his self-control before this ended sooner than it really began.

"You good?" he croaked out, his fingers digging into Colin's abs.

"You feel..." Colin couldn't even say the words, he was too far gone.

"Don't come," Nick ordered, more to himself than to Colin—or maybe to both of them. Because once he started to move, it felt like every tiny shift of his hips had Colin's dick, long and hard, brushing right against his prostate. It felt so good he never wanted it to end, and at the same time, it was too good to last.

Colin's hands clamped around his hips, fingers digging into the flesh, and they both moaned as he experimentally flexed his hips, pumping up into Nick as he was moving downwards.

It took a few thrusts to get the rhythm right, but once they did, it was a hard, steady, wild ride to the end, Colin moaning a nonstop litany of how tight and hot Nick was around him. The physical pleasure was almost enough to tip Nick over the edge, but when Colin started babbling, that was all Nick needed to push him right over.

He grasped his cock once, then he was gone, pleasure exploding along his nerves, a white-hot supernova sparking over him.

Colin pumped once and then twice and then bellowed long and loud, burying his face into Nick's shoulder, his teeth probably leaving marks that wouldn't fade for a while.

Nick collapsed onto Colin's chest and they lay there for several long minutes, before Colin gently moved him to the bed, getting up to get a damp washcloth.

Colin might have been a virgin, but he was a considerate one. Then he settled back next to Nick, and pulled his head back to his chest. Nick made a contented sound and snuggled in closer.

"I hurt you," Colin said softly, his fingers tracing the red oval his teeth had made in the heat of the moment, his voice concerned but tinged with a hint of awe. Like he couldn't believe he had done it, and that Nick had let him.

The truth was, Nick would have let him do that and a lot more. But the care and the gentleness was nice too, something he'd never enjoyed before. "I'll heal," he said, stretching his legs out on the bed, trying to find a dry spot. "The sheets are gross. We should get up. Aren't you starving?"

"I was going to bring you breakfast in bed," Colin confessed. "But then you distracted me."

Nick quirked an eyebrow. "It seemed a fairly mutual distraction to me."

Colin was quiet for a long moment. "It's still hard for me to believe that."

Nick's hand, slowly stroking Colin's side, hesitated. He wondered what he could say that might convince Colin how incredible he was—as a football player, a friend, a *lover*. He was wrapped up in a loyal, kind package, with the added benefit of being hot enough to make men weep. But Colin had heard all those things before, and they'd clearly not resonated.

"Do you want me to tell you what I'm going to write in the article?" Nick tried to keep his tone casual, but it was tough with the *L* word clanging around in his head, demanding to be heard. Demanding to be *said*.

Colin shrugged, the sort of expression on his face one that Nick had deciphered weeks ago. It meant he desperately wanted to know, but also didn't want to hold anyone to an obligation.

Nick was perfectly happy to be held to all sorts of obligations.

"Well, a lot of things, really. But the gist of it is that you've been subjected to the sort of past that would've changed anybody else. Bitterness, egotism, resentment, callousness, jealousy—it would have been so easy to embody those. Nobody could have blamed you. But unlike almost every professional athlete I've ever encountered, you care more about what you can do for people than what they think of you. And that's extraordinary."

Nick felt as Colin grew tenser and tenser as he continued to speak. When he finally finished, Colin didn't say anything right away.

When he did speak, it wasn't what Nick had expected to hear. "All of that and nothing about my *Sports Illustrated* cover," Colin said wryly.

Nick buried the pulse of hurt he felt. He told himself that some people didn't know how to accept compliments. He almost believed it. *Almost.* Maybe if he hadn't been so tied up personally, he could have.

"Well, you're fucking hot, too," Nick said flippantly, burying the last bit of hurt away. He slid a hand down Colin's abs, tracing each groove with a fingertip. "And I definitely plan to appreciate every last inch."

And instead of climbing out of bed and eating breakfast, they stayed in for another hour, finally leaving the temptation of the fluffy covers and each other to eat mangos and pineapples over the sink, juice dripping down their chins.

"This is a perfect day," Nick pronounced from his lounger. It was late afternoon and the sun was shining mercilessly on the beach, except for the patch of shade where Nick had dragged his chair earlier in the day.

"You're just saying that because you literally went from the bed to that lounger," Colin retorted without heat. "I had to leave to find sustenance."

"Your idea," Nick pointed out. "I'd have been happy enough to subsist on fruit and champagne. Oh, and sex." He didn't have to glance over at where Colin was sitting to know he was blushing.

"Well, I didn't manage breakfast in bed, so I figured pizza on the beach was a good alternative."

"I'm definitely not complaining."

"The opposite, actually," Colin said, his tone full of amusement and affection. Nick wanted to soak up every bit like the sun and store it away for the inevitable rainy day.

"I'm just saying it was perfect," Nick said, "but tomorrow we should maybe do something less...sedentary."

"We could take the boat out. Teddy emailed me a list of fishing guides he uses."

"Ugh. Fishing."

"Isn't that what athletes do in the Keys? Go deep sea fishing?"

Nick sat up in the lounger, and slipped his sunglasses onto his head, shooting Colin a very frank stare. "I don't care what the fuck athletes do, neither of us has any interest in fishing, unless you have a secret kink you're not telling me about."

Colin flushed again. And Nick was almost certain it wasn't a sunburn because he'd rubbed in the sunscreen himself, at regular intervals. It had been his best entertainment of the day. At least since they'd managed to leave the bed behind.

"So that's a no-go on the fishing," Colin said ruefully.

"Feel free to tell me to go to hell, but maybe you should worry less about what everyone else wants and do what *you* want. Be upfront about it."

"I'll take it under advisement."

Nick hoped he would. Colin could get hung up on his idea of what he "should" be doing, probably because he spent his waking hours desperately wishing to flaunt the rules. The residual guilt over this rule-breaking seemed to lead to an attempt to toe the line the rest of the time.

The thing was, Nick wasn't certain Colin would be truly free until he could let go of the guilt and tell the world to fuck off.

"But the boat, though, that's a good idea. Let's do that. Beer and sandwiches and lots of loud, obnoxious music. Maybe Pitbull."

Colin laughed, which was all Nick had been trying to accomplish. "I thought we weren't trying to be cliché."

Nick settled back into his lounger. "I like Pitbull," he insisted, and Colin laughed harder.

It was really a perfect day.

Despite plans to leave earlier, they didn't drag themselves out of bed until nearly noon the next day. Colin bemoaned his muscle tone because he hadn't done a single physical activity in two days. Nick raised his eyebrow and didn't have to open his mouth to remind Colin that they'd done *plenty* of physical activity in the last two days.

Just not jogging or weight lifting.

"I'm not saying that I didn't enjoy what we've been doing more than a twenty-mile jog," Colin said earnestly as they were lying on the deck of the boat, the sun drying their trunks after their last dip in the ocean. "I just want you to know that."

Nick chuckled. "If you preferred the twenty-mile jog, I'd have been really concerned for your mental stability."

"Right, well, I don't want to lose anything you've come to appreciate, either," Colin retorted.

Nick was ninety-five percent comfortable, a state of relaxation that was difficult to achieve, and he groaned as he hefted himself up. He wanted to smack whomever had given Colin O'Connor the idea that he wasn't good enough the way he was—six-pack abs or not.

"You sound annoyed," Colin said, and there was a thread of alarm in his voice.

Nick scrubbed a hand over his eyes and opened them despite not having any idea where his sunglasses had disappeared to and the flaming ball of fire that was currently directly above them. "I'm annoyed," he confirmed. "But not with you."

"I don't get it."

The worst part of this was that it was clear that Colin really didn't.

"Believe me, I love the way you look. I've made that plenty clear over the last few weeks, especially the last forty-eight hours. *Many* times," he said with emphasis. "But that isn't why I'm here with you right now."

Colin still looked befuddled. "Was it Jemma?" Nick demanded, his annoyance growing. "Was it her that made you feel like this?" Because if it was, they were going to have *words* when he got back to LA.

"Jemma?"

Nick groaned and fell back to the cushion. "Did she," he enunciated carefully, "ever make you feel like you weren't good enough to be with? Not hot enough? Not accomplished enough? Or was that someone else? That kid from high school maybe?"

Colin's voice was even more careful than Nick's had been—if that was even possible. "I'm not sure I understand what you're trying to say. You're here because you were *assigned* to be here. As for me feeling the way I do, of course it wasn't Jemma or *that kid from high school.*"

Nick opened one eye and glared in Colin's general direction. He thought that maybe this was their first fight ever, and he wasn't even sure why that was happening. Because Colin had expressed concern that if he lost his gorgeous abs, that Nick wouldn't be around anymore? That was just plain fucking offensive, and the more Nick stewed on it, the more it bothered him.

"I'm not *here* because I was assigned, you asshat," Nick grumbled. "Yes, in the general Floridian area, but not *here*. This is actually the opposite of what I should be doing if we're talking about my assignment."

"Oh." Colin's voice was small and still bewildered.

Suddenly it was too hot, even for Nick, and because he could, he leveraged himself upright and took a dive into the balmy water of the Atlantic Ocean.

It did both things Nick needed desperately: one, it cooled him down, and two, it stopped an increasingly non-productive conversation in its tracks.

Except when he finally finished swimming around—cooling off his blood and his brain, and climbed back onto the boat, dripping water everywhere—Colin, who'd dug into the cooler of sandwiches and was currently nursing a beer, said, "I feel like we're having two different conversations here."

How had he managed to forget that Colin was one of the most stubborn people he'd ever met?

Nick stuck his hand into the cooler and dragged out a beer. Popping the top, he took a long drink. And then another. "Probably because we are."

"I thought that was just men and women that did that. Aren't we supposed to understand each other better than that? You know, because we're both from Mars?"

Barely restraining his eye roll, Nick dug around in the cooler for his sandwich. Pulling it out, he focused on unwrapping it, anything not to throttle Colin sideways. There were a lot of great things about spending time with Colin. It turned out his dogged persistence was not really one of them.

"What nobody tells you is that it doesn't matter," Nick finally said between bites of meat and bread. "Personal relationships are still fucking hard. You still speak a hundred different languages, no matter what sex you are, or who you're banging."

"Hard, but not impossible," Colin said, because of course he'd chosen to focus on that.

This time, Nick didn't bother to hold back his eye roll. He might be head over heels for this dork, but that didn't mean he wasn't completely aware of his shortcomings.

"Did you mean what you said?" Colin asked after a few moments of silence had passed. "About you being here being the opposite of what you should be doing for your assignment?"

Nick swallowed hard. "Think about it," he said, not unkindly. It also turned out that it was really hard to stay mad at Colin. "Jemma didn't get assigned to write your story because she was too close to you—and that was *platonic*. This sure as hell isn't platonic." Nick barely managed to rein in all the additional word vomit he could have said about his feelings. *Sure as hell isn't platonic* was about as mild as he could manage.

"You don't think you can be objective?" Colin's voice had finally lost that puzzled edge, and he seemed particularly pleased about Nick's confession.

Chuckling wryly, Nick grabbed another beer and settled next to where Colin was sprawled on the deck. He smelled like sunscreen, clean sweat, and salt. Nick wanted to eat him up and never stop gorging. It was a problem. He wrapped an arm around Colin's much broader shoulders and rested his head against his bicep. "Not a chance," he admitted quietly.

"I trust you," Colin said, that intense fondness creeping back in his voice. "Probably more than if you'd stayed objective."

What Colin didn't understand was that no matter how he tried, Nick knew his article was going to read like he had a huge crush on Colin O'Connor. And not like all those bro articles, like on his perfect spiral or his footwork or his vision on the field, but on the *man*. It was going to be all right there, between the lines. Nick didn't think he could help it, it was so big sometimes it felt like his feelings were going to swallow him whole.

Nick didn't know if it was good or not that Colin seemed to have similar feelings. He'd turned off the logical, forward-thinking part of his brain the moment their lips had touched for the first time, and he was terrified to return back to LA and reality.

Maybe it was time to take a step in that direction, no matter how much it killed him. "The day after we get back to Miami, I have to fly back to LA."

Nick knew by the way Colin stayed relaxed against him, a hand carding through his salt-crusted hair, that he didn't realize the implications of this.

Maybe that was for the best.

When they returned to Miami, Nick knew he needed to say *something*.

The problem was that the words had gone from difficult to practically impossible.

It was never going to be easy to say, *Hey, listen, we had a great time together, but this isn't going to work. Not like you want it to.* As they'd driven back to Miami, Nick had run the variations through his head so many times he was sick of himself by the time they drove up to Colin's house. Towards the end, he'd begun to add, *Not like I want it to.*

Even though he'd known he was in deep shit for at least a week, it was even more painful than he'd imagined to admit to himself that he wanted more, that he wanted *Colin,* while acknowledging that it was possibly impossible to actually achieve.

They'd gotten another late start, which Nick would fully admit later was his own idea to make this shitty thing a little easier on himself and on the man next to him, and so they didn't get back to Miami until late in the day. And his flight was first thing in the morning.

He faced his suitcase in the room he'd pretty much abandoned, and started to pack as Colin puttered around downstairs, calling in a grocery order to his PA.

At some inevitable point, Colin would stop delaying the inevitable, and he'd come upstairs and start the conversation that Nick really, really did not want to finish.

As he moved clothes from the dresser to his suitcase, he tried to tell himself that he was being overdramatic, that Colin would accept Nick's decision easily. That he'd just gotten carried away while being locked away with Colin, and when he went back to LA, the feelings wouldn't follow.

Except Nick already knew that wasn't going to happen, unless he carved out his heart and left it as a bloody gift for Colin's housekeeper.

Yeah, definitely not overdramatic at all.

He'd pretty much finished packing and was in the bathroom pretending to gather his toiletries, but in reality was avoiding looking himself in the eye, when Colin walked in.

Nick knew from his awkward stance, the way he'd shoved his hands in his pockets, and that he also couldn't look Nick in the eye, that the time had come.

He fought the urge to manufacture a reason to leave *now*, before everything that had been good between them soured completely. But instead, he felt rooted to the floor, frozen in place, unable to dodge the bullet that was absolutely coming his direction.

Definitely overdramatic, he tried to remind himself, but even his usual snide comment made him want to cry.

"I keep telling myself," Colin said, "that there's a reason why you haven't said anything about what happens when you go back to LA. But the truth is, I can't figure it out. I know you like me, *I know you do,* and I know you're not with anyone else. We had such a great time these last few weeks, it would be nuts not to want this to continue."

He paused, and Nick knew it was going to be worse than he could ever have imagined it.

"So I'm going to be the one saying it to you. What happens now?"

Nick took a steadying breath, even though he didn't feel even remotely steady. "Now, I go back to LA."

Colin shot him a look like he was crazy. And he probably was. He'd finally found this great guy—*the* guy, really, if he could stop reminding himself of this particular fact—and he was going to tell him that it was over.

And that was the *nice* version. Nick had already thought of and dismissed another half dozen lies that he didn't think he could force past his lips. Besides the idea that Colin deserved better and deep down, the thing Nick wanted most was for Colin to get what he deserved.

Nick ignored the voice in his head that told him that sort of insanely self-sacrificial behavior was almost certainly love.

"You know I was talking about us," Colin said, a perplexed look on his face.

"Right." Nick leaned back on the counter. "Well, I go back to my life, and you go back to yours. I write the article. You come out."

Realization was beginning to dawn on Colin's face and it was so much worse than Nick could ever have dreamed.

"You really mean that."

"I...I don't want to. But I don't see that this is a legitimate option. You're a football player. I *report* on you, on and off the field. It's a huge conflict of interest."

Colin's jaw took on a stubborn angle, and Nick wanted to tell him to *leave it alone, it'll be so much easier if you just accept it.* "Were you or were you not a reporter when you came to my house? Was I not a football player then?"

Nick wanted to cry. "I was. You were. I know, it was *stupid*, I was so goddamned stupid. I just...I couldn't *not*. I tried really hard not to, God knows I did."

"I would never ask you to change what you do for a living. I know you love it." Colin sounded wretched, and Nick was there every step of the way. "Isn't there something we can work out? Something we can do to move forward. I..." Colin hesitated and Nick prayed, *fervently*, that he would not choose this moment to try to tell him how he felt, in a last-ditch effort to change Nick's mind. Because that might actually work. "I care a lot about you," he said instead, and that was bad enough, but not as bad as it could have been.

Nick knew what he was supposed to say. What he had intended to say. Instead, at the last moment, his uncooperative lips stuttered out with, "I don't know. I care about you, too. A lot."

And that was just enough of a reprieve that Colin reached out and grabbed Nick, wrapping him up in those big arms, holding him tight and close, like he couldn't bear the thought of losing him. And Nick was right there, his face buried in the cotton of Colin's t-shirt, holding back the tears.

He was supposed to say, "*No*," and that was supposed to make Colin so angry and so hurt that it was inevitably over. A wound, undoubtedly, but one that they'd both cauterized when Nick flew back to LA.

Now it was open and bleeding and painful as fuck.

It was worse, if that were even possible, in the gray, early morning light outside the Miami airport.

They sat in Departures, and Nick knew Colin wasn't supposed to just sit here, parked at the curb, but he hadn't moved in five minutes, and so neither had Nick.

Colin's bottom lip was trembling when he finally turned his head Nick's direction. Nick felt a new wash of guilt and pain and he just wanted it to *stop*. When this thing with Colin had started, it had felt so goddamn good. He'd not even considered the possibility that when it ended, it could cut back with just as much power.

That had been incurably stupid of him. He was thirty years old, he'd been in relationships before, unlike Colin. He should have known.

"Promise me you'll call me in LA. Promise me you won't just stop talking," Colin begged, and each word felt like the knife in Rio, plunging in over and over again. The knife in Rio might have hurt less.

Nick had already hurt both of them enough by his inability to just *end it*, but he couldn't do it again. He leaned over and pressed one last kiss to Colin's mouth. The same burst of heat, the same happiness bubbled up inside of him. But it wasn't really the same. He pulled away before he could start bawling into Colin's shoulder.

"I promise," Nick said, and he opened the car door.

Chapter Nine

"You look like shit," Gabe said, shoveling eggs and hash browns into his mouth like he was starving to death. And maybe he was; god only knew what sort of sustenance he needed to keep up with Jemma.

The thought edged too close to the pain Nick was still trying to pretend didn't hurt so bad, so he dropped it like a hot potato. Glowering into his coffee cup, he didn't even look up at his best friend. "Thanks."

"You should tell me what happened in Miami," Gabe suggested, though his tone hinted it was more like an order than an option. "You barely even texted me when you were there. I think Jemma talked to you more than I did."

"That's because Jemma actually *talks on the phone*, unlike some people," Nick retorted. He was fully aware he was heading towards full-on grouch territory, curling up the raggedy edges of himself like a blanket to ward off everyone.

If Gabe hadn't showed up at his loft, threatening him with physically carting him to the diner they frequented, Nick would have stayed, wrapped in his favorite comforter, feet tucked underneath him, at his desk, where he'd been for the last four days. Ostensibly, he was working on deadline—he had the article on Colin to write, which was just about as painful as he'd guessed it would be—but even he usually needed fresh air after forty-eight hours.

"Did O'Connor fuck with you?" Gabe asked—no, *demanded*.

"Gratifyingly and many times," Nick said, because even though he knew the details wouldn't bother Gabe, he still childishly wanted to punish him for asking.

"Then why did I find you moodily staring out the window, buried under days of gross coffee cups?"

"And you say *I'm* dramatic," Nick muttered.

"You *are*, which is why you're sitting over there like a 2010 Panic at the Disco! album instead of telling me what the fuck happened."

Nick glowered. "You're the absolute worst. If I want to marinate in my own pain, who are you to stop me?"

Annoyingly, this only made Gabe grin. "Maybe the sort of person who wouldn't let *me*?"

"I'd just been stabbed. I was on heavy medication. Normally I would have just let you stew." Which they both knew was a lie. While Gabriel was Nick's best friend, he'd also grown close to Jemma, and when Gabe had fucked up early in their relationship, Nick had instantly called Gabe on his bullshit.

"So you like him. O'Connor," Gabe clarified, since he'd apparently figured out that Nick wasn't going to volunteer anything.

"Yes." The word *like* seemed too mild and too small to even come close to encompassing how Nick felt. He'd gone without Colin O'Connor's presence in his life for most of his thirty years, and somehow, after a few weeks, he couldn't handle even a break. If this was even what this was.

Colin had texted twice, the first to make sure Nick had made it home to LA safely, and the second time to remind Nick that he'd *promised*. Nick had returned the texts because he'd given his word he would. Not because he was dying to. That definitely had nothing to do with it.

"And he likes you."

Nick ground his teeth together and forced himself to nod.

Gabe jauntily pointed his fork in Nick's direction. "And yet this does not seem to be a positive development."

"For a detective, you're not very good at this interrogation thing," Nick said.

Gabe's sympathetic glance back was galling. "Right. So you're basically crazy about each other."

The problem was there was no *basically* about it.

"And," Gabe continued, "you're still sitting here, with hair that has permanently scared our waitress away and a pissed-off expression that nearly scared *me* away."

Nick scoffed. "You're made of stronger shit than that."

Gabe just kept smiling. He leaned over the stained, chipped, linoleum tabletop. "You're afraid to be happy."

Even Nick could only take so much. "He is the *worst* person for me to get involved with," he practically wailed.

"Because he's a player and you're a reporter? Come on, don't use that tired excuse. You're afraid of your goddamned feelings. I was too, which is why I can spot it a mile away. Did you piss him off enough that you can't fix it?"

"It's *not* a tired excuse. When he comes out, it's gonna be the biggest fucking story on the planet. And *his new boyfriend* wrote the article about it?"

"You're afraid of the implications overshadowing what he's trying to do," Gabe guessed.

"Closer," Nick grumbled.

"So wait a few months before going official. There's ways around this, you don't need me to tell you that. This is what you're good at, Nicky. You invent the story, it's yours to control."

"I really hate when you start spouting my Forrest Gump pseudo-media psychology back at me."

Gabe shrugged his shoulders, like *what are you gonna do about it?*

Unfortunately, Nick was pretty certain that Gabe wasn't just talking about his Forrest Gump pseudo-media psychology. He was talking about Colin. And frankly, Nick wasn't sure yet.

"Do I even want to ask how the article's coming?"

It was horrifically difficult to write while also being alarmingly easy. Like Nick had been waiting his whole life to talk about the brave new world that Colin O'Connor was creating. But every word yanked on the band-aid he'd attempted to use to contain both his feelings and his fear that in the end, they wouldn't matter.

"Not terrible, actually," Nick confessed. "I mean it sounds like I'm in love with him, which I guess I am, but other than that, it's fine."

Gabe leaned back, crossing his considerable arms across his considerable chest. His brown eyes gleamed. "Are you now?"

"You fucking know I am."

"Just glad you can admit it."

"Admitting it to you is a lot different than writing it in an article that millions of people are gonna read."

Gabe looked suddenly thoughtful, which was never a good thing. "Maybe you should tell Colin about it first. He shouldn't have to read about it with the millions."

It wasn't like Nick hadn't *thought* about it. He had. Pretty much every moment of every minute of every day since he'd gotten on the plane back to LA. Part of that problem was the profile he was supposed to be writing. The other part definitely wasn't because he'd been a melodramatic asshole.

Except he'd definitely been a melodramatic asshole—much harder to deal with than the writing itself, which was never easy, but this time around, it flowed easily and excitingly from his fingertips.

At the very least, Nick thought, as he spun around in his desk chair, the dim lights and tightly drawn shades in his loft promising either 7 pm or 7 am, what he'd feared hadn't come to pass. He could still write, voraciously apparently, about Colin O'Connor.

The article had taken shape in record time, which made sense because he'd barely left this desk in days. He couldn't remember being so driven to get something perfect before, and he'd made more than one underling cry over his type A-plus asshole ways over the years.

Ultimately, he'd been a lousy affair for Colin to have—fantastic and thrilling in the moment, shitty at the end—and Nick wanted, at the very least, to create something lasting and good. This profile would become part of Colin O'Connor's legacy, and no matter what had happened between them, Colin deserved Nick's very best.

His phone rang.

It was Jemma. He'd ignored about a hundred of her calls over the last two days, ever since he'd had breakfast with her boyfriend and *his* best friend, Gabe.

No doubt she'd tried to pump Gabe for information, and came up alarmingly short. Gabe, when he wanted to be, could be locked tighter than a drum. He was also certain Jemma was desperate to talk to him so she could properly guilt him for how he'd left things with Colin. He was already overflowing with guilt and *really* didn't want to do a play-by-play over their last few hours together, so he ignored this call, too.

He returned to his keyboard, fingers sitting lightly over the plastic, drumming rhythmically as he thought of how he wanted to rephrase a particular concept.

The phone rang again, and Nick let out a silent oath. He grabbed it without checking the caller ID and barked into the receiver, "Jem, for the love of god, *leave me alone.*"

There was a conspicuous silence on the other end. Nick realized belatedly that the next caller had probably not been Jemma.

"I guess I should be relieved that you're screening everyone's calls," Colin said slowly. He sounded about how Nick felt—heartsick and miserable.

The nauseous roll of guilt in the pit of his stomach doubled in size.

"I haven't been screening your calls." It wasn't a lie; Colin hadn't called and Nick had scrupulously, if succinctly, answered every text Colin had sent. He'd kept his promise, and not left Colin in the dark.

"I heard you had to be aired out a few days ago."

Nick did not particularly like the spin either Gabe or Jemma—almost certainly *Jemma*, if he was being honest—had put on that particular encounter. He'd showered, *fuck you very much.*

"I've been writing. I get in a zone."

Nick clamped back all his questions on how Colin was doing, on how he was handling the ramp-up to his media blitz, if Helen and Mark were behaving themselves.

"How's it going, then?" Nick could tell Colin had attempted to phrase it casually, but Nick wasn't sure an expert actor would have been able to pull that off.

"Great, actually." He hesitated. He didn't think Colin would assume he'd write anything less than flattering because they were undergoing...*personal* difficulties currently. But he wanted to make certain Colin knew. "I'm not...I wouldn't...it's all really good. I promise."

Colin chuckled and it was like the first breath of warmth after a long winter. *God, you really are a melodramatic asshole,* Nick chastised himself. "No references to my smelly feet or my addiction to bad nineties pinball machines?"

Nick was so head over heels that he honestly hadn't minded the smelly feet. They'd made him feel affectionate and touched that Colin liked and trusted him enough to see him at his worst.

He was really *so* fucked.

"I think you'll like it. I'll send it to you before I send it to Duncan."

"You'd send it to me before your boss?"

Nick could hardly fault Colin for his incredulous tone. Duncan would have his head if he knew what he was saying, but Nick knew it was more important what Colin thought than what his boss thought. "It *is* about you, after all," Nick said defensively.

"Right."

There was an infinite pause. Nick's heart jumped to his throat. There was so much he wanted to say and he didn't know how to say it. Or what he could say to fix what he'd messed up. Then Colin broke the quiet. "Teddy's here. I gotta go. I just wanted to make sure you weren't dead or insane with writer's block."

"Still in one piece," Nick said, which was *mostly* true.

"Talk to you later," Colin said and hung up. Nick had to put the phone down so he didn't do something stupid like *dial him right back.*

Colin set his phone down on the desk with a soft plastic click. Nick might be in one piece, but Colin wasn't sure he was anymore.

He didn't know what he'd expected after Nick left for LA, but he hadn't anticipated the sudden distance between them. Even though Nick's reasons made logical sense, there was a completely non-logical part of Colin that rejected reason and instead wanted to embrace the chaos of emotion.

The house was silent around him, Teddy's presence nothing more than a convenient excuse to end a phone call that he shouldn't have made in the first place. Colin had known even as he'd dialed that he was incapable of telling Nick the real reason he'd called, but he'd made the attempt anyway because something about the other man's voice still calmed him, despite all the emotional upheaval.

Colin stood, grabbed his gym bag off the floor, and headed to his car. Putting this off wouldn't do him any favors. Besides, it was pointless to wait until he could talk to Nick about this, because Colin knew he couldn't. Not now.

The drive to the Piranhas' practice facility was quick. Quicker than Colin wanted it to be, even though he'd bought the island explicitly because it was the closest to Coral Springs and the Piranhas' compound.

He parked in the garage, taking the spot that had been specifically and *embarrassingly* set aside for his use exclusively, and ducked into the elevator. He was one of the first players here, which he'd done on purpose.

Coach's office was high above the practice field, with one wall of floor-to-ceiling windows that looked over the field.

Colin still had difficulty reading Daniel Mortensen, even a year after joining the Piranhas, and when he entered the room, he wished he could see something of what the man felt on his face.

Except he couldn't. Coach was a blank slate; he would be, Colin was certain, a hell of a poker player.

"Sit," Coach said, gesturing vaguely to one of the chairs opposite his big desk.

Colin sat, forcing himself to relax into the chair. He never could have brought Nick to this meeting, but even knowing he *knew* about it would have made it easier. Instead, Colin was all alone, the first step in this brave new world he'd insisted on creating.

"Helen tells me you're telling the other players today before practice," Coach said, his voice carefully neutral.

Colin nodded. Thankfully, he'd not been the one to inform Coach Mortensen about his sexual preference, that had happened a year ago, when he'd told Mark and Mark had been tasked with negotiating what would eventually become the Rainbow Clause with the Piranhas.

Colin hadn't noticed any different treatment over the last year, but he wasn't sure that meant anything. Coach was sort of a closed book.

Coach leaned back in his chair, his expression morphing into something more contemplative. "It's funny, isn't it, the requirement to be in this world is a certain uniqueness, but as soon as people discover you're different, they're all over you like flies on shit."

Colin could hear the echoes of the Southern twang in Coach's voice. He'd done his research and learned that Daniel Mortensen was originally from Georgia, and had gone to the University of Alabama. You could still hear his roots in his voice when he grew angry or excited.

He was neither now, and Colin tried to even out his breathing, counting his breaths as a way to force himself to relax. He'd taught himself this technique in high school before his first starts at quarterback, and it had also come in handy when he'd had to face his crush in the locker room.

"Are you saying I'm shit, sir?"

Coach's chuckle was rueful but not unpleasant. "It's the nature of the game to be the shit when you're the first, O'Connor. You know that."

The chair suddenly swung to the side and Coach stared out onto the field, still empty. "When they first told me, I didn't think you'd ever actually do this. I should have known better."

Colin told himself firmly that he could play for a homophobic dick, if that's what Coach turned out to be. He *could*. He just didn't want to. He wanted Coach to be different. Colin just wasn't sure which side he was going to tip over to.

"You've never backed down from a challenge in your entire life," Coach continued, his gaze swinging abruptly back to Colin. "It was stupid of me to assume that you'd chicken out. Instead you're going to be the fucking bravest asshole I've ever known." Coach looked him straight in the eye, for once leaving no doubt about his feelings. "I want you to know I've got your back. In the locker room. On the field. In the press. But I doubt you'll need it because you're the gutsiest player I've ever coached, and Helen is stupid good at her job."

"Sir?" Colin couldn't quite get the word out. It came out a little garbled. Relief flooded through him in a cascade and he still sat there, shocked and disbelieving.

"Oh, come on, O'Connor, you didn't think I was going to be a dick, did you?" Coach laughed a little. "I treated you the same as anyone else the last year, didn't I?"

Colin couldn't nod fast enough. "Of course, you did. Of course. I just..." Colin hesitated. "Sometimes it's better to prepare yourself for the worst in these situations. And to be honest, I'm not very good at telling people yet."

Coach stood, pulling proudly up to his full six-foot-three height. "Then let's go get you some practice, son."

It should have been easier, after the nightmare in Coach's office didn't end up being a nightmare after all. But as Colin stood in the middle of the room and met the hardened, somewhat uncaring stares of the players around him, he still couldn't help but wish that Nick had been around in some capacity.

He could do this without Nick. What he was learning was that he didn't want to.

Colin met Teddy's eyes, and he gave an encouraging little nod.

It was inevitable some of these men would hate him in a minute. Inviting it seemed like the most foolish thing he'd ever done. He'd stood in so many locker rooms over the years, terrified to take one glance above the floor. Always afraid he'd be discovered. And now he was standing in one, ready to lay his soul bare.

"In a month, there's going to be a big feature article on me," Colin said. He knew how to give the impression of confidence, all smooth and effortless, with no cracks, but inside he was trembling. "In it, I'm going to talk about my bisexuality."

There were rumbles immediately. A few poorly hidden grimaces and expressions of disgust. But not as many as he'd guessed there might be.

"I know it's going to cause a lot of media talk and speculation about what happens in this locker room," Colin continued. "But I'm the same football player I was last year. I'm still as committed as I was last year to winning games, to taking the Piranhas to the playoffs. Reporters sniffing around isn't enough of a reason to distract us from what's really important."

It was all he'd planned to say. Short, sweet, and to the point. Direct, just like he was. It got the job done, but Colin still wished that Nick had been around to help plan these words that would change his life. He'd done this before; surely he knew the best way to do it. But Colin felt like he'd done a decent enough job muddling through.

Still, there was a solid, impenetrable hush falling around the room, and Colin, who'd never liked the unvarnished attention he tended to attract, froze.

Corey Armstrong, one of their veteran safeties, stepped forward. They'd barely spoken before this moment, even though they'd been on the same team for a season. Colin tried not to flinch when Corey laid a heavy hand around his shoulder.

Corey's face took on the determination of a very protective bulldog. "Anyone who has a problem with what O'Connor just said, they can come talk to me."

This was not something Colin had expected, but he relaxed a fraction as Corey's arm stayed stubbornly around his upper body. "Is that clear?" Corey repeated.

"That's right," Coach said briskly, clapping his hands. "We're here to play football. So let's focus on that."

Colin was plenty happy to focus on that, and turned towards his locker, but not before he caught Teddy's approving gaze.

He'd dreaded this, but it hadn't turned out too badly, after all. Colin thought of his phone, tucked into the pocket of his jeans. He should text Nick and tell him that telling his teammates had gone okay. As good as could be expected, anyway. But even though he knew he wanted Nick involved with more certainty than he'd felt since Nick had left, he didn't know how to approach someone who had made himself so unapproachable.

Duncan emailed Nick later that night, insisting that Nick come into the office the next morning. "You've had your uninterrupted writing time," he'd said, but what would have been more accurate was, "*You've had your uninterrupted pity party.*"

Nick took himself to bed at a decent hour, and lay awake for what felt like an eternity, replaying his last conversation with Colin, their last kiss, the phone call he'd had with him, all the texts he should have sent and hadn't.

By the time he showed up to the *Five Points* office at eight, venti coffee in one hand and his sunglasses on, the last thing he wanted to do was to talk about Colin O'Connor.

The problem was, Colin was all anybody wanted to talk about.

"You look tan," was the first thing Jemma said, sliding into the chair opposite his desk. Nick was hunched over his laptop, sunglasses *still* on, and what he knew was a semi-permanent grimace on his face.

"Brilliant investigative journalism," Nick retorted dryly. "I was in *Miami*."

"Yeah, sunning yourself on the beach with Colin. A real drag of an assignment." Jemma's challenging stare made him want to crawl under the desk and take cover. Considering Colin was her best friend, it wasn't a surprise she was pissed off.

Nick raised a hand of surrender. "Can we just...not do this right now?"

Her glare shifted to something more speculative. "Despite the tan, you do look like shit, though. Gabe was right."

"Gabe is rarely wrong."

"Fine." Jemma tapped her nails on the desk impatiently, as if she had many better things to do than to talk to him. And she probably did. "You can take me to lunch. Twelve thirty, I've got a call at eleven."

Even though she did leave after Nick agreed, her presence was replaced ten minutes later by Duncan's.

"You look good," Duncan said, leaning back in the chair, regarding Nick opaquely.

Even though Nick had worked for Duncan Snyder for six years—he'd been Duncan's first full-time hire, way back at the start of *Five Points*, when all Duncan had had was a vision and a name that reminded him of his hometown of Atlanta—there were still plenty of times when he had no idea what his boss was thinking.

"You're the only one who seems to think so," Nick grumbled.

"Helen called this morning," Duncan said. He'd always preferred the direct route, and while the lack of bullshit masquerading as tact intimidated others, Nick had always thrived in such an honest environment. Which was probably why, despite being offered a variety of different opportunities over the years, Nick had stayed at *Five Points*.

Also, there was definitely something to be said about being the most senior writer on the staff.

"They've nailed down the final timing?" Nick asked, even though he already knew. He'd been sitting in the Piranhas' conference room when they'd finalized it. But Duncan didn't need to know that particular detail. He definitely didn't need to know how close he and Colin had grown over the last month, even though he would almost certainly guess when he read Nick's profile.

Duncan nodded. "We need to finish the profile and get it over to Helen's people. Of course, they want to do a final polish."

Nick rolled his eyes. He'd known Helen for years—and Helen had known *him* for years. When was the last time he'd not gotten something this important right? The truth was almost certainly that Helen had guessed correctly that he and Colin were sleeping together and wanted to make sure this fact hadn't adversely affected Nick's performance.

"Here," Nick said brusquely, rotating his laptop and gesturing to the screen. "Read it."

It was hard to sit there and watch Duncan slowly make his way through his words. *Putting his heart into it* was a horrible cliché, but probably not completely off base. Nick paced around some, went to grab more coffee from the break room, and when he came back, Duncan was sitting back in his chair, looking terrifyingly thoughtful.

Duncan skewered Nick with a look so pointed it might have been crafted as a weapon. "You do realize you weren't exactly being subtle, right?" he asked with a raised eyebrow.

Nick took a long sip of coffee. "I do realize."

"Do I want to ask what you being so deliberately obvious means?"

He thought for a long minute. "I haven't decided yet what being so deliberately obvious means," Nick admitted. He couldn't yet admit, especially to Duncan, that Colin was probably going to decide that for him.

"It's one of the best things you've written," Duncan said. "But I'd have expected nothing less. You've been waiting for this opportunity for a long time."

Nick nodded, but Duncan continued. "I didn't know what to think when Helen called me last week and told me she was pretty sure that you and O'Connor were having…I think she termed it…a *hot affair*. I wanted to tell her that you didn't do that. I didn't, though, because I wanted to talk to you first."

"I know it's…not smart." Nick winced at his own choice of words. "I've always been so careful to avoid even a hint of subjective journalism. But, well, Colin is a fairly determined person. Which you know, already."

"As are you," Duncan retorted with dark amusement.

"Right," Nick said uncertainly. He hadn't expected that Duncan might find this development funny, even in an ironic light.

"I'm not mad. Helen isn't mad. We're more in the…*cautious* column, I suppose. I told her that if you were in fact having an 'affair' with O'Connor that you'd be smart about it, and that you probably wouldn't want to turn it into a media circus."

"I don't. I don't want to take away from what Colin is doing."

"I didn't think you would. So I've marked a few spots I'd like to…we'll say *tone down*, before we send this to Helen."

"Right, of course. Not a problem." Nick couldn't remember the last time he'd just accepted an editorial change from Duncan without arguing, but in this particular scenario, Duncan was probably right. If he didn't want to make a big deal out of this, there were definitely some spots that could use some fine adjustment.

Duncan stood. "Also, I lied earlier. You don't look good. You look like you haven't slept in a week. Get your head on straight." And with that final jab, he was gone.

Jemma picked at her sandwich, casting a speculative glance over at Nick, who hadn't even made a half-hearted attempt to eat his own lunch. "Have you talked to Colin recently?" she asked casually.

Nick glared. "I really don't want to talk about this."

Unfortunately, his glares must have either softened in Florida, or Jemma was no longer as intimidated by them as she'd been before Rio. "Too bad," she said with a frankness that scared him. "So, did you?"

"Yesterday," Nick mumbled into a bite of potato salad.

"Oh," she said, her voice growing more casual, and yet more suspicious by the moment, "so you know then."

His head snapped back up. "Know *what?*" Nick demanded. He knew it was unreasonable to make demands, considering that he'd just made his own to *not talk about this*, but if something had happened to Colin, good, bad, or otherwise, he *needed* to know.

Jemma shot him the frankest stare yet. "He told his teammates yesterday."

Suddenly, Colin's phone call out of the blue made so much more sense. He'd *wanted* to tell him, Nick realized belatedly, he just...*h adn't*. Probably because Nick had been a grade A asshole who was too busy pretending he was okay to notice if Colin was.

"And?" Nick barked, mind whirling. There were so many ways that announcement could have gone. He'd sort of hoped he'd be there to help support Colin when he took this step. Instead, he'd been on the other side of the country and about as absent emotionally as he could.

"He said it went well," Jemma said, clearly enjoying his discomfort. "I mean, obviously not everyone was happy about it. Expecting everyone to be is unrealistic. But he said his coach was supportive and one of the defensive players said something to the rest of the team about not creating an issue over it."

"I should have been there." The words popped out before he could stop them. Jemma looked over at him, galling sympathy in her eyes.

"Yeah, you should have," she said.

"You're not going to take it easy on this, are you?" Nick asked.

Jemma sat her sandwich down on the plate, making no pretense of even attempting to eat it. "Of course, I'm not. Colin is my best friend. He's pretty much the greatest guy I've ever met, barring my boyfriend. He's loyal and kind and funny and *hot*, even if he doesn't do anything for me personally, and you just left him in the middle of one of the most important times of his life, because—" She hesitated. "To be honest, I'm *still* not sure why you left."

"I had to write the article," Nick said, and the excuse sounded pathetically flimsy, even to his ears.

Her gaze back was stern. "You didn't have to leave the way you did."

"No, I didn't."

"You're going to fix this," Jemma ordered.

"I'm going to try," Nick said, which was the first time he'd let himself admit that he needed to. It wasn't a *want* at this point, it was verging on a dire, nearly insatiable need.

Later that night, Nick sat at his computer, staring at the screen, at the spots that Duncan had marked to be "toned down." They were all sections that Nick would have picked. Still, when he went to make the changes, he could only stare at the screen, putting off the inevitable as long as possible. It turned out that instead of just fucking *talking* to Colin, he'd written this article, and it said everything that he'd never been able to verbalize. And the idea of toning it down, even though it was smart and logical, ruined the Hail Mary pass that he hadn't even meant to throw.

Nick realized that when Duncan had asked *why* he'd been so damn obvious, he'd lied. He *did* know. He'd written it this way on purpose.

Before he could think it through and convince himself to change his mind, Nick typed out a quick email to Colin and attached the original version of the article. *You're just doing what you promised,* he justified, but the truth was, he didn't want Colin to read the safe version. He wanted Colin to read the version where he'd gone *balls to the wall, crazy in love* journalist.

Even if what Nick really meant wasn't *let's be boyfriends and make everyone completely jealous of our epic love* but rather, *let's figure out how we can work with this situation because I miss you like crazy,* Colin still deserved to know how he felt.

What he needed was Colin to hold on a month or so and be patient, while Nick worked out an awesome plan that didn't create a massive clusterfuck around Colin's coming out party. The flaw in this thinking was that Colin wasn't really a "wait and see" sort of guy, and Nick, wrapped up in his own flair for the dramatic, forgot about that completely.

It was two days later when he was lounging on the couch, eating his weight in pizza because that's what men did when they were three quarters of the way to heartbroken, there was a knock on his door.

Wiping his mouth on the hem of his old t-shirt, Nick shuffled to the doorway, fully expecting to see Jemma or Gabe on the other side, probably claiming he'd missed some outing so they could have a good excuse to drag him out of his loft. But when he yanked the door open, it wasn't Gabe or Jemma standing there. It was Colin, a duffel slung over one shoulder, and apprehension in his tired blue eyes. Like he didn't really expect Nick to let him in.

And *fuck that.* Like Nick was ever going to leave this man on the doorstep.

"You're here," Nick said stupidly. So much for the groveling he'd fully meant to do the next time they met.

"I'm here." Colin paused. "I hope it's okay. Jemma gave me your address."

"Of course she did," Nick grumbled. He held the door out. "Come on in. It's not your fault Jemma doesn't have any personal boundaries."

The edges of Colin's mouth tilted up into a smile. A bittersweet smile, but a smile nonetheless. Nick could work with that.

"I got your email," Colin said.

"Oh." Nick wanted to pretend he'd forgotten that he'd sent it while he'd been in the middle of agonizing over Duncan's requested edits, but the truth was, he'd been even more of a wreck when Colin hadn't replied.

Colin dropped the duffel on the hardwood floor and Nick, feeling jumpy, flinched at the sound. He took a step closer to Nick and shoved his hands in his pockets. "I wanted to give you my feedback in person," he said.

"I'm sure you saw the new version," Nick said awkwardly, because he knew Helen had sent it around after Duncan had approved it. "I'm sorry. I didn't get to keep it the way it was."

Colin shook his head. "It's okay, I understand why they wanted you to cut some things. It's still perfect."

"Perfect?" Nick squeaked, his voice going embarrassingly high. He was just realizing he was in a stained t-shirt and old, threadbare sweatpants that he wouldn't even wear to the gym. His hair was probably a wreck, and there was a definite possibility that he still had tomato sauce on his chin. And there Colin was, looking tall and handsome and...

"Perfect," Colin said with all that certainty that he had. Nick envied him that tone of voice, and also the strength it took to *be* so sure. "Perfect enough that I came here to tell you that I finally figured out what I want. Not what anyone else wants. What *I* want."

Nick felt breathless, because the way Colin was looking at him left very little room for doubt as to what he meant. "I hope you mean me," he said, "because I was going to grovel, but I'm no good at it. And if you tell me it's Teddy or Mark or someone else, I'll probably have to try, and that'll just be ugly."

Colin laughed, and reached out for him, pulling him close despite the sweatpants and the greasy t-shirt and the tomato sauce. Nick felt his body relax in a way that it hadn't in the last two weeks, something between a sigh and a moan, Colin's hand stroking tender and sure along his spine.

"I missed you," Nick murmured into Colin's cotton-covered shoulder.

"I missed you, too." Colin's voice was even more soothing than his hands. "Though I wasn't sure you'd admit it."

Nick opened his mouth to argue, to try to *explain*, but Colin continued before he could. "I know, I know, it's not a good idea, it's bad timing. But *this*, this right here, this is why I'm doing this. It seemed really stupid to let it go."

Sniffing, Nick buried his nose further into Colin's shoulder, his own fingers digging into Colin's hips. "It would've been. We've still got to figure some stuff out."

Colin pulled back, and Nick glanced up to see two very blue eyes, looking fondly at him. "But it makes it a lot easier to do it together, doesn't it?"

Nick let out an unsteady breath. "And that's what you want? To be...*together?*"

Amusement glimmered in those eyes. "I sort of thought we already were, until you announced we couldn't be."

"God," Nick groaned. "I am so stupid."

Amusement shifted into a blinding smile. Nick had forgotten, even though it had only been two weeks, how powerfully attractive Colin could be. "Yeah, that's my *boyfriend* you're insulting there," Colin said with a playful poke in his hip. "Don't talk about him that way."

Chapter Ten

"I HEAR CONGRATULATIONS ARE in order," was the first thing Helen said after Nick let her and Mark into Colin's dressing room on the set of *The Ellen DeGeneres Show.*

Colin watched in the mirror as Nick shot her a half-hearted glare. He'd definitely expected Mark to tell Helen about his newly-official relationship with Nick, but that didn't mean Colin had to like it—like so many of the day's events.

They were at *Ellen* to film his first interview, post-coming out, even though he hadn't actually announced anything yet.

"They always film these things early," Helen had informed him when he'd questioned the order of the detailed and color-coded schedule she'd emailed over last week.

"You look...*great*," Helen concluded as her eyes scanned his body. The hair and makeup artist had just left, leaving him feeling nothing like himself. Add to that the strangely tight, stylish clothes they'd insisted he wear, and he was currently feeling like puking might be an inevitability.

Colin considered complaining again about the wardrobe his new stylist had selected, but after catching Nick's gaze lingering on his body more than once, he decided to stay quiet. The clothes might not be his style, but he loved the way his boyfriend's gaze heated every time he looked his direction.

"You feeling ready, bud?" Mark said, propping himself up against the counter and blocking Colin's view of himself in the mirror.

"I guess," Colin said. What was he supposed to say? *Sorry, I've changed my mind.* Too many pieces had already been put in place, dominoes to tip over at the right moment, one after another. And he really didn't *want* to change his mind. He still wanted to come out. He still wanted—*very much so*—to tell everyone that he and Nick were dating.

Talking to Ellen today was an important first step that couldn't be avoided.

"It'll be easy, you already know the questions," Helen inserted.

The truth was, it was easy enough to practice his answers with Nick when they were sitting tangled up on his couch; it was a different proposition to do it with Ellen, in front of a camera, knowing that millions of people would eventually be watching.

"A lot easier than winning a Heisman Trophy, or facing down the Raiders' defensive line," Mark chortled, annoyingly.

Nick had told him last night that while he'd come with Colin to the taping, he was going to stay uninvolved in the proceedings. Colin had doubted this, but had kept quiet, because he'd learned quickly it was easier to let Nick believe he didn't have a protective streak a mile wide.

Nick lasted exactly one shitty comment from Mark, which was just about how long Colin imagined he would.

Nick pushed away from the wall he was leaning against and stalked over to Colin's chair. Wrapping an arm around Colin's shoulders, Nick glared at Mark. "Can you two give us the room, please?"

Mark spluttered something about just getting here. Helen sniffed and claimed they'd just stopped by to wish Colin luck. The good news was they *did* leave, with the jut of Nick's chin practically slamming the door shut behind them.

"Thank god, I thought they'd never leave," Nick said. His other arm wrapped Colin's neck and he slumped against the back of his chair, his chin resting on Colin's shoulder.

"They just got here," Colin pointed out, amusement overruling the nerves for a precious few moments.

"Yeah, even five minutes was five minutes too long," Nick said. "Anyway, they're going to be here for you any moment."

Nick's gaze met Colin's in the mirror. "I won't ask you if you're ready," he continued. "I've done this before, way too many times, and I'm not stupid enough to believe you're ever really ready."

"It seems so silly," Colin admitted quietly. "I did those things Mark said. Impossible things, or at least they seemed at the time. And this is just sitting on a couch and saying a few words, I should be embarrassed at how nervous I am."

Nick's fingers flexed against him and Colin relaxed into his touch. "You've spent your whole life avoiding talking about yourself," he said. "I can imagine it might be pretty tough to change that. But you told your teammates, and it went okay. This'll be easy." He quirked a tilted smile, which was so charmingly hot Colin felt his insides liquefy. He wished that instead of going onstage in a few minutes that they'd be going back to Nick's loft instead. "Bet you wished that you'd picked a smaller secret to start with."

"Before you," Colin admitted, "I didn't *have* another secret."

For a split second, Nick's expression was pained. They hadn't talked much about Nick's insistence they not reveal their relationship yet—only keeping the focus on Colin for now—just that Nick believed it was necessary and that Mark and Helen were on the same page. "I'm sorry. I promise that this is the right way to do this."

The right time to discuss this wasn't less than five minutes away from his first coming out interview, but Colin wanted Nick to know that the conversation wasn't over. So he reached out and cupped his cheek, his stubble delightfully scratchy against his skin. "We'll talk about it later," he promised, which definitely wasn't what Nick wanted to hear, because he grimaced. "Seriously," Colin insisted in a light tone, even though he was serious as shit.

"Stop talking so I can give you a good luck kiss," Nick said bossily, moving around and rearranging his body over the chair. Colin had expected a rather chaste kiss for luck, but Nick leaned in and slid his tongue right into Colin's mouth. His muscles tensed and his nerves buzzed, and by the time Nick pulled away, lips red and wet, it was all Colin could do not to grab hold and pull him right back in.

Of course, that's when the knock on the door sounded, and the voice of the PA responsible for bringing him to the set echoed through the dressing room, letting him know it was time.

Colin's nerves dissolved, the way they usually did in his first huddle of a game. Focus took over. Nick slid off his lap, and Colin glanced down at his own half-hard dick. "That was the plan," Nick announced smugly.

"So mean," Colin said, but he couldn't stop smiling.

It really annoyed Colin, but over the next twenty minutes, he discovered that Helen had been right. It *was* easy. Sitting on Ellen's couch, knowing the questions she'd ask and his own answers as well as he knew the plays in the Piranhas' playbook, it all felt rather anticlimactic. It had been so much tougher to negotiate the Rainbow Clause, arguing with Mark every time the Piranhas had come back with a compromise on a point that he refused to negotiate on. Mark making nervous noises about a contract standoff. The media's viciousness over his supposed greed.

Colin hadn't realized *that* was the fight. He'd been so focused on making sure he wouldn't be forced to compromise down the line. At that time, he hadn't even been considering coming out. Hadn't even contemplated when he might want to, when he might be ready to take that step. He'd still held out hope that he and Jemma might date, though those days were numbered, and deep down he'd known it.

Even with a career of unknown importance and length ahead of him, and even the dying possibility of being with Jemma, he'd still fought against Mark's apprehension, the Piranhas' ignorance and his own fear, all because he'd believed that his identity was too important to concede.

Sitting on Ellen's couch didn't feel like the fight; it felt like the victory lap.

He hadn't realized how light he would feel like when he could say on a show soon-to-be televised internationally, "I like women and I like men, and I want to make sure *everyone* knows there's no shame in that fact."

Nick had inferred, but not outright stated in his profile, that he believed Colin fighting his own inner demons of shame and anxiety over his sexuality had led to his ability to persevere in football. Colin had never believed that was true, but feeling the weight lift off his shoulders as he said the words, he realized he'd been wrong. Nick had known him better than he'd ever known himself.

"Have you spoken to Michael Sam?" Ellen asked, her eyes warm and supportive. Colin wasn't stupid; he knew part of why this felt so easy was that she and so many others, especially the man she was asking about, had paved the way.

"I've never met him," Colin admitted, "but if I did, I would thank him for being the first. For being a trailblazer, and for giving the game of football the jolt it needed. We can't continue pretending that heterosexuality is the norm and shouldn't change. Growing up feeling different is tough enough. We need to let kids know they're not alone."

That had *not* been the answer he'd practiced with Nick, or with Helen. Or with anyone. But as Colin spoke, it felt *right*. If he had been on TV, telling himself at the age of twelve that there was nothing to be afraid of, that he would be alright, his life might have been so different.

Maybe he wouldn't have gone around with a burning need to prove he was good enough to belong.

"Is that why you're taking this step now?" Ellen asked. A question that had not been on the list. Something else he'd not practiced ahead of time, but it still felt easy. The rest of his life had been the fight. Twelve, when he'd started noticing boys, that had been the fight. Sixteen, when the boy he'd liked had told him they couldn't see each other anymore, that had been the fight. Eighteen, when he'd seen Jemma for the first time and realized he didn't just like boys. Twenty-two, just about to be drafted into the NFL and the look on his brand-new agent's face when he'd told him he was bisexual.

"Actually," he laughed a little self-deprecatingly, "I'll be honest. I started this because I want to be able to date. Like, really date, and not worry about who sees us. Not sneak around. And that's going to be either men or women, and so it seemed sort of important to tell everyone."

Ellen laughed. "So really, this is Colin O'Connor being selfish."

He gave her and the camera a wide smile. The widest he could. He knew Nick was watching, after all. "Absolutely."

"And are you dating anyone?"

He blushed and even though he knew hiding it was probably impossible, he didn't even try. "No comment?"

"Oh, that's cute. You're cute," Ellen gushed. "I like you."

When Colin returned to the dressing room, Mark and Helen were back, this time with a bottle of champagne Mark was currently opening.

Nick was leaning against the chair, eyes on the phone in his hand, when Colin opened the door. His head snapped up instantly, a smile breaking over his features, an undeniable pride in his eyes.

"I would like to know," he said, throwing his arms around Colin with no hesitation, "why when you finally decide to be an open book with an interviewer, it's Ellen DeGeneres? If it hadn't been so brilliant, I'd be a little jealous right now."

"It was brilliant?" Colin asked, because he couldn't help it. Nick's praise was so sweet and if he was being selfish, he might as well keep it up.

"You fucking know it was brilliant," Nick scoffed. "Maybe I *am* jealous."

"You shouldn't be," Helen soothed, a big smile on her face, too. "Your article is going to get plenty of praise. The best written piece on Colin that's ever been done. You *know* that."

"Right. I do," Nick said smugly, and Colin couldn't love him more than he did in this moment.

"Let's have some champagne and celebrate," Mark said, handing out glasses.

Usually this close to training camp, Colin didn't drink, but he took a glass anyway. He already felt like the bubbles rising through the liquid; light and effervescent with freedom.

"Happy coming out," Nick said, raising his own glass and giving Colin that charming, slanted half-smile that had owned him since they'd first met.

The next morning, cuddled up in bed together, Colin murmured into Nick's shoulder, his bare skin soft and warm and perfect, "I showed you all over Miami. I think it's time you return the favor. What do you like to do here?"

Nick gave a muffled giggle. Colin's heart stuttered in his chest. He'd never known it could feel this way, your happiness expanding every moment you spent with someone. But he felt it every second he was with Nick. "You do realize Los Angeles is the seventh level of hell, right?"

"Then why do you choose to live here?" Colin asked incredulously. "You work from home at least three quarters of the time."

Nick shrugged, his body moving under the weight of Colin's. Colin, who was at least semi-interested in his answer, tried to ignore the way that felt against his dick.

"I'm serious," Colin insisted again. "Show me around. You were so afraid I was a recluse when we were in Miami, you always wanted to go out. Now we're here, and I discover you're practically a hermit."

"Traitor," Nick scoffed. "I think you're conspiring with Gabe."

Now *that* was hilarious. Gabriel still looked at him like he was a tiny bit afraid Colin was going to punch him in the face. Before, it had been because of Jemma. Now, it was hard to say if it was because of Jemma or because of Nick. Basically, Colin despaired of ever getting on the man's good side.

Colin thought his pointed silence was a good enough answer, and it must have been, because Nick let out an amused little chuckle. "Okay, point taken. Probably not going to happen. Um, well, we haven't been going out because it's so nice here with you."

"And because Helen probably told you not to be seen with me," Colin said before he could stop himself.

He felt Nick take a shaky breath, and then another. "I guess we should talk about it," he finally said quietly. "But you should know, I do agree with her. We don't often agree, but I do think right now is not the best time to be out when the whole world is shortly going to be speculating on who you're dating."

"What if I really don't care? I mean, the world is gonna find out eventually. Why can't it be sooner?" Colin was definitely aware he was pleading; begging even, a little. But he *wanted* this. He wanted the whole world and to get the whole world, they couldn't hide. He was *done* hiding.

"It just...it looks bad, okay? I wrote your coming out profile. I'm a journalist. Albeit one that isn't known for objective commentary, but *still*. We've got to be smart about this."

"What about Samantha Ponder?"

Nick made a cute laugh-groan, and buried his head in the pillow. "Please don't compare yourself to Christian Ponder."

"Okay, what about Jack Bennett? He married the woman who was the sideline reporter *for his own team*."

"That's baseball," Nick said dismissively. "Everyone knows there's no objectivity there."

"I'm being serious."

"So am I." Nick paused, and Colin could feel his hesitation in the air between them. "It's not that I *don't* want to do this, I do. Very much. All I ask is we take a breath after you come out, and think about the best way to approach the situation."

Colin reached out and turned Nick over, maybe not as gently as he could have. Nick's gray eyes blinked blurrily up at him. It took a split second longer for him to speak his mind, because while not a professional athlete, Nick still had a chest and abs that were defined enough to tie Colin's tongue right up. "We are not a *situation*," he gritted out. "I want to be able to go jogging or go get food. Or just...*hang out*. We don't even have to *touch*, for god's sake, even though I always want to touch you. I'm not going to pretend the world isn't out there until you and Helen can figure out how to turn an announcement of our relationship into advantageous PR!"

Nick's expression grew thoughtful and a little sad. "I didn't mean to coop you up," he said softly. "I'm sorry. I do like you here. I'm selfish, too. Like keeping you where I can still touch. Where you're mine."

If Colin ever needed evidence that he was weak in the form of Nick's persuasive charm, he had it. He melted, like a god-damned snowstorm in the middle of summer. "I'm always yours," he said, pulling Nick closer, his arms moving lower, cradling his hips. "I don't want to fight about it. But I do want you to know how I feel about it."

"I know," Nick admitted, his breath warm against Colin's chest. "It might seem easy now, but it won't always be easy. There will always be dicks. Especially if you end up dating a guy, and not a girl."

"Isn't that what bisexual *means*?" Colin asked, mystified.

Nick laughed, but didn't seem very amused. "It's a different story; you announcing you *might* date a man, and then actually dating a man. I know it shouldn't. But the world is dumb."

Colin groaned. "This is why I let you deal with the hard stuff, and I just throw a ball around a field."

"The hard stuff?" Nick asked slyly, his hand slipping down Colin's chest and cupping his dick in his palm.

Colin let his fingertips dig harder into Nick's hips. "Are we going to have make-up sex now? I've always heard it's great."

"I think you're gonna like it," Nick said confidently, shimmying down the bed, his lips coasting down Colin's abs, making the muscles twitch. "In fact, I think you're gonna *love* it."

"First time outside in what feels like a week, and you take me *jogging*," Colin complained as Nick maneuvered his car into a parking spot close to the beach.

"No, we're going to the *beach*. I asked you what you normally do at the beach, and you told me jogging. So jogging it is."

"I'm pretty sure that was a trick question," Colin insisted, like he didn't jog on the beach just about every single morning. Like he didn't *enjoy* jogging on the beach.

The trick wasn't to outsmart Nick, because Colin had dis-covered that was nearly impossible. The trick was to make him smile, maybe even laugh, while holding his own against Nick's tricky, witty brain.

"I'm pretty sure you knew that when you answered." Nick flashed him a particularly filthy smirk as they climbed out of the car.

"And if I'd said I like to hold hands on the beach?" Colin asked, because he couldn't seem to help himself. One little taste of freedom and he wanted it all, damn the consequences.

Colin fully expected a hint of impatience, or even annoyance from his boyfriend. They'd come to a truce of sorts, but he couldn't stop pushing. That was his problem; spend your whole life being told to push for what you wanted and the instinct was nearly impossible to contain. But instead, Nick just glanced over, serious as he'd ever been. "Then I'd find you a beach we could hold hands on."

Swallowing away the sudden lump in his throat, Colin said, "I'm sorry."

"Don't be sorry," Nick said, as they crossed over to the board-walk. He'd brought them to Venice, which he said was great for a casual workout and serious people-watching. "I'm only sorry we can't do it yet."

"But I keep...pushing." Colin leaned over and braced his hands against the stone wall edging the wide concrete path, stretching his back and his calves.

But Nick just laughed. "It's like you think I don't know you at all. I've spent *years* studying you. I don't expect you to change. I'd be pretty stupid to be angry."

"Years?" Colin had suspected that he'd jumped at the chance to interview him. He vaguely remembered some pretty blatant flirting in that first sit-down, but to hear that Nick had *studied* him was different. Flattering, but also troubling, because how could Colin ever hope to live up to the man Nick had formed in his head?

Maybe Nick had come to Miami primed to fall into Colin's bed. Maybe he hadn't had to do much at all to win Nick's attention. He'd just had to be Colin O'Connor. A thread of doubt he'd never expected wormed its way into thoughts it had no business infiltrating. Colin knew it and he still couldn't stop it.

Nick's sideways glance was confused. "You *did* read the article, right?"

"I mean, *of course* I did." He had, but he'd done it in a haze of anxiety over whether he might have fallen alone. Most of what Nick had written, besides the few passages that *really* proved he hadn't, blurred together.

They'd finished stretching, but instead of beginning their jog, Nick just stared at him incredulously. Like he suddenly wasn't sure. Anxiety bloomed in Colin's stomach. He'd never have considered the worst-case scenarios flashing through his head, but then, he'd never really thought through Nick's admitted obsession with his career.

Now, he couldn't help himself.

"I told you," Colin said, "what all this comes down to for me. *Someone.* That was what I wanted. So maybe I read the article wondering, with a pit the size of the Pacific Ocean in my stomach, if I'd been wrong about how you felt."

Nick openly gaped now. "*That* was what you read it for? Clues about how I felt about you? Didn't you care about coming out at all?"

"You'd just left me in Miami!" Colin said, both more defensively and at a much louder volume than was probably smart if they were trying to not fight and not let the greater Los Angeles area know they were involved in more than just a platonic relationship.

"For the greater good," Nick retorted. "I told you why us becoming involved was a bad idea. It's *still* a bad idea."

For the last few years, Colin had heard a thousand times how much people must want to be with him. He'd been propositioned more times than he ever wanted to remember. People looked at him and saw a handsome man, an accomplished man, a rich man. A man everyone wanted. But the funny thing seemed to be, he thought with a bitter sense of irony, that only people who he'd ever wanted could never just accept him and *be* with him.

"And yet, here we are," Colin retorted. "So forgive me if I want to find some happiness in a brand-new relationship, instead of constantly worrying that it's going to fuck up everyone's plans."

"Are you saying I'm not happy about us?" Nick's voice edged upwards.

"I'm saying you can't seem to make up your mind! One minute you're happy, the next, you're worried that you're going to ruin my career. Guess what, you don't have that much power." Colin knew that thread of doubt was talking, but he couldn't quite shut it up.

"Well next time, do me a favor," Nick said in clipped tones, "and don't reduce yourself to a romantic relationship. You're way more than that." He spun on his heels and started stalking down the Venice boardwalk like it had done something to personally attack him, his feet slapping insistently on the concrete.

"Dude," a man panhandling near them said, his long limbs arranged on a ratty blanket, his dreads swirled in an enormous bun on his head. "You should probably go after him."

"Yes, *thanks*," Colin snapped in the man's general direction.

"Just saying," the man said, holding his hands up. Colin knew the second he recognized him, because his eyes widened comically. "*Dude*, you're Colin O'Connor."

Colin gave a short, clipped nod, hoping to cut this whole interaction off. Normally he might have chatted with him a bit, left him a few bills. Instead this time, he jabbed a hand in his pocket, pulled out his wallet, and peeled off two twenties and leaned over, stuffing them in the chipped tin cup on the blanket and turned to leave. Not so he could go after Nick. Not yet. But so he could go *somewhere*. Maybe in Nick's general direction. The man's voice stopped him in his tracks.

"I hate your guts, you know. Went to Stanford so of course that was brutal every year. And then you came out here last year, kicked the Rams' ass. First home game back in LA and you couldn't even let us have that."

Colin sighed. That Rams game would forever haunt him. Not many games where he'd thrown three touchdown passes also made him want to crawl in his bed and never leave. "You're not the only one."

"You mean, snotty boy over there, trying to pretend he isn't trying to listen to what we're saying?"

Colin glanced up and saw that Nick *had* stopped walking away, and was currently loitering under the next palm tree down.

"I think we just had our first fight," Colin admitted, because *fuck it.*

"Here's the thing," the man said, leaning over and poking his finger into the cup filled with change and Colin's bills, "he wouldn't give a shit if he didn't care."

"I...I...I hadn't thought of it that way before," Colin said. He hadn't. Whether or not Nick had come to Miami, wanting to hook up with Colin or not, it was difficult to argue that Nick didn't care.

Nick cared enough that he'd locked himself in his apartment after he'd left Colin in Miami, drowning himself in bad coffee and a hideously bad mood. Cared enough that he'd given every-thing he had to write the best possible profile he could about Colin. Cared enough that he'd find a beach where they could hold hands if that was what Colin really wanted.

"You gave me money. It would be shitty to give you bad advice, even if I hate your guts."

Colin laughed, the sound startled right out of him. "I appreci-ate that."

The man waved a hand. "Go get your boy before he has an aneurism."

When Colin approached Nick's palm tree, the anxious look on his face went a long way to soothing Colin's anxiety. Nick *cared* about him. He wouldn't be so worried if he didn't.

He wouldn't get so frustrated if he didn't.

"I'm sorry," Colin said. "I got...I don't know if I'd call it cold feet exactly. I'm not really proud of being afraid, but I was. I *am*."

Nick's eyes softened. "Relationships are terrifying. I think you're allowed to be afraid once in a while. I'm sorry, too. You're not a mistake or a bad idea."

Colin sat down on the low stone ledge. Nick joined him, dangling his foot close to Colin's. Out here in public they couldn't kiss—not yet anyway—and so Colin bumped Nick's sneaker-clad foot with his own.

"What are you afraid of?" he finally asked.

"Lots of things. People hating my writing; people hating *me*. Which is the same thing, I guess. You deciding that I'm nobody. You deciding I'm a reporter. You deciding I'm not worth waiting for. Coming out being too hard for you."

If the man with the dreadlocks had overheard this conversation, Colin would have guessed he'd have pointed out that one of the things Nick was most afraid of was something Colin was currently going through. And didn't that say it all?

"I'm sorry I don't remember that first interview," Colin admitted. "Not just because it bothers you. But because that was the first time we met, and I *missed it*."

"I get why you don't," Nick said, reaching out and grasping Colin's knee in a quick, immensely reassuring touch. Something that others might not see, but that Colin felt deep, down in the marrow of his bones.

"I don't remember anything except the game. The whole game, I remember every damn touchdown. And Gabe's face, the first time I met him. And I remember how much I wanted to punch him in the face."

Nick let out a shocked bark of laughter. "Really? I guess I'm not surprised. I should consider myself lucky you didn't want to punch me in the face, too."

"I definitely didn't want to punch you in the face."

"True love," Nick said so casually that Colin might have missed how much it meant, if he hadn't seen the little tremor in Nick's hand as he went to stand up. Joy exploded in Colin in one big sparkly burst. Nick didn't just care; Nick *loved* him.

It was hard containing all that surprised delight inside his body, but he managed it. Maybe spending so much time with Nick, his snarkiness was finally rubbing off. "Are we going to jog or fight?" Colin asked, standing too.

"Not sure we have much to fight about."

"Jogging it is. You just love me for my body," Colin retorted flippantly but watched Nick's face closely, not that he could have missed the bright, answering smile blooming across Nick's face.

"Damn straight."

Chapter Eleven

Nick woke up after the sun crept across the room and snuck up the comforter. It took him a second to remember why he hadn't set any sort of alarm the night before, or why Colin, still sleeping next to him, hadn't either. Then he remembered. They'd not only not set any alarms, they'd turned their phones off. Deliberately.

This was the morning the article and the press release were both published. As of this moment, Colin was no longer in the closet. The entire world was rapidly discovering the truth of Colin O'Connor.

Nick lay there for a long moment, wondering if he should wake Colin. He'd agreed, at least at first, to let Helen and Mark filter the press coverage through them. Initially, Colin had claimed it wouldn't be necessary, that any negative responses he could handle himself, but he'd finally capitulated. Mostly because Nick had taken him aside and practically begged.

"The thing is," Nick had said, "it doesn't matter how strong you are, the first time someone sneers at you or says a nasty word because of who you are, what you've revealed, it *hurts*. If people want to help spare you that, let them."

Colin hadn't looked particularly convinced, but he had agreed, mostly, Nick feared, not because of himself but because Nick had wanted him to.

"I can hear you over there, stewing," Colin said lazily, a deep yawn punctuating his words. He rolled over, his blue eyes bright in the morning light, completely unconcerned and undeniably happy. A man finally free of the last shackle holding him back.

Nick knew this should be reassuring, but the less Colin seemed to worry, the more he seemed to. An unfortunate side effect of being head over heels in love.

"I'm not stewing," Nick said, sliding closer and tucking his head under Colin's chin, his hands reaching out and stroking warm skin. Colin looked so good in the morning, half-naked and sleep-tousled, it was nearly a crime and it was actually impossible to keep his hands to himself.

"No?" Colin asked, clearly amused. "Are you sure? 'Cause I can practically hear you from here. What's worrying you now? And don't tell me it's what people *might* say, because I could honestly not give a shit."

"I know," Nick mumbled into Colin's chest. "You have zero self-preservation."

"I've spent my whole life being cautious," Colin said softly. "It never got me a damn thing."

"Only a Heisman Trophy and a National Championship and millions of dollars." Nick rolled his eyes, even if Colin couldn't see.

"And I've never been happier than I am right now," Colin insisted, his lips brushing the crown of Nick's head. "Funny how that works."

It was hard to remove his cheek from that wide expanse of warm pectoral muscle, but Nick persevered and pulled back, just far enough that he could see the soft gaze of Colin's eyes. If even a tiny part of him had doubted the truth of Colin's statement, Nick couldn't now. It was all right there, shining in those damn beautiful eyes.

"You're an unbelievable sap," Nick muttered, though it was tough to deny just how thrilled he was, deep down.

"Yeah, yeah, you love it," Colin said, wriggling out of Nick's grasp. "I'm hitting the toilet, then you can come up with a way to distract me from my inevitable breakdown." The way Colin's eyebrows waggled left very little mystery about how exactly he wanted to be distracted.

Nick flopped back against the bed, trying to calm the insistent racing of his blood. Even just the thought of sex with Colin set every nerve in his body buzzing. He felt sixteen again, despite that it felt like they'd barely left the bed the last two weeks.

He heard the toilet flush and a moment later, the bed shifted as Colin returned.

"I think you must be getting bored. One mention of sex and you fall right back asleep," Colin teased, leaning over Nick, and brushing a kiss across his lips.

Nick grinned lazily as Colin's mouth moved to his neck and his ear, coasting downwards. "I thought I was supposed to be distracting *you*," he teased right back.

"Right," Colin said, and he pulled back, leaving the blood buzzing insistently beneath Nick's skin with no additional stimulation.

Nick pouted. "You left," he said, opening his eyes. Colin was kneeling on the bed, the bottle of lube and a condom from Nick's bedside drawer in his hands.

"You promised," Colin reminded, a blush staining his cheeks. He still tended to get embarrassed when he asked for things, and while they'd had a lot of sex, and Nick had fingered Colin plenty of times, he had yet to fuck him.

"Whatever you want," Nick said, sitting up and reaching up for Colin, fingers gripping the back of his neck, tugging him closer so he could kiss him. "You know I'd give you anything."

Colin flushed more. "Then give me this."

It wasn't even a request that needed an answer, at least a verbal one. Nick kissed him, pouring everything he felt and couldn't quite say into Colin, hoping he would understand.

They settled back onto the bed, Nick between Colin's legs, as he fumbled for the lube. His heart pounded with a sort of possessive love that might have scared him, if he'd had the mind to consider it logically. He only cared about making this good for Colin, branding him with his body so that he'd never need anyone else.

But Colin already knew what Nick was afraid of, because he'd told him, and he let him, opening his legs wider, as Nick pressed slicked-up fingers down his taint and into his hole.

"More," Colin panted, the tendons on his neck flexing, his fingers buried in the sheets. The muscles of his thighs tensed and relaxed, once then twice. "I need *more*."

"Bossy," Nick tried to quip, but with Colin's heat around his fingers, pulsing and tight, his voice was breathless. He slid a third finger in, trying to be careful even as lust barreled through him in successively bigger waves. At some point, they were going to knock him right over, and Colin with him.

Colin threw his head back and let out a guttural moan, and Nick had to swallow hard. He was right on the tenuous edge of his control, but he wasn't sure Colin was ready. They'd done this plenty, but never gone all the way, and the last thing Nick wanted to do was hurt the man he loved.

But Colin took that decision right out of his hands, pulling away and reaching for the condom package. He ripped it with his teeth and reached for Nick's dick. "No more waiting," he panted out. "I'm ready."

Nick took the condom before Colin could tease him any further and rolled it on, slicking himself up. "Okay," he breathed out. "It'll be easier on your front, honestly."

Colin frowned. "I want to kiss you."

Nick leaned over and kissed him thoroughly. "I know," he said, his hands resting on Colin's chest. "But do this for me, okay?"

Nick had quickly learned that the easiest way to get Colin to go along with something was to pretend it was something he wanted. It was manipulative, maybe, but Nick also knew he was right. It *would* be easier like this.

Colin rolled over and Nick took a single deep breath, his fingers trembling on Colin's flank. "You ready?" he asked, one last time, his other hand wrapped around the base of his cock, praying he wouldn't lose control too quickly. It had been so long since he'd done this with someone he really cared about, and it would be stupid to think that it wouldn't matter.

It already mattered.

"I'm going to fall asleep if you wait any longer," Colin ground out, and Nick let out a choked laugh as he pressed in, Colin closing tight and hot around him.

Nick felt Colin tense, and hesitated. "Am I allowed to ask if you're okay?"

Colin's voice was soft. "I'm okay. Just need a little...adjustment."

Nick waited a breathless moment, and then another, before Colin shifted back, and pressed Nick all the way in, a long, slick slide that left Nick lightheaded and grasping for restraint.

"God," Colin grunted, guttural and intense, and that sound alone was nearly Nick's undoing.

Trying to keep it slow and steady, Nick set a rhythm, hands sliding along Colin's hips, trying to hit the angle that kept him swearing, low and strained, but of course, Colin demanded more. "Faster," he panted, the muscles in his back straining, his biceps flexing as he fisted his own cock in time with Nick's thrusts. It was an undeniable image that sucked Nick right down—he couldn't ignore it even if he closed his eyes. He'd see it in his sleep, in his dreams, and it shot him right over the edge, right as Colin gave a yell and squeezed around his cock.

"I think it's safe to say, I really like dick," Colin said, a bright grin enveloping his features, as they lay in bed, finally clean, and tucked back in.

Nick choked on the water he was drinking. "I didn't realize that was up for discussion still."

"It wasn't, not really, but it's not a bad thing to verify the morning I tell everyone that I do."

"Little late to take it back now," Nick reminded him.

"As if I would," Colin grumbled, throwing an arm around Nick's shoulders and pulling him close. "I've never been happier."

Nick's heart throbbed and felt like it was expanding another half-size. He'd never be able to keep his marshmallow side hidden if this guy kept going on this way. "You said that already this morning."

The expression on Colin's face was earnest and affectionate. So goddamned *open*. Nick still wasn't sure if it was a blessing or a curse. "It's worth saying twice."

Helen called at eleven, her voice perennially cheery as Colin put her on speakerphone. "So much positive coverage," she chirped. "Everyone is so proud and happy. I'm emailing you over a selection of articles."

But of course Colin wasn't happy at that. "What about Twitter and social media?"

Helen's half-second of hesitation was enough of an answer. "Mostly positive," she said, which Nick knew she would've said even if it had been 95% negative. "There's some disbelief and ignorance, of course, but then we knew that was inevitable. There's ugly people everywhere."

"Right," Colin said, and Nick wished he could throw himself physically in front of every single person who would say something nasty to him. But that was not only ridiculous, it was impossible.

"I'm still recommending you stay off the grid, at least for another day or two," Helen continued.

"We're going to the *Five Points* offices tomorrow afternoon, but nothing planned before then," Nick interrupted, like Helen didn't already have the schedule memorized.

Helen's voice was careful. "I was talking more about social media, but that's good, too."

"I want to make a post tonight," Colin said. "Something basic, like to thank everyone for their support."

Nick knew, because Colin had already tried to convince him twice, that he'd *actually* been hoping that Nick would appear in the post with him, as his official partner. But they didn't need to bring that up to Helen, who'd have a coronary.

"Run the post by me first," Helen said.

Colin rolled his eyes. "I'm perfectly able of making a social media post without your explicit permission," he said.

"As you're aware," she said with a tone of steel, "any account with as many followers as you do has all their posts vetted first. That's social media one-oh-one, and you know that."

As Nick expected, Colin grumbled, but ultimately agreed to send her the post first.

Duncan emailed over some preliminary numbers mid-afternoon, when they were in the middle of their *Indiana Jones* marathon.

"How are they?" Colin asked, looking more interested in those than in the articles Helen had emailed over earlier.

Nick rolled his eyes. "Spectacular, of course. You're big news. And we're sort of the experts on you, right now, anyway."

"The other articles were just shallow copies of what you'd already said," Colin said, and for the first time all day, there was a testy note in his voice. "If Helen had given them the press release and your article even twelve hours earlier, there might have been more original thought in them."

Colin knew exactly why Helen hadn't pre-distributed the material to the media, but he continued to pretend ignorance that his story wasn't the biggest one sports had seen in *years*.

"Just dying for people to judge you?" Nick asked drily. "Calm down, O'Connor. This isn't a game to win. You've already won."

"I just...part of me really wants to know what people think. Not because it changes my own perception, but I'm curious."

Nick pushed on Colin's chest, pinning him to the couch. Colin went easily, even though they both knew he could have overpowered Nick in a second. "Just sit down and watch the damn movie."

Colin shot him an annoyed look.

"Believe it or not," Nick insisted, "this is actually me helping you. Besides, you agreed to the media blackout. I'd imagine that in a week, when you've done all those interviews you hate so much, you'll wish you were back here anyway."

"Probably," Colin admitted grudgingly.

"Then sit your ass down and watch the damn movie," Nick said.

Around seven, Jemma and Gabe showed up with pizza and beer.

Nick tried to pretend there was a fleck of dust in his eye when Jemma wrapped her arms around Colin and didn't let him go for a long moment.

"How're you hanging in there?" Gabe asked when they went into the kitchen to give Jemma and Colin a moment alone together.

"I'm fine," Nick said as casually as he could.

"You're a nervous wreck," Gabe corrected. "I'm not sure who's worse off in this media blackout, you or O'Connor. He's looking increasingly cornered, like he just got blitzed, and you look as cranky as I've ever seen you."

"I'm not cranky," Nick said, pulling plates down from the cupboard. "I just hate not knowing what's going on. Colin hates it, too."

"Then let him fucking look at it. It's not like twenty-four hours is going to change anyone's mind about him. They either think he's the bravest thing since Michael Sam, or they think he's a fairy who shouldn't be playing ball. Time isn't going to make him *more* ready or the world more accepting."

"I know," Nick said lowly, resting his elbows against the counter. "I *know* that."

"There's a lot of supportive people in the world. And even if there weren't, not knowing is killing both of you."

Nick had hoped they could at least hold off until tomorrow morning. But he already knew that they'd go through some of the material online after Gabe and Jemma left. Maybe then this horrible knot of terror would loosen a little.

"I remember when you told me you were gay," Gabe continued. "And you just *said it*. You didn't know me, didn't know how I'd react, and you just said it to some guy you'd just met at the gym, totally matter-of-fact. Don't tell me that O'Connor can't do that. He *could*. He *can*. You know he can. You've let your feelings cloud your judgement of what he's capable of."

Nick frowned. "I know he's capable. That isn't the issue."

"I *know*. You're afraid for him. But you keep forgetting, this is the dude that stared down the Alabama defensive line. The Raiders. The Ravens. The fuckin' *Steelers*, man. He's stone cold in a zone. You can't shake him."

An uncomfortable feeling crawled up Nick's neck. "He's a lot more than a football player."

Gabe shot him a grim look as he grabbed a beer from the fridge. "Maybe, but he's still got that inside him. And you shouldn't forget it."

Nick took a long drink of his beer and resisted the urge to find something harder. "I'm trying not to."

"The hardest thing in the world is to support the person you love, but not smother them."

Nick laughed, even though Gabe had a really fucking good point. "When did you become some sort of love expert?"

Gabe glowered, but Nick was pretty sure he caught a hint of a smile as Gabe turned and headed back to the living room. *You know when* was the unspoken, extremely self-explanatory answer. Since Jemma.

Nick had never experienced the desire to provide more than a token support for any of his past partners, and never the intense need to protect (aka smother) if he was using Gabe's terminology, and he didn't particularly want to. Nick had known very early on during his trip to Miami that he was on new, undiscovered ground. He'd believed himself in love once or twice before this, but it had never been like it was with Colin. Colin felt like a whole new universe.

It was after midnight when Jemma and Gabe left. Colin had had a few beers—most of a six-pack if he was being totally honest—and so when he walked into Nick's bedroom, he was feeling pleasantly buzzed and more relaxed than he had in at least a week.

Nick was lying in bed, head propped up on a handful of pillows, his tablet on his lap, and he looked up when Colin walked in.

He extended the tablet silently, and Colin took it.

It was what he'd wanted *all damn day*, but still looking at it, at the Twitter icon at the top of the screen, was almost too much. He saw enough to know that Nick had specifically filtered out results with his name.

Not just replies to the tweet he had written earlier this afternoon and Helen had vetted personally, and then posted. No, just a general search. The widest search with the most possibility there could be something Colin wouldn't want to read.

"I thought you weren't supposed to do this," Colin said.

Nick gave a helpless shrug. "I keep forgetting how tough you are. Apparently my natural inclination is to wrap you in cotton wool. I'm sorry."

"And Helen?"

"Helen's just afraid you're going to see something bad and have trouble with your interviews in the next few days."

"Oh, so she's worried about herself," Colin said wryly. "Per usual."

"She means well," Nick said, but Colin noticed that he hadn't disagreed. "But this is your choice. If you want to read what people are saying, you should. It's your right."

Colin stared down at the screen, but he couldn't look at it. Not yet. "This is all I've wanted to see all day," he said slowly, "and I thought I'd be ready, but I'm fucking terrified."

Nick's face softened. He tapped the bed next to him. "Come sit with me, and I'll read you a few. Break the ice." He plucked the tablet right out of Colin's grip. "You can still be tough and ask for help, you know."

Colin slid onto the bed, lying on his back, hands tucked behind his head, his eyes closed. "I know," he mumbled.

"Okay, well, now that we got that out of the way," Nick teased, keeping his voice light. "You just tell me when you're ready."

Colin took a deep, mostly steady breath. Let it out, took in another. Let that one out. "Okay. I'm ready."

"Hmmm, let's see. Here's a good one. MrsAlice45 says: Colin O'Connor says he's bisexual. Apparently that means some people don't think he can play football. Too bad he's already proved them wrong."

Colin couldn't help but chuckle a little at that one. "I think that might be Helen in disguise."

"Too bad her name wasn't MrsHelen45. We could have exposed her so easily."

"I *knew* she was too smart for us," Nick hissed conspiratorially and that was all it took to unearth a laugh from somewhere Colin thought he'd lost in the last week.

"Go on," he said. "And don't take it too easy on me and only read the good ones."

"How about I read all the *fair* ones?" Nick asked and Colin made a grumbling noise of assent. "Okay, here's one. "Vikings-Fan4Ever says: Definitely knew something was off about Colin O'Connor when he passed for almost three hundred yards against the Vikings."

"Three hundred yards and *two touchdowns*," Colin corrected, amused.

"EverShade wants to know what the downside is. According to her, everyone should be thrilled because you're fair game for both sexes."

Colin laughed again. "If they only knew."

"Yeah, yeah," Nick teased. "Oh, this is good. This gentleman says, Colin O'Connor joins Michael Sam as the only two football players with enough sense to be honest about who they are."

Nick read tweets out loud for almost an hour, and by the end, Colin had laughed and he'd cried. There had been a few that had set his teeth on edge, but he knew Nick had carefully edited out anything really bad. They would be out there, and someday he'd read them. But not today. Today, he felt just about light and free as a helium balloon, floating towards the endless horizon.

"Thank you," Colin said softly, reaching out and stroking Nick's leg. "Thank you really isn't enough, but it's all I've got."

Nick sniffed suspiciously. "It's plenty."

"It'll have to do until I can tell the world how amazing my boyfriend is."

Nick rolled his eyes, but Colin hadn't missed the gleam in the gray depths. As protective as Nick was, Colin definitely suspected that Nick would *really* enjoy informing the world that not only was Colin O'Connor off the market, he was *his*.

Someday.

The next afternoon, Nick took Colin to the *Five Points* office, where he signed a gigantic blown-up copy of the second *Sports Illustrated* cover that he'd posed for. This time, instead of a bare chest, he was wearing a t-shirt emblazoned with a rainbow, and he might not to be a real expert—not like Nick, anyway—but he was almost certain that he looked nothing like a cardboard cutout.

"This one is for my office," Nick said, unrolling another enormous poster-sized version onto his desk. "Make sure the signature is *nice and big*."

"Has anybody ever told you that you're sort of embarrassing?" Colin teased as he signed in a huge swath across his own torso.

"I tell him all the time," Jemma piped up.

Colin threw her a bright smile. The helium feeling that had bloomed inside him last night still hadn't faded, and he felt like he was walking lighter than air today.

"You're both the worst," Nick grumbled. "Ganging up on me."

Next on the agenda, and the *real* reason he'd come to the *Five Points* office, was a live Q&A session, via their Facebook page.

The questions were heavily moderated, but Colin wasn't really surprised to get one about his love life. He'd been getting questions about his love life the whole time the world had believed he only liked women; he didn't really expect that would change now that he'd opened it up to *both* men and women.

"I saw the *Ellen* interview," the girl asked nervously, "and you said *no comment* when she asked you about a partner. Are you single?"

Helen shot him a look that could cut from ten yards away, but again, Colin let his flush do all the talking for him. "I'm not ready to say," he said, which was most definitely not true. But what he was absolutely not going to do was lie outright and pretend that Nick didn't exist.

Helen threw up her hands in mock defeat, and Colin was pretty sure he could see Nick, behind the scenes, smirking, clearly not as upset as he might have been. Colin wasn't sure when Nick would finally say it was okay for them to be honest about their relationship, but he liked to believe that he was slowly but surely wearing his boyfriend down, and that day was a lot sooner than Nick tried to pretend it was.

When the Q&A was over, Helen pulled him aside. Colin knew from her expression that her patience was wearing thin. "First *Ellen* and now this?" she nearly shrieked. "Do you have any idea how much pressure I'm getting from the media about your love life?"

But nothing could really kill Colin's good mood today, even Helen in a snit. "So, not much different than normal," he said smoothly.

"You're *encouraging* them!" Helen insisted, which wasn't so far from the truth.

Colin fully expected Nick to bring it up later, and he was glad he hadn't bet against his gut instinct, because he did on their way home from the *Five Points* office.

"You know, you can't half-out me as a way to convince me," Nick said, his words the opposite of the wide grin on his face.

Sure I can't, Colin thought. The truth was, they were both flying high, the intoxicating taste of freedom burning in their mouths, and he gave it only a few more days until Nick caved. The response to Colin's coming out had been even better than either of them had believed it could be, and Colin could practically *see* Nick mentally wrestling with how much he just wanted to say *fuck it* and throw caution to the wind.

During Colin's next interview, the interviewer inevitably asked if he was dating anyone. Colin gave a single bright grin to the camera and wouldn't answer at all. Supposition and rumors raged like wildfire. Helen told him he was giving her an ulcer.

But the soft smile on Nick's face was worth Helen's annoyance, and he kept going, pushing as much as he dared.

A week after the press release, Helen forwarded him an invite to a major NFL player's big children's fundraiser that he was holding in LA in a few days. Colin had been not-so-subtly pushing for an invite for a while because he not only wanted to do what he could for the kids, but because he had heard *great* things about this particular player's charity and he wanted an inside look for his own burgeoning folder of ideas.

I knew it would come through, Helen wrote. *You can take a plus one—but not Nick. Maybe Jemma?*

Of course, the first thing Colin thought when he saw it was that now that the invitation had finally materialized, he *needed* Nick to come with him.

"Absolutely fucking not," Nick said bluntly, as he shoved plates into the dishwasher. Colin had made breakfast—well, more like *brunch*—and Nick had offered to clean up.

Colin was flabbergasted. He'd not expected Nick to instantaneously agree, but he'd expected more hesitation, and less absolute certainty than *no*, he would *not* be going as Colin's plus one to the fundraiser.

He'd done everything he could to guarantee a positive response from his boyfriend, including dragging his butt out of bed way too early in the morning and grabbing donuts from Randy's, because that was Nick's favorite.

"Don't get me wrong," Nick continued, "I'd love to go with you. But it's a bad idea."

"Why? Because you wrote about me coming out? By the fundraiser, nobody will care."

"That's probably not entirely true," Nick said slowly, "but that's not really why."

"Then what?" Colin demanded, a little more harshly than he'd intended. He'd come out, to way more positive fanfare than anyone had ever predicted. Why *couldn't* he go with his boyfriend to an important fundraiser?

"People were way nicer than any of us expected, yeah, but that's only because you haven't publicly dated a man yet. The moment you do that, everyone who reserved judgement, who sort of expected you to end up with a woman, is going to come down on you like a ton of bricks."

"That is what being bisexual *means*," Colin said. He'd heard this argument from Nick before, but he still found it hard to swallow. He'd absolutely picked up on Nick's protective streak. It wasn't that he believed Nick's concerns weren't valid; more like the situation wasn't nearly as grave as Nick was presenting it as.

Nick turned back to the sink and shrugged, his shoulders tense under his loose t-shirt. "I don't have to like it to know it happens."

"It doesn't even have to be a date," Colin said, hating how desperate he sounded.

Nick glanced back at him, expression tinged with bitterness. "But we *are* dating. I'm not going to go to an event and pretend otherwise. I'd rather not go than lie."

Normally Colin might have agreed with him, but he hated the idea that he'd been through all of this damn publicity and personal exposure and he still couldn't take his boyfriend as a date to an event.

"Fine. But don't expect me to like it," Colin said, hearing a bitterness in his own voice that echoed Nick's.

Nick sighed, and dropped the dish towel on the counter. He walked around it and wrapped his arms around Colin's middle, laying his head on his chest. Colin resisted for about half a second, then gave in, his own hands sliding across Nick's shoulders. "I don't like it, either," Nick murmured. "I hate it. But we'll figure it out. Just give it a little more time."

Patience had never really been one of Colin's strong suits, despite all claims to the contrary. He'd had to teach himself, through intense repetition and mental control, the patience to wait through his progressions without just throwing the ball down field to the first receiver.

Learning patience had sucked, and exercising it now felt even tougher, but then Nick—the culmination of so many hopes that Colin had carried through the hard years—was worth it, and more.

Colin let out a sigh, trying to empty the frustration out of him along with the extra air. It nearly worked. "You've got your time. I'm sorry I keep trying to push."

He wasn't really sorry, and Colin knew by the way Nick chuckled that he knew it, too. "No, you're not," Nick pointed out wryly.

"No, I'm not," Colin admitted.

Later that afternoon, they met up with Gabe and Jemma at Nick's favorite taco stand outside the city, along the 101.

The sun was setting as they sat on the wide veranda, drinking beers and shooting the shit. And if Colin scooted a little closer to Nick, let his arm drape over his shoulders, Colin told himself that Nick *knew* he was pushing and if he didn't like it, all he had to tell him was to stop.

Nick didn't tell him to stop and so when he got up to get another round, it felt natural to lean in and brush a quick kiss across Nick's lips. It wasn't anything different than what Gabe had done with Jemma just a few minutes before.

The problem was that neither Gabe nor Jemma were an NFL quarterback who had just come out of the closet, and who had spent the last two weeks inciting a fury of gossip on just who he was dating.

It was the witching hour, just between dark and dawn, when Colin's phone rang. He picked it up on the third ring, vaguely sensing through his sleepy brain that Helen calling him at 2:39 am was probably not the best sign.

"Secret's out of the bag," Helen said shortly. "There's pics of you kissing Nick. And Deadspin found some other clubbing pics, from that place you went in Miami, and they've published it all. Everybody knows."

"Oh," Colin said stupidly, still mostly asleep.

"Buckle up," Helen said, "we're in for a shit storm."

Chapter Twelve

Any chance Helen might have been exaggerating ended after Nick hesitantly shook Colin awake.

He wore a truly impressive scowl on his face, his hair standing straight up on one side. "*What?*" he asked first, then turned to grab his phone, then tablet, muttering to himself. Finally after a tense minute, he swung his feet to the floor and stalked off in the vicinity of the second bedroom he'd set up as his office.

Colin lay in bed, staring up at the ceiling, replaying that single moment at the taco stand, when he'd leaned in and kissed Nick. It had been less than a second, and the sort of off-handed kiss you gave someone when you weren't thinking about it.

Had he really been thinking about it? He went back and tried his best to remember what had been in his head at the time. Would he have done it if he'd known there were paparazzi stalking them? If he'd known there was a fan with a camera only a few tables away?

Before Colin could decide for sure one way or the other, Nick returned, laptop under one arm, a frown marring his handsome features. "I'm not mad," he said. "I'm mostly confused."

"Why?" Colin wasn't confused at all. He'd whipped the media into a frenzy of speculation about his love life, which was why he'd spent the last six years of his life avoiding personal subjects. He'd been asking to get bitten; it didn't really seem fair to complain about the pain after the fact.

Nick glanced up from his laptop, which he'd settled back in his lap. Colin glanced around and saw Nick's phone, tablet, and now the laptop arranged in a semi-circle around him. A veritable wall. "Deadspin can be dicks, yeah, but they're usually dicks with an agenda. And permission, of a kind."

"Do you think *Helen* okayed this?"

Nick looked unsure. "I'm sure she wasn't happy about it."

"She wasn't," Colin interrupted. "She said, *get ready for a shit storm.* Shit storms are not typically things you invite."

"I don't think she invited it. I think they came to her with the story and something worse and she agreed to publish this to bury the bad."

Colin continued to stare a hole in the ceiling. If his eyes were lasers, he'd be halfway to the sun by now. "Helen traded some pictures of us for a story about one of the Piranhas fucking up," he stated baldly.

"It's a strong possibility. But we'll probably never know for sure." Nick shrugged. "I guess it really doesn't matter. Everyone knows now."

"Some player beat his wife or crashed his car or needed his stomach pumped. And I pay for it."

Nick shot him an inscrutable look. "Wasn't this what you *wanted?*"

"Not like this," Colin said, trying to contain the anger that was threatening to boil over. He'd never considered himself to have any kind of temper, but now he understood how people punched walls. It was impossible, feeling helpless this way, like he wasn't even in charge of his own damn life.

Nick was typing madly on his laptop, and his fingers barely missed a beat. "We could still do something else, if you wanted to."

"Helen would kill me," Colin said, even though the thought of pissing Helen off wasn't exactly a negative possibility right now.

Nick's shrug said, *So?*

"What I really wanted," Colin said, "was to just post a picture. Nothing too ridiculous. Nothing too suggestive. Just something that showed how much I care about you."

"Okay, let's do it."

Colin couldn't help it; he just gaped.

"Everyone *already knows*," Nick retorted to Colin's silent protest.

"Won't Duncan be pissed?"

"You're kidding, right? Duncan is fucking thrilled. The hits on my profile have reached an all-time high. He's worried about our servers being able to handle all the extra traffic. Now that everyone knows we're involved, they want to know exactly what I said about you."

"What do you want?"

That was the only thing Colin had said in the last five minutes that had even given Nick pause or had broken his furious typing rhythm for a moment. He glanced up at Colin, gray eyes contemplative. "You know what I want."

"I know, but I need you to say it out loud. I couldn't stand misunderstanding you now."

Nick hesitated for a split second, then pushed the laptop away, and cleared the electronics between them with a single sweep of his hand. He scooted closer to Colin, curling up next to him like he never wanted to be anywhere else. Resting a hand on Colin's chest, right over his heart, Nick's smile was bittersweet. "You. Now. Today. Tomorrow. As long as you let me stick around."

Colin reached up and let his fingers twist through Nick's sleep-matted hair, doing his best to smooth it down. "Then you've got me," he said as he worked, his voice not quite steady.

"There's no going back from this." Nick's voice wasn't steady either.

Colin looked down and saw the quiver of Nick's upper lip. He rarely gave away his nerves, but he could see them now, lurking in the depths of his eyes. "I don't want to. I wouldn't change this, even if I could." Suddenly it felt very stupid that they'd spent the last three weeks talking in code. Even though he knew how Nick felt about him, it still felt terrifying to take that last step off the cliff. "You know, I love you."

The corners of Nick's lips tilted into a wide, bright smile. Suddenly, he was luminous. "You know, I love you, too."

"Then let's do this," Colin said, grabbing his phone and leaning back a little, capturing the remnants of that smile, and the crazy hair that would fool nobody. He stared at the picture for a split second, suddenly regretting that he had to share this version of Nick with the world. But it was just one moment, he realized, he'd get dozens and hundreds and thousands more.

He'd make sure of it.

Typing out the caption before he could lose his nerve, he quickly uploaded the picture to his social media. It was the first post he'd ever made without Helen's consent, and as it finished posting, Colin felt the last chain holding him back fall away.

Woke @NickWheeler up to tell him the cat's out of the bag. He doesn't look too disappointed.

"It was incredibly irresponsible," Helen said sternly.

"In Colin's defense—" Nick began, but Helen cut him right off.

"Mr. Wheeler, we all know you're willing to defend him to the ends of the earth, but that isn't the point here."

"In *my* defense," Colin said, perfectly ready to defend himself if Nick wasn't allowed to, "the chances of someone catching a photo of us at some hole-in-the-wall taco stand was extremely slim."

"The photographer who took the picture was tracking you," Helen said. "Which is a possibility I *know* I warned you about."

"You also said that almost every paparazzi is *paid* to take photos with full permission of the person they're photographing. I assumed, because of what you said, that someone going rogue with almost no guarantee of a payoff, wasn't worth worrying about."

Helen sighed. "It wouldn't have been...except you spent all those weeks teasing everyone with the idea you were dating someone. The paparazzi had a very good idea what a photo confirmation would be worth.

"Then when Deadspin bought the pictures, they were smart enough to comb through pictures of you from when Nick would have been in Miami," she continued. "And they hit pay dirt."

Colin leaned back in his chair. He hated the way this felt; like he'd been caught doing something wrong and he'd been brought to the principal's office for punishment to be doled out. "I thought the point of me coming out was so I *could* date a man."

"We just don't want to turn what's been a surprisingly positive experience into something else," Helen said. "I know it doesn't sound like it sometimes, but we're on your side."

"Then don't call me in here, and start lecturing me," Colin snapped. "From what you say, it was a thousand to one chance someone might find out I was dating Nick, but it *happened*."

"We're trying to figure out what to do about it," Helen said, and the minute trace of apology in her tone placated but didn't really calm his temper.

"What to do about it?" Colin questioned. "There's nothing to *do* about it. We're dating. We'll continue to date."

"We thought maybe some official paparazzi photos, you know, you and Nick out shopping in Malibu or maybe even back in Miami, holding hands, looking cute and marketable. That gives us control back of the media cycle and means that everyone stops circulating those blurry pics that Deadspin owns."

Colin leaned forward, giving Helen the same look he often gave his receivers when he was challenging them to catch more balls. "Then let me bring Nick to the fundraiser."

"No," Helen and Nick chimed in simultaneously.

Colin threw his hands in the air. "Why the *hell* not? It's the perfect opportunity. We'd look just as cute there as we'd look holding hands pretending to shop, and at least it would be for a good cause."

Nick reached over and brushed one of Colin's hands with his own. "Then the event becomes about us and not about the kids," he said, and at least he sounded more apologetic than Helen.

Switching his attention to his boyfriend, Colin asked him softly, "What do you think about these other pictures?" He'd promised himself—and *Nick*—that they'd get equal say in whatever Helen was going to ask them to do, going forward. Colin had insisted on not being the deciding factor, even though he was the one with the PR consultant. Nick had merely looked at him like he was crazy, and told Colin that he could take perfectly good care of himself when it came to the media. Which was undoubtedly true because Nick *was* the media.

One of the things Colin was rapidly learning about relationships was that even when you had the other person's best interests at heart, that wasn't always how it was interpreted by them.

"It's not a bad idea," Nick said and Colin groaned out loud.

"Faking a shopping trip? Ugh, I hate those staged photos."

"We could go frolic on the beach," Nick said, a glimmer of a smile ghosting around his lips.

"Absolutely not," Colin retorted.

"You could even go shirtless. The photos would be a wild success."

Colin shot his boyfriend a glare. Helen cleared her throat. "Why don't we discuss possible photo opportunities later and agree now that the idea in general is a good one?"

"Probably because I don't think it's a good idea in general," Colin said in what he knew was an uncharacteristically grumpy voice.

Helen threw her hands up and shot Nick a look, which probably meant something along the lines of, *talk to him because I give up trying.*

"We'll talk about it and get back to you," Nick said diplomatically.

Ultimately, the problem with what Colin had tried to promise Nick was that the opposite wasn't really true at all. The moment Nick expressed his opinion about something, Colin couldn't even help it—he wanted to say yes, to give him exactly what he wanted. Which was how he knew when they ended up having the conversation, Nick would tell him (again) that it was a good idea, and Colin would say, *okay, let's take these stupid pictures.*

Another part of being in a relationship, Colin had discovered, was learning when to gracefully compromise.

"We'll do the pictures," Colin said. "But at the taco stand."

Helen looked pleased but puzzled. "The taco stand?"

"The same one we were discovered at," Colin said. "I want to do something we'd actually do, so we'll do something that we've already done."

He could tell Helen wasn't a huge fan of the idea, but she'd also gotten what she wanted with very little coaxing on her end. He watched her internal struggle and knew he'd get his way.

Which was how, the next day, Colin and Nick and Gabe and Jemma all took the day off to recreate a double date at their favorite taco stand.

"Do you think they're getting my good angle?" Gabe asked, between bites of *al pastor*.

"I really hate you," Colin grimaced, his annoyance by no means eradicated by the way Nick was giggling next to him.

"Don't look that way," Jemma said, "they're going to think you're already having a fight with Nick."

"Yeah, that's all we need," Nick said. "*Trouble in Paradise Already?* headlines."

"Don't be ridiculous," Colin said, trying not to frown, "what am I supposed to do? Smile constantly? This is supposed to seem *natural*."

"I hate to break it to you," Gabe said. "But none of this is very natural."

"You don't say," Colin retorted sarcastically.

"Just try not to look so *angry*," Jemma soothed. "You're supposed to be having a nice day with friends, with your *boyfriend*, who you're crazy about."

Colin morosely poked at his uneaten tacos. He was too afraid to get a picture taken with a mouthful of half-eaten food. It turned out that it was a *lot* easier to do this when you didn't know there was a photographer hiding in the bushes by the salsa bar.

"O'Connor," Nick said quietly, and Colin glanced up, everything in him magnetically drawn to the man next to him. Nick reached up and put a hand on his shoulder, scooting a half-inch closer. "I'm going to kiss you now," he said, "and then the guy can leave and we can all enjoy our lunch."

"Better make it a good one," Colin said.

Nick's eyes lit up, and Colin thought he liked the look of that long, slow smile with the diabolical edge.

He wasn't wrong. It was a smile that promised, and delivered, fantastic things.

The pictures of Colin and Nick kissing at the taco stand came out on a Tuesday, and the fundraiser was that Friday. The pictures even made the cover of *People* magazine, which meant that when Nick ran to the store to grab milk and bread and some other necessities, they taunted him from the rack next to the checkout.

From the way the checker eyed him up and then down again, Nick was pretty sure she'd recognized him, but the lady didn't say a word. He wasn't sure if he was grateful or not. He'd meant to keep the kissing rather tame, but then Colin had struggled so much with the whole experience, and it had been hard for Nick to control himself when he'd discovered such a great way to distract him.

Nick steeled his resolve and offered a smile in exchange for her suspicious glances. So much of this was an unpleasant reminder of what coming out the first time had been like, but he knew it was so much more fraught for Colin than for himself, so he kept quiet. And, he kept telling himself, it would calm down. Right now, Colin was the biggest story in the sports world. That wouldn't last. They just had to make it through the next few weeks and something else would crop up and the scrutiny on their every move would end.

Nick had already decided that he would go for a long run while Colin was at the fundraiser. It would keep him from moping around the house, wishing that things were different and that he'd been able to come along.

The problem was that if Nick even showed a fraction of how much he wanted to go, Colin would never let it go. So Nick had taken a hard line of *it's impossible*, which was further bolstered by Helen's certainty it was a bad idea. Still, he was looking forward to the day when he could be a little selfish and let Colin drag him to all these events.

Plus, Nick had heard some...contradictory things about this particular NFL player's personal beliefs, and he wasn't sure Colin receiving the invitation after coming out was a good or a bad thing. Nick was hoping the rumors were lies, and it wouldn't be an issue. After all, if this player was indeed a homophobic bag of dicks, it didn't make any sense for him to invite Colin *after* he came out of the closet.

He'd just heard wrong, Nick decided as he climbed the stairs to the loft, grocery bags in hand. Nothing else made sense.

"Hi there, handsome," Nick said as he walked into the loft and found Colin primping in his tuxedo.

Colin's face lit up as he caught sight of him. Nick didn't think that was ever going to get old, and it helped take some of the sting out of his grocery store run.

"You look great," Nick said, because he could see Colin gearing up for yet another round of *you should really be coming with me*. The problem was if Colin kept asking, Nick was going to eventually say yes. The trick was to make sure they never got there.

"It's James Bond theme," Colin said proudly. "Sounds really fun for the kids. I think I'm going to do themed fundraiser events every year."

"A wonderful idea," Nick said, reaching up and smoothing down Colin's already smooth lapels.

"What are you going to do while I'm gone?"

"Go for a little beach run, probably. I like it when it's dark."

Colin's face scrunched up adorably. "You're so weird. Only person I know who enjoys running at night."

"Better than running at the ass crack of dawn," Nick retorted with a grin.

"Yeah, who's the weirdo who likes to do that?"

Nick kissed him in lieu of actually answering. So enthusiastically, in fact, that when they finally broke apart, Colin was breathing a little heavy and his erection was poking a hole in Nick's leg. "What was that for?" he asked.

Ignoring the clammy tendril of fear, Nick reached up and grasped his cheeks between his palms. "Because I love you."

Nick told himself, after Colin left in the hired car, that he'd made the right choice to send Colin off with love and not with some shady gossip that would only worry him.

He still ran hard and long, pushing his body and his brain, trying to shut up that little voice at the back of his head that kept telling him that he'd made a mistake by not telling Colin about his fears—or that he'd made a mistake by not going with him.

By the time he got back to his building, he was dripping sweat and shaky on his legs. He unlocked the door and found all the lights still off, which made sense. He didn't anticipate seeing Colin until much later. Nick decided he'd take a shower and order a pizza for dinner, maybe catch the Lakers game on TV. He stopped by the fridge to grab some water, chugging it as he moved from the kitchen to the bedroom. He flipped the light on, and nearly dropped the bottle.

Colin was sitting on the edge of the bed, the bowtie of his tuxedo hastily undone, his head in his hands. He looked up slowly now that Nick had turned the lights on.

"What are you doing here?" Nick said, that horrible hateful fear that he'd been trying to push away all night billowing exponentially inside of him.

"It was a mistake," Colin said dully.

"What happened?" Nick said, forgetting about his sweat, sitting right down next to Colin, pulling him tight against him. Colin was usually a huge cuddler, loving any and every touch that Nick could give him, but he went so easily tonight, like a puppet with its strings cut.

"As soon as I got there, the lady checking us in said they wanted to see me personally. You know, the organizer and his buddies. I assumed it was to thank me personally for coming on such short notice." Colin laughed bitterly and Nick felt a chill run up his spine.

"What did they say?" he asked quietly, though he had a good idea already. Maybe that gossip hadn't been shady. Maybe he'd known all along, and he'd sent Colin out there, unprepared and naïve, expecting everyone to be accepting and loving of who he was when Nick already knew the truth.

"Oh, he did thank me for coming," Colin said. "And said when they'd read about me a few weeks ago, they'd been *disappointed*, but hoped that I'd not make a huge mistake and make a spectacle of such an embarrassing secret."

Nick soothed as best he could, a shaky hand stroking Colin's broad back. He could feel a shudder run through him, and had never wanted to kill anyone the way he wanted to tonight.

"They used a bunch of other, much worse words. I won't repeat them," Colin said dully. "But you get the idea."

"That's what they'd invited you for? You weren't even there for the kids?" Nick had worried, but he'd never expected that this would turn out so badly.

"No." Colin's voice cracked. "To quote him, *can't have some fucking queer influencing the kids.*"

Rage was a white-hot living thing boiling inside Nick. "What an asshole."

Colin laughed again, the sound so bitter Nick could taste it as he swallowed. "He only invited me to the fundraiser because he didn't think I'd meet him if he just asked. Said something about you knowing what he thought and that you'd warn me off."

"God, I...I am so fucking sorry. I did hear that he was like this. I thought...I mean...I *wanted* to be wrong. And I wasn't sure. It was all rumors. I didn't know for sure. If I'd known, I would have told you. I wouldn't have let you walk into his trap."

"I believe you," Colin said, and the forgiveness in his voice nearly broke Nick's control over the tears threatening. And he'd been *upset* over the way the checker at the grocery store had looked at him! "I told him that he didn't intimidate me on a football field, and he didn't intimidate me in his street clothes, either."

Nick cried then, and he was fairly certain Colin was crying, too. They stayed there like that for long, drawn-out minutes, just holding onto each other.

"You warned me so many times," Colin finally said.

"I never wanted to be right," was all Nick could say.

"Some people are just assholes," Colin said with finality. "And I know you've been struggling too and not telling me. This hasn't been easy for you either."

"Don't go working yourself up about how I'm doing. I'm fine. I'm more worried about you."

"Actually," Colin said. "I'm better than I thought I'd be. I mean, it was just as horrible as I'd ever imagined. But that was probably the worst it'll ever be. I can't imagine anything worse, anyway. And now I won't be wondering what it might be like. I've already had it happen, and I got through it, and I came home to you."

Nick choked on a sob and gripped Colin's shoulders harder. "You're too good."

"No, I'm not," Colin said wryly.

"No, you *are*. You believe in the best in people. Most of the time, it's my job to look for the worst, whose comeback is going to fail. Who's a bust in their league. So much focus on the negative. It makes us such an improbable match."

"Are you breaking up with me? If you are, can you just...I don't know...not do it tonight?"

Nick couldn't help but laugh a little through his tears. "Hell no. I'm saying it's not always going to be easy."

"Easy? You think I've ever wanted things *easy*? It's like you don't know me at all."

"I know you pretty well."

"I want you because I love you," Colin's voice rang with certainty. The same certainty that Nick remembered hearing so many years ago at a press conference after Colin's very first start at quarterback in college. He'd been so sure that even though he'd had a rough day on the field, the next *would* be better. "I don't care if it's easy or it's hard or it's something the entire world hates. It's you and me, I hope for a very long time."

It might not have been as easy for someone else, someone who hadn't made such a study of Colin's career, but Nick knew that voice, knew that bone-deep vein of absolutism that ran through Colin. Knew what he would do to make his promises a reality. And so it was the easiest thing Nick had ever done to believe.

It had been many, many years since he'd been able to put aside every apprehension and trust in the unshakeable. And he'd never been able to do it with a lover; he'd always held back, a tiny part of him waiting for the other shoe to drop.

Nick finally understood that with Colin, it never would. It didn't matter how many fellow players were dicks. It didn't matter what Nick did for a living. It didn't matter how many covers of *People* they ended up on. "You've got yourself a deal," he said. "A very long time or forever, whichever comes first."

Chapter Thirteen

Four months later

Miami was still stupidly hot.

Nick stood at the curb at Arrivals and this time wasn't surprised to see Colin's black Audi pull up. He'd nearly expected to see it. Would secretly have been disappointed if it hadn't shown. Still, that didn't mean he needed to let his boyfriend get away with sneaking off to pick him up when he had a perfectly good PA to do stuff like fetching people from the airport.

Which is what he said when he opened the door and slid into the passenger seat. Not before giving Colin a good long kiss, though, resulting in more than one impatient honk from the cars waiting behind them.

"But you're not just *anyone*," Colin retorted with the cutest grin on his face as they pulled onto the freeway. "You're my boyfriend. Can't lump you in with the rest of the world."

Nick rolled his eyes, because the notion of Colin *ever* doing that was ridiculous. Six months into their relationship, Colin still hadn't gotten over the thrill of finding someone to love who loved him back. Ninety-nine percent of the time, it was adorable as hell, because anything that made Colin sappy, emotional and/or sentimental—especially when it was over *him*—was definitely okay by Nick.

Then there was the remaining one percent, which were almost always things that Nick teased Colin for relentlessly.

"Someday," Nick said, "you're actually going to act like an NFL quarterback."

Colin's grin could have lit a flotilla of solar panels for a hundred years. "I thought you liked that I don't." He pasted on a pretend little pout that both of them knew wouldn't fool Nick for a second.

Whenever Nick thought about how preposterously in love Colin was, he couldn't help but think about how head over heels he was, too. He reached over and stroked Colin's hand with his thumb. He'd only been gone for a few days, but they had still seemed interminable. "I love that you don't," he admitted. "I love *you*."

"I missed you," Colin exhaled in the quiet as he pulled off the main highway, taking the exit that led to what had initially been his own little slice of private heaven. Now it was *their* little slice of private heaven. Every time Nick had to leave, it got harder, even when it was never for very long.

Unfortunately there was only so much freelance journalism work Nick could do from a private island off Miami's coast. At some point, he always had to hop on a plane and fly away to get his hands dirty.

"I know I sent you about a million texts," Colin continued, a tinge of self-consciousness in his voice now. "I hope I didn't bother you too much while you were working."

Nick of a year ago probably would have made a sarcastic quip, burying deep the truth of how he'd felt every time his phone had vibrated in his pocket. Not even for any sort of good reason, either. Just because he'd been caught up in a web of semi-jaded cynicism.

Since meeting Colin, Nick had learned to care less about that carefully cultivated front and more about what lay behind it. At first, he'd felt naked and exposed, but as he got used to it, he realized how much happier he was, now that he allowed himself to really *wallow* in his feelings instead of always trying to hide them.

"You didn't bother me," he said with a little chuckle. "In fact, I loved reading each one, even though I couldn't always respond. Aaron Rodgers thinks we're pretty cute, by the way."

"Could you convince him to throw less spectacularly against the Piranhas in week twelve?" Colin asked.

"Unfortunately, we're not that cute. At least not you, anyway."

"Asshole," Colin accused playfully.

"Me or Aaron?"

"Like I'd ever malign Aaron Rodgers that way." Colin pulled up the driveway and turned off the car, getting out before Nick could even throw out a decent comeback.

Not that there really *was* a decent comeback. Aaron Rodgers being Aaron Rodgers, after all.

Colin had popped the trunk and was in the process of retrieving Nick's bag. Nick took in the scene in a second. Conscientious and fucking adorably hot boyfriend that he hadn't seen in days. *Check.* Smoking fast car. *Check.* Complete privacy. *Check.*

It wasn't even really a decision to pin Colin to the bumper and wrap himself around Colin like he was his favorite tree.

"You're my favorite tree," Nick murmured as he reached up to kiss him.

The sweet pressure of Colin's mouth roared back into Nick's brain, reminding him of everything he'd lost out on while he'd been away. Their lips met and caught, again and again, sliding together without missing a single beat. There was a constancy and a certainty that Nick had with Colin that he'd never had with anyone else before, and it was easy to lose himself in the idea that what they'd begun to build together was permanent and unshakeable.

Of course, forever didn't have to be boring or predictable, either.

Nick caught Colin's gasp as his hands made quick work of his pants and then his boxer briefs, shoving them to his knees as Nick sank to his. The concrete might be hard and a little uncomfortable, but it was hard to remember when Colin's dick was hard and a little wet at the tip, mesmerizingly close.

Colin's breath was uneven and rushed as Nick ran his tongue up the underside, pausing to curl around the pulsing head. "You...*y ou*," Colin exhaled shakily.

Nick didn't pause, didn't even hesitate at Colin's breathless litany of variations of his name, just sucked him down, pushing himself because even five days was too many days without this dick in his life.

Hands sliding down into his hair, Colin began to pump his hips restlessly and Nick went still and soft, letting him. A swear word wrenched itself out of Colin's throat.

It felt so good like this, even with gravel digging into his knees, that Nick had to palm himself through his jeans, rubbing mindlessly against the swamping pleasure.

"Yeah, yeah," Colin begged, even more mindless as he thrust into Nick's mouth, and Nick ground against his hand.

Colin came half a beat before Nick did, bitter cum flooding his mouth as he swallowed. He almost choked as his own orgasm hit, a blinding flash of light and heat.

When he opened his eyes, Colin was tucking himself back into his pants messily, and Nick was painfully aware of a growing wet spot and his thirty-year-old knees protesting.

Colin must have known because he reached down and gently helped Nick up. "You're a menace," Colin said playfully as they walked into the house. "I'm never going to be able to think about Aaron Rodgers again without getting a hard-on."

Nick grabbed a bottle of water from the fridge and leaned against the counter, knowing he should go upstairs to shower and change, but not wanting to leave Colin's presence for the time it would take. Every time he left, coming back felt even better.

"Maybe that was the plan," Nick said slyly.

Colin groaned.

"I'm going to go shower. When are Jemma and Gabe getting here again?" Now that the endorphin rush was fading, Nick felt rather gross.

"Wouldn't that have been an important thing to find out *before* you went down on me in the driveway?"

Nick shrugged. "Might have been educational."

Colin just shook his head, the giggles practically spilling out of him. "They arrived a few hours ago." And because that didn't get the shocked concern he'd probably expected, continued. "I put them up at the Four Seasons, with instructions to Lindsay that she makes sure they're spoiled."

Colin looked really proud of himself, like he'd solved a problem that Nick hadn't even discovered yet. What Colin had yet to truly figure out was that Nick could not give a crap if they had loud reunion sex with Gabe and Jemma just down the hall. Nick was so in love, he was totally shameless with it.

But hey, if Colin wanted to spoil Gabe and Jemma so he could get some privacy, that was fine by Nick, too.

"Are we going out or staying in?" Nick asked, pausing at the bottom of the stairs. Like he didn't already know the answer. It was Friday night. The game was on Sunday afternoon. Gabe and Jemma were in town. And since Nick basically moved to Florida, he'd discovered one of his favorite things to do with his boyfriend was to spend the night in, watching his house-husband-slash-NFL-quarterback in front of the grill and a guilty pleasure show on Netflix.

"Staying in. I'm grilling."

If Nick spent his entire shower grinning like an idiot, then nobody needed to know but him and the tile walls.

After digesting dinner, Colin suggested they go for a midnight swim just as Nick was gearing up for another episode of *Leverage*. He valiantly didn't pout and followed Colin out to the veranda instead, stripping off their clothes and sinking into the cool water. It was September but it was still damn hot.

"Are you nervous?" Nick asked, as Colin swam circles around him. Nick felt too lazy to swim. He'd dragged his butt to the pool because tomorrow Colin would go to bed early, and they'd not get to enjoy this. But that didn't mean Nick had to turn it into actual physical exercise. Colin couldn't seem to help himself because he was Colin O'Connor.

Colin shrugged. Even though he'd asked in the capacity of Colin's significant other, Nick found it hard to not shift into journalist mode, watching Colin's face carefully for any sign he wasn't being honest. It turned out, it was difficult to turn off his inquisitive instincts, even when they weren't necessary. But the truth was, Nick as a boyfriend had spent the last six months discovering that if Colin was truly anxious about tomorrow, he'd tell him.

"People have been shitty. People have been nice. If I let them get to me, I can't change their minds." Since the horrible night at the fundraiser, Colin had developed a plan to deal with the assholes who couldn't accept who he was: ignore, and if ignoring was impossible, don't ever sink to their level.

Nick hadn't thought he could be prouder than he'd been in those weeks after Colin's coming out, but after spending the last six months watching his boyfriend confront ignorance and homophobia, he discovered new levels of pride every day.

Every time he was confronted with a dickhead, Colin had made it his personal mantra to rise.

To his surprise, the entire Piranhas team, who had not been *entirely* supportive, but close enough, had adopted the slogan for the upcoming season.

Three months ago, Nick had taken a few weeks of leave to help Colin found The Rise Foundation, which helped LGBTA+ kids with resources, shelter, and medical care.

Still, it was hard to forget the boos during the preseason games. It was hard to unhear what Nick had heard some fans shout in Colin's direction. It was hard to un-see some of the signs he'd seen in the stands. It was hard to forget the rumors he'd heard about a particularly virulent group of homophobic players.

Basically, Nick still worried about Colin, and he didn't know if he would ever stop because even though he knew Colin could handle it, Nick didn't *want* him to handle it. He didn't want him to have to experience it at all. Every instance still made him burn with rage.

Rising was a choice that Nick had to make each and every time. It didn't come naturally to him the way it did to Colin.

"I sent an email to Helen. She said she'd try to alert security about signs and disruptive fans in the stands."

Colin shook his head, amused. "I know they bother you. They don't bother me. They've exposed themselves through their own hatred."

Nick found his fists clenching impotently in the water. Was it so wrong that he still found the instinct to protect the man he loved the strongest of all? Would Colin feel differently if their positions were reversed?

"I'm not worried about them," Colin continued. "Even if the whole stadium chose to boo me."

"You would care," Nick insisted.

"No, because it wouldn't be the whole stadium. I know you're there. Jemma's there. Gabe's there. Teddy and Boomer are there. Teddy's wife and their kids. They're not going to boo me. And that's who really matters."

Colin floated over to where Nick was trying to relax, one uncooperative muscle at a time, against the edge of the pool. He reached down and took Nick's hands in his. "It's okay. I know you worry because you love me. But I hate to see you this upset."

Nick hadn't even known he was upset until he'd considered the possibility that Colin could face a whole stadium of hatred on Sunday.

"I'm not upset," Nick said, which they both knew was a lie. But he tried to make it true, gradually calming his breathing, and calming his mind and then forcing each muscle to unknot.

"You're not upset," Colin confirmed, when Nick had finally sagged against Colin's big, broad body. "You're good."

No, nothing was perfect, but they still had each other.

"You look like you're about to puke," Jemma said critically, eyeing him sideways from their position at the front of the luxury box suite at the Piranhas' stadium.

"I'm fine," Nick ground out. He figured the more emphatically he said it, the more accurate it might become.

"No, you're a nervous wreck." Jemma tossed her ponytail. "I know you've been to a ridiculous number of games in your life. But it's not really the same when it's Colin, is it?"

Nick clenched the beer bottle in his fist. "It's not the same," he had to agree.

"He's solid. He looked fantastic in preseason. Great footwork. Even better arm."

"You don't need to preach his skills to me," Nick said with an eye roll.

Gabe wandered over. "I've been drafted to stop you from launching yourself out of the box and attacking anyone who looks at O'Connor sideways," he announced.

Nick glared at Jemma. "I'm not that bad."

She threw her hands up. "I didn't say you were. For the record, I'm not the one who talked to him."

"Oh. *Oh.*" Nick flushed, embarrassed that he'd been so transparent that Colin had actually been worried enough to talk to Gabe about it.

"You," Jemma said, jabbing a finger Nick's direction, "need to chill. And Colin needs less chill."

"Yeah, that's not happening, not with all this." Gabe gestured around the stadium. It was draped in flags and banners proclaiming, "Rise," many of them in rainbow colors.

The first time Colin had brought Nick to see them, a few weeks ago, Nick had choked up. He'd never, even in his wildest dreams, imagined a modern-day football team embracing LGBTA+ rights this way. But that was before the preseason had started. Before Nick had gotten too caught up in the signs and the boos and before he'd started hearing the echoed insults in his nightmares.

"It's not that easy," Nick said quietly. "I worry because I love him."

"And nobody would doubt you cared if you let some things go," Jemma said, her voice kind. "I've got to talk to Mark, I'll be right back.

Nick and Gabe watched Jemma wander over to where Colin's manager was currently holding court. "You know she didn't need to talk to him, right?" Gabe asked.

Nick rolled his eyes. "As if anyone ever wants to talk to that guy."

"I have a feeling she wants me to tell you that you can still worry without letting it overtake you."

"So Jemma *did* conscript you," Nick said wryly.

But Gabe's gaze remained steady and serious, not amused in the slightest. Nick hadn't even realized how much he was falling back into his old habits of using humor as a shield until this moment.

"I conscripted myself," Gabe said. "You didn't think Colin was the only one worrying himself sick over you?"

Nick was embarrassed that he'd never really considered the possibility.

"When Jemma and I were in Rio, I behaved like the Terminator, and not in a good way. I was a wreck, because all I could see was your blood. I had to re-learn that you were plenty capable and worrying about you so much it impacted my normal life wouldn't save you from jack shit."

Nick took a long drink of beer. "You've never told me the Terminator thing before."

"Yeah, well, I was embarrassing as fuck. I'm lucky Jemma waited around until I got my head screwed on straight."

"So you're saying I need to get my head screwed on straight?" It wasn't like Nick didn't abstractly *know* this, but it was different somehow, coming from his best friend.

"I sorta think that's the message Colin was sending by asking me to stop you from attacking anyone in the stands."

Nick considered this. "Point."

Jemma wandered back over, clearly having decided that they'd had the conversation they needed to have. Nick intended to ask Colin later if she had always been this nosy.

The answer was probably yes. After all, she was a journalist for a reason.

"It's starting," Jemma exclaimed happily, as the confetti cannons on either side of the tunnel began to explode, showering the field in rainbow glitter.

The music reached a crescendo. Colin stepped forward on the field, flanked by two enormous Piranhas flags, and Nick heard a roar that he wasn't quite sure he understood.

"What's that?" he had to yell to be heard.

Jemma looked over, tears in her eyes. "It's the crowd."

They weren't booing. They were screaming their support and their love for him, a standing ovation for their starting quarterback who had done the bravest thing in the modern age of professional football. There might have been some nasty comments, but they were drowned out completely by the sound of a stadium full of supporters.

Gabe nudged Nick with an elbow. "Don't think I'm going to be stopping you from jumping out of the suite."

Nick blinked back tears. "No. No, you won't." He paused, taking in a deep, steadying breath, his eyes never leaving his boyfriend, down on the field, who was waving like crazy, jogging towards the sideline. "He did it."

"He'd want you to have at least partial credit," Jemma said, as the screams finally began to die down.

"I wouldn't accept it," Nick said.

She shook her head, a smile glimmering on her face. "Which is how I know you're perfect for each other."

Don't miss the bonus scene! What happens when the Piranhas make the playoffs and Colin's superstitions rear their ugly head?

And make sure to check out the Piranhas series, about the next generation of Miami Piranhas players, available on Amazon and Audible.

INTERESTED IN READING MORE OF
BETH'S BOOKS?

CHECK OUT A FULL LIST OF TILES
BY SCANNING THE QR CODE
OR VISITING HER WEBSITE

WWW.BETHBOLDEN.COM/BOOKLIST

WANT TO FOLLOW BETH?

MAKE SURE YOU NEVER
MISS A RELEASE?

SCAN THE QR CODE BELOW
OR VISIT HER WEBSITE
FOR A SOCIAL MEDIA LIST,
NEWSLETTER SIGNUP,
AND SO MUCH MORE!

WWW.BETHBOLDEN.COM/ABOUT